Wildest Winter

ALAINA ROSE

ALSO BY ALAINA ROSE

STARLING HILLS

Relative Fiction
Happy Accidents

* * *

Next Chapter of Us

AUTHOR'S NOTE

Thank you so much for picking up *Wildest Winter*. I want every reader to have a safe and enjoyable experience, so I have included this list of content/trigger warnings.

Wildest Winter includes graphic, on-page, consensual sex (including oral sex, vaginal penetration, toy use, mutual masturbation, the use of an anal plug), processing grief, parental death (past, lung cancer), problematic binge drinking, swearing, flight/travel anxiety, driving in a blizzard, massage induced orgasm, marijuana use.

I endeavored to make this list as inclusive as possible. If you feel anything else should be included, or if you have any questions or concerns, please contact me.

this one's for me

PROLOGUE

ARI

IT'S JUST *some random day in November.*

The refrain repeated over and over in Ari's head. Except she couldn't fool herself. Her body kept telling the story.

The shivering while wearing fuzzy thigh-high leg warmers and an extra cashmere sweater. A constant headache despite perfect hydration. Memories that wouldn't stop playing on loop in her brain over the mind-numbing electronic music in her noise cancelling head-phones. Dry, itching eyes as she stared at her lecture notes, willing herself to remember a single goddamn thing for tomorrow's exam.

Mom, Thomas, Danny, and Ari had breakfast that morning at Callaghan's Coney Island; Dad's signature pancakes for everyone. Afterward, everyone hugged and Ari went to the graduate library to study. A nice thing to commemorate the one-year anniversary of Dad's death, but not a big deal.

After all, they had years of his sickness to grieve. No one ever thought Dad was going to survive lung cancer. Everyone knew that eventually, the sickness would take him, despite his extra-long battle. In the end, he made the decision to stop his treatments last summer and by the end of fall, he was gone.

Now, Ari kept her phone on Do Not Disturb, unwilling and uninterested in dialoguing with anyone today. Breakfast had been hard enough. She hadn't said much at all with the grief lingering like a shroud over her shoulders.

But why now? Why, a year later, did the loss of her dad send her emotions into an absolute tailspin?

She needed a drink. In fact, she wouldn't mind getting black out wasted. Something, anything to hide from the emotions that writhed under her skin like creepy crawlies.

The words on the page of her notebook blurred and twisted. Lecture notes, perfectly outlined, tabulated, high-lighted—and for what? As if Ari really cared about supply chain management.

Not for the first time, the ridiculousness, the useless-ness, of her Master in Business Administration struck her right in the middle of her chest. At twenty-six, she was halfway done with the program at Everdale College, and she had never been more apathetic.

Sitting in her study cubicle, the sun streamed in the massive window. A perfectly blue sky stretched over the campus, the best kind of November day: cold with a crisp wind, but warmer in the sun. It reminded her of all the times her dad brought her to Blake's Cider Mill out in Armada, a half-hour drive in the country, away from the hustle and bustle of Metro Detroit.

Her stomach clenched at the memories. She needed that drink. She could finish studying at her apartment. As she packed up her bag, Ari convinced herself she'd be more productive there anyway because it was more comfortable.

Deep down, she knew she was lying to herself.

IT WAS THE SWEET SPOT; Ari drank the first bottle of wine fast enough that all she wanted was another. Good thing she had a little stockpile of the nice pinot noir that Thomas bought for her every holiday. But as she popped the cork from bottle number two, she got another idea.

"Pop-Tart," she mumbled to herself, tripping toward the snack cupboard above her head.

Her phone buzzed in her pocket. Groaning at the thing, she took it out and looked briefly at the name before tossing it onto the counter.

Gid. Her best friend and dance partner and the only guy she knew that would dress up as a hot dog at their annual summer barbecue just because he thought it was funny.

Even as she topped off her glass of wine, she knew it was an awful idea. And yet, she couldn't stop. There always was that gluttonous streak in her, the black hole in the center of her chest that she could never fill.

In high school, it was dance. Pushing her body and mental capacity as hard as she could while in those pointe shoes. But she could never be a perfect enough ballerina. Never small enough, flexible enough, never turned out enough.

Starting in college, she began collecting different dance styles. Ballroom, pole, burlesque. Less exact styles where she could discharge some of her excess energy. It all worked as a distraction. For a while.

That's why she went back to school, too. She'd be the first in her family to have a master's degree and goddamn that feather in her cap was alluring. Everdale College's prestigious business school was know from their strict admissions criteria, but she'd managed it with ease.

But now, especially since one year ago *today*, alcohol and weed had become her favored distractions of choice.

Which, she thought as she ripped open the package of Pop-Tarts, would explain a lot.

It was no thanks to all the other young professionals that she met in Chicago during her internship, who seemed to prefer stronger stuff anyway.

No thanks to her grief that never seemed to lessen—it only grew heavier and more opaque.

No thanks to her therapist, who Ari still wouldn't fully open up to.

She certainly didn't want Gid to know that she was on her way to blacking out the night before an exam. And that's why she didn't pick up his phone call.

A new text came through on her screen.

No need to call back. Just wanted to wish you good luck tomorrow.

Tomorrow, tomorrow, tomorrow. That's right—

"Exam time tomorrow," Ari boomed, raising her drink and toasting the air.

And that was her last conscious thought.

ONE
ARI

THE FAMILIAR OPENING jingle bells to Mariah Carey's *All I Want for Christmas Is You* tinkled through Folklore as Ari took another sip of her Gingerbrute Winter Stout from Last Glass Ales.

She knew that her best friend Zahra had a soft spot for this song. It was on her bookstore-coffeehouse-pub holiday playlist a record ten times for maximum repeats.

In the last hour, it came on five times, which would make even the most festive person grumpy. Except for Zahra, who still waltzed behind the bar slinging pints with the widest grin on her face, the golden tinsel in her micro braids twinkling as it caught in the light. The effect of the sparkling gold against her dark brown skin was stunning. Zahra knew it, too. That girl was gorgeous.

"Damn it," Isa growled as he stalked from the shelves

in the back of the store, a couple books clutched in hand. "I've heard this song too many times today!"

Zahra's older brother, co-owner of Folklore and certifiable Scrooge, distinctly did not have tinsel anywhere close to his person. He came to a halt at Ari's table, dropping the mini-tower of paperbacks there and putting his hands on his hips.

"Hi Ari," he said while glaring at his sister across the bar area: she was now singing along at full volume.

"Hey Isa." Ari smiled up at the flannel-wearing grump in front of her. He continued to frown at his sister. "Happy Holidays?"

"Yeah, Happy Holidays and all that...but someone's gotta rein that girl in."

"I do not volunteer as tribute. She takes her holiday cheer very seriously."

"And it seems to get more intense every year." Isa's frown, if possible, deepened. "Does it have to be *this* song?"

"Your patrons seem to be loving it."

Across the bar area and the bookstore section, everyone was smiling and laughing. Some were even singing along with Mariah and Zahra. The joy was, quite literally, palpable.

If only Ari could absorb some of it. She knew her grades were going to be awful. Earlier in the semester, her college advisor put her on academic probation after she missed her exam the day after the one-year anniversary of her dad's death. Instead of getting a good night's sleep the night before, she drank two bottles of red wine, took a hot bath, and passed out on the couch. The exam was at nine AM and she slept through all ten alarms she'd set. Her stomach swooped at the memory of waking up to the sun shining through her living room window.

Yep, at the very least that class would be a fail. There was no way she could redeem her grade afterward. Her professor had been immovable on the subject.

"I recognize that one," Ari said, flicking the spine of a T. Callaghan book, her older brother Thomas's most recent release.

Isa looked down at the stack, still frowning, but seemingly grateful for the distraction from Mariah Carey.

"Thomas has been selling pretty well since he came back to Michigan and took over at the Coney Island. Turns out folks love a local celebrity."

Ari snorted. *Celebrity*.

To her, T was still the overbearing older brother who had disappeared for years. He was a dick sometimes, yet he was always down for a romcom movie marathon or a game of Uno Death or getting stoned and having philosophical discussions. She couldn't help but love the guy.

And there was Danny, her middle brother who would do anything for anyone—to a fault—and always had a quiet word of advice.

She loved their little Callaghan clan down to the

bones. For better or worse. And, frankly, they'd all been a little worse for the wear since Dad's death last year.

Finally, *All I Want for Christmas Is You* made it to its stunning end, the choir fading out and Isa breathed a sigh of relief. But it was short lived as the music crossfaded right into the same chiming bells, marking the seventh time the song came on in the last hour.

"Holy shit," Isa groaned. "I gotta take care of this," he said, stomping off.

From behind the bar, Zahra's protests were drowned out as Ari hit refresh once more on her computer, desperate for her fate. And there they were: her stunningly, shockingly, though not surprisingly, dismal results for this last semester: C-, C, C-, and—to cap it all off—a flaming D- in her supply chain logistics class.

As if perfectly timed, her phone lit up with a notification in the Callaghan family group chat. They still hadn't taken Dad's number out of it, despite the fact that he'd never send a text again. Three messages arrived in rapid succession.

Mom: *Ari, did you get your grades yet?*

Danny: **eyes emoji**

Thomas: *Eyes emoji? Is that a thing?*

Thomas: *Sorry, don't mean to change the subject. How'd the semester go Ari?*

It was almost like a coordinated plan of attack. Were the three of them sitting around the dining room table at

Mom's sipping whiskey from the nice crystal glasses? Likely.

Ari's grades were the last thing she wanted to talk about right now. Or ever, really. She'd managed to keep her epic failures a secret so far.

She groaned, trying to think of a noncommittal answer that would be enough. Eventually, she'd have to tell them what was going on. Especially if her academic probation turned into academic recess and she couldn't take classes next semester. Which, given her dismal performance, was looking very likely.

Ari could think of little more humiliating than telling her family and friends that she'd *failed*.

And despite Ari and her advisor's best efforts, apparently, she couldn't do better than a C- average these days.

These days... These days without Dad. These days when, after spending the summer at an internship in Chicago, she just couldn't see the point anymore. These days when the devastating dichotomy of her cushy small-town life was so at odds with the atrocities going on elsewhere in the world.

After getting a taste of the real world—what the rest of her life would look like—she wasn't having it. And she just couldn't care about her business degree anymore.

Frowning at her phone, she composed a text. Not a blatant lie, but a white lie, about how her semester ended. She didn't need the spotlight on her. It should be on Thomas and Julia for the rest of the week anyway. As the baby sibling, and resident simmering trainwreck, she really just wanted everyone to ignore her.

Fine. It's fine. Everything is fine. Stop worrying about me. I'm fine

No, that wouldn't work. Too many "fines." Ari backspaced the whole thing as she took her last sip of beer.

Good! Really good! Nearly 4.0!

Alright, reel it in, girlfriend.

Not bad. Glad it's over, at least

Hmm. Vague, mysterious, maybe satisfying enough that they wouldn't question it. She hit send. Within a few moments, her mom responded.

Mom: *Yay! We can cheers you this weekend, too*

That was the last thing Ari wanted. She locked her phone and put it down before she did something else irresponsible, like throw it outside into a snowbank.

Zahra plopped down in the seat across from her. "You ready for your trip?" she asked.

Their conversations were like one continuous stream of consciousness, as if they never actually stopped talking to one another. It had been like that since they met when the Callaghans moved to Starling Hills when Ari was ten years old. The two had spent that summer together, starting their own, quite lucrative, dog-walking business. It was both of their first foray into the business world. By the time sixth grade started that fall, they were best friends.

Ari closed her eyes, pressing her fingertips into her eyeballs until she saw stars. "Sorta."

"Ooh. Packing tonight?"

"Tomorrow morning probably."

"Sounds about right."

"You on break?" Ari asked.

Zahra rolled her eyes and pulled her braids over her shoulder, playing with the ends.

"Isa vetoed the Christmas music, despite the fact that Christmas is *next week*. So I vetoed working behind the bar." She smiled her shit-eating grin, the one she used when she got her way. "I told him it's called balance. He told me which shelves still needed stocking. Why did I decide to open this place with him?"

Ari laughed, happy for the distraction. "Well, for one thing, it's been your dream since you were twelve. You wrote it in your diary and made a dream board about it, remember?"

"Yes, but *with my brother*?" Zahra laughed. Though she joked, she loved her brother, much like Ari loved hers, despite how annoying they were.

"You didn't let me finish—for two, he was the financial backer."

Isa had a short but lucrative career in the tech field when he developed and sold an app that was essentially matchmaking for people looking for bandmates. He loved the idea and development part, but wasn't meant for life in Silicon Valley.

"You're right, you're right." Zahra stretched her legs under the table. "And I guess he's not always such a douchebag!"

She yelled the last part loud enough that Isa could hear it over the acid rock playlist he'd put on. He flashed his middle finger across the bar. Some patrons laughed along with them, but most ignored the siblings: their bickering banter had become commonplace in Folklore.

"But back to your *trip*," Zahra sang the last word. "Wedding time!"

"Yeah," Ari sighed, deeply aware that she needed to muster some enthusiasm for Thomas and Julia before tomorrow's flight. "I've just got a lot going on."

"What do you mean? It's the end of the semester, right? Freedom for the next month!" Zahra's golden-brown eyes sparkled, because usually freedom meant the two of them got up to trouble together. "We need to have another wine and pole night."

Ari sighed, slouching down on the bench side of the table and smiled thinly. Splitting a bottle of wine and choreographing new pole dancing routines in absurdly high platform stilettos was innocent enough *trouble*, and it kept her distracted from things like studying.

Her chest heated. She hadn't so much as breathed a word to Zahra about her crisis. The holiday season was particularly stressful for her friend too, being a full-time small business owner. The last thing Ari needed was to be a burden on anyone else. She could deal with the consequences all by herself, thank you very much.

Bile soured her throat and she coughed to clear the taste. She needed to change the subject.

"Freedom, yes, but you know traveling with Gideon isn't the easiest thing in the best of times," she said, leaning across the table conspiratorially.

"Oh god, the poor boy," Zahra laughed, covering her mouth with her Christmas-colored manicured nails. "I'm surprised he agreed to go with you, especially this time of year."

"Not poor boy, poor *me*. His travel anxiety is next level. I'm sure he's been packed for weeks."

Zahra clicked her tongue thoughtfully. "You're probably right."

"If anything goes wrong with our travel plans, we will be so screwed."

"You better knock on wood, girl," Zahra said, one eyebrow raised.

With one tightly-clenched fist, Ari knocked twice on the table, hoping to hell that she didn't just jinx their entire trip.

TWO
GID

GID WHISTLED *All I Want for Christmas Is You* as he double checked his pre-holiday closure checklist. Contrakale Logistics shut down for the week between Christmas and New Year and he wanted to square away every task possible before heading to Ireland with Ari and the rest of the Callaghans.

The thought, not for the first time, sent sparks of heat down his neck.

He wasn't nervous to be around the Callaghans for a long weekend, nor did spending a couple days with Ari at a Christmas tree farm inspire fear, it was more like generalized travel anxiety that set him on edge. He was, after all, quite familiar with the Callaghans. Every couple months, Ari invited him to their Friday dinner. He'd read Thomas's books, helped Danny around Handy Danny's Workshop when things got hectic, chatted with their mom, Molly, at Callaghan's Coney Island on a weekly basis. Ari's dad, Sean, had even helped Gid buy his first used car after college.

And Gid had been best friends and dance partners with Ari since freshman year of college. What? Eight years ago now? He found it hard to believe it had been that long.

Gideon Sims felt more embraced by the Callaghans than his own family some days.

Okay, most days. The holidays always made it worse.

But he'd held out hope that he'd hear something else from his parents. Not that holidays with them were particularly endearing. His scientist parents were more dedicated to their research lab at Everdale College than anything else.

Though his parents lived a town over in Everdale, it might as well be oceans away. Gid spent more time in Everdale with Ari than at his parents', though the dance partners mostly met up in Starling Hills if they could. That was where their studio was anyway, Rosales School of Dance, tucked right above Salt Cellar Distillery on Main Street.

Gid clicked through his last emails tucked away in his cubicle. All of his work tasks were finally cleared away and he could leave for the holidays with nothing on his mind. At least, nothing work related.

"Hey," Julia breathed, popping her head over the side of his cubicle.

Gid jumped, placing a hand on his heart. "You scared me."

"I could hear your whistling from miles away. Someone's in the holiday spirit, eh?" She smiled, her cheeks a peachy pink.

Of course she was flushed, the woman was getting married to the boy she'd loved in high school, lost, and got back again twelve years later. It really was a romantic story. One that Gid, on his most jaded days, refused to believe actually happened. But here she was, his coworker and best friend's soon to be sister-in-law, in the flesh. Proof that true love existed.

Gid reminded himself not to visibly recoil at his inner thoughts.

Engage, Gid. Engage. It was like a game to him. The more he could socially interact, the more points he got in the imaginary column against himself.

"Just checking off the last things on my to-do list and then meeting Ari downtown."

"Oh?"

"It's our dance date. One cocktail at Salt Cellar, then we go upstairs to Rosales and dance."

"God I love that you two still dance together after all these years."

"It's the best exercise I get all week," Gid said.

And sometimes the only exercise he got. His job as a packaging engineer at Contrakale Logistics was great but all the social interaction depleted him too much most days to go to the gym afterward.

"You'll have to show us some moves this weekend." Julia raised her eyebrows expectantly.

Gid laughed and shocked his head. "Speaking of, what are you still doing here?"

Julia flipped her hand in the air as if to say, *it ain't no thang*. Gid highly doubted that planning a destination elopement over Christmas weekend was hardly *no thang*.

"Thomas has got all the logistics figured out, bless him." She half-frowned, half-smiled.

When Gid threw her a questioning glance, Julia elaborated. "He's dealing with a little bit of writer's block. The wedding planning has been a good distraction."

He nodded, totally understanding what she meant.

Where Ari and Gid had dance and a little just-for-fun TikTok account, Julia and Thomas had writing.

Writing was a full-time career for T. Callaghan, a well-known romance author, and Julia had a respectable following for her smutty fan fiction. A creative block could be devastating in any field, but he was thankful that he had Ari, who could bust him out of most of his funks. That's what partners were for, he guessed.

The alarm on his phone went off, making them both jump.

"Sorry," he said. "It's my half hour warning to get my butt across town to meet Ari." Gid stood, stretching his 5'9" frame, arms high in the air.

Julia smiled, crossing her arms as she leaned against the cubicle wall.

"And don't *you* need to be somewhere, miss?" Susan, Julia's work-friend-turned-best-friend, popped over her shoulder.

Julia clicked her tongue as Gid laughed.

"I just said the same thing," he said, shrugging into his puffer coat and pulling his navy beanie over his fluffy, dark hair.

"Jeez, you two, micromanage much? I'm just tying up loose ends. I'm sure Thomas has us both packed and my dress tucked away already."

Gid laughed, knowing better from Ari what her brothers were likely up to tonight. "Yeah, if he's not at Molly's house drinking whiskey with Danny."

Julia narrowed her eyes, considering. "You make a fair point, Sims. I'll have to tell your supervisors you were a good hire. Keen intellect and worthy deduction skills." She walked across the aisle to her own cubicle and shut down her computer.

"Wait!" Susan hollered, pulling out three mini bottles of Buttershots.

Somehow, wherever he went, Gid's infamous drink of choice always managed to catch up to him. Drink of choice was a bit of a stretch, but it was rare that he was without a little pocket flask of the butterscotch flavored schnapps. Particularly in winter. He smiled, appreciating that his teammates already knew him so well.

"We're toasting to the bride," Susan said, her voice uncharacteristically thick with emotion.

Julia pouted. "Don't get all sappy on me now, old Suse."

Gid laughed, putting out a hand for his tiny drink. Four months ago, he hired into Contrakale and was pleasantly surprised to be assigned to Julia's team. Julia and Susan came as a bundled deal, not that he was complaining. The familiarity of Julia and her best friend helped him settle in quickly. Like his own little work family.

"I," Susan sniffled, her eyes just slightly watery, "am entitled to be sappy. Since I have been by your side as you suffered that fucking peckerhead, and fucking Michelle," she growled.

"Be nice," Julia said.

"I will never be nice and I don't know how you do it."

"Because I found true love, remember."

"Right, right, that's why we're here. To Julia and Thomas, many blissful years, and blessed be the fruit."

"Oh my god get out of here, old Suse." Julia knocked into her friend's shoulder.

"And," Susan cleared her throat, "to Gideon here, who's completed our little tripod, the second best thing that Contrakale gave us this year, only after our hefty bonuses last quarter."

Now it was Gid's turn to be unexpectedly emotional. He never thought that getting a job at Contrakale Logistics would be anything more than a way to pay the bills and move closer to Ari.

Okay, that sounded a little creepy. But he wanted to be near his best friend, and this job got him as close as he could get. Since she lived a town over in Everdale near the college, Starling Hills checked all of his boxes. Gid's own parents just outside Everdale hadn't factored into his decision at all.

After graduating Michigan State University with a packaging science degree, Gid floundered a bit after college, working in entry-level roles, trying to find some kind of groove.

Turns out, the only groove that felt right was being near Ari. Everything else was gravy, as long as he could make rent and pay his student loans since they had started up again. Once he figured out what he wanted, the job at Contrakale basically fell in his lap.

"Right," Gid said, when he realized that both Julia and Susan were waiting on him to say something too. When it came to expressing his emotions, he got as clogged up as his nose in hay fever season. "You two are great. And... I'm glad I work here. Thank you for welcoming me to your team."

He smiled, a straight, awkward line of his lips and hoped that would be enough to appease them.

Susan nodded curtly and patted him on the back, her eyes showing that she understood exactly what he meant.

"We're glad you work here, too, Gid," Julia said, before raising her mini-shot.

They tapped the lips of their plastic bottles together before downing the syrupy sweet liqueur. The irony wasn't lost on Gid that his little work cell was quickly becoming more connected than his blood relatives.

And he didn't hate it. Not one bit.

* * *

GID HATED BEING LATE.

Late in the sense that he wasn't early.

And, really, he was still early but he didn't leave work right when that first alarm went off and even though he knew that Ari would *actually* be late, he hated that now he felt rushed. Feeling rushed meant he started to sweat. Since he was still in his work clothes, sweating was less than ideal.

Thankfully he quickly found a parking spot in the lot behind Salt Cellar. Stepping outside his car, he inhaled the cold air, clearing his head of his anxieties. It had started to snow on his drive into downtown Starling Hills, a beautiful snow globe kind of snow. Perfect for Christmas, right around the corner.

He wondered if there would be snow in Ireland. From what he'd read, they didn't typically have snowy winters and the country would come to a full-stop with the rare big storm. Like it did during the blizzard back in 2018.

Yes, he Googled it.

But there wasn't anything to worry about now. He was on a holiday shutdown, about to be on vacation, and Ari would be here soon. As long as he didn't think about the flight tomorrow, everything would be fine.

The very long flight crossing over the Atlantic Ocean. Where he'd be trapped for six and a half hours after their layover at JFK airport.

Don't think about it.

For someone who loved to travel, and spent time abroad in college, his flight anxiety was really something else. But armed with *The Office* on his tablet, his noise cancelling headphones, and an extra dose of Xanax, he should be able to manage it.

At least, that was the plan he'd worked out with his therapist. Gid refused to ruin this trip for Ari, so he had to manage it.

The downtown holiday lights twinkled as he grabbed his dance bag from the back. When he stumbled upon the Ballroom Club at MSU during freshman year, he hoped that he'd found something to replace the structured dance classes of his youth and his forgotten dream of professional dance. He'd been right; and he also found a partner and best friend in Ari Callaghan, who just also happened to be his hallmate in the dorms.

Gid kicked his way through the soft, fluffy snow as flakes settled on the tips of his brown loafers. He pulled open the door to Salt Cellar, greeted by the noise of happy hour and the bounding chorus of *All I Want for Christmas Is You* by Mariah Carey.

There was no escaping the damn song this time of year, so Gid counted himself lucky that he loved it. Years ago, Ari and Gid had come up with a swing routine for it. Could they dig it up out of their brains and practice it tonight? He'd suggest it. It would be a perfect routine to put up on their TikTok.

With a smile on his face, he swung into a big, cushy seat at the bar and placed his bag on the open one next to him, reserving it for Ari. Despite his fears of being late, he still managed to arrive five minutes early.

"Gideon!" Camden called, drawing out each vowel of his name as she slid in front of him across the bar, slinging down two holiday drinks menus without asking.

As best friend to Ari's middle brother and manager of Salt Cellar, Camden Kirby was well familiar with the duo's weekly routine.

"How's it going, Cam?" Gid asked, picking up a menu and giving it a quick scan.

"Great." She shrugged, gesturing around at the bar packed full of folks decked out in varying shades of ugly sweaters. "Ugly Sweater Night is a hit. I can't complain."

"It's genius. I wish I had thought to wear mine," he said, thinking of his *Die Hard* themed sweater that Ari had gifted him the year before. "These cocktails all look delicious. I'll do the Egg Noggin' Martini and a Hot-Mamacita-Chocolate Martini for Ari. Punny names."

"I know." Cam rolled her eyes as she began pulling together the drink ingredients. "For some unknown reason, I let Angus help me name the holiday drinks. The man named his food truck *Bovine Intervention* for crying out loud. I should have known what I was getting myself into. But people seem to like them anyway." She laughed. "You all set for the trip?"

The trip, the trip, the trip. There were so many ways to answer that question.

In a theoretical sense, he'd been ready for this trip for years, dying to go abroad with Ari since he spent a semester in London during their junior year.

Practically, he'd been completely packed for at least a week.

In reality, his travel anxiety made it so that, no, he was never "all set" for any trip. Not really.

"Danny hasn't shut up about it for weeks," Camden continued, ignoring, or completely missing, Gid's pause. "Neither has Lacey. When your two best friends start dating each other, you get to hear everything twice."

"Lucky you," Gid said, happy that she moved on quickly from her question.

"Lucky me alright." Cam slid the two drinks across the bar. A frosted gingerbread cookie poked out of his martini, while a Pirouette cookie straw stuck out of Ari's.

"Let me know if you need anything else," she said with a wink before sliding down the bar to the next patron.

Gid lifted his drink and took a sip, pleasantly surprised at how well the flavors balanced. His phone vibrated, the final reminder for the evening. He picked it up to cancel the alarm then immediately called Ari.

THREE
ARI

WHOOSH. Ari's phone buzzed just as she picked it up from the cupholder in the middle console of her ancient Toyota Corolla.

The little words flashed across the screen: **Notification of Academic Probation Conference.**

Well, that was quick. It hadn't even been a couple hours since her grades populated in the online portal and already they were summoning her. While her academic advisor had prepared her for this, it didn't soften the blow.

"Jesus, Mary, and Joseph," Ari swore, as she dropped her phone in her lap and banged her steering wheel. The curse came from her Catholic grandmother and was the only thing that truly hit the spot when she was upset.

Ari's vision danced with pulsing black spots. *This can't be fucking happening.*

This, in that she couldn't believe she was on the edge of getting kicked out of her MBA program.

This inconvenient little panic attack thing she couldn't shake since the one-year anniversary of her dad's death.

Just over a year now and, *god*, that wound was still so fresh. Ari curled her hands around the wheel, willing away the pain as usual. She wasn't ready to heal. Healing meant moving on and she wasn't fucking ready for that.

A tense laugh clawed its way up her throat before it curdled on her tongue. The sour taste of bile followed close behind like clockwork. She coughed. Swallowed. Took a sip of water from her emotional support water bottle. Still, tart.

A tinny alarm blared to life on her phone—*Dance Gid*, it announced—the perky little reminder of where she was meant to be at this moment. In the next second, her phone rang.

Her contact picture of Gid—eating a hot dog while dressed in that hot dog costume at last summer's Fourth of July Fireworks and Barbecue Bonanza—burned her retinas before she swiped to answer.

"You're late," he said on the other end.

"I'm fixing my lipstick in the parking lot."

Sorta true. Her signature berry-colored lipstick did need fixing. Emotional breakdown came first though.

"Come on, Ari, I'm waiting for you. I've got a chair and a drink both with your name on it," Gid sang into the phone.

She opened her mouth, on the cusp of spilling the beans to him. Telling him everything.

Except the words got lost along the way. She hadn't told anyone about her spectacular academic failures and now wasn't the time, the evening before their first trip abroad and Thomas's wedding weekend. No way. The last thing Ari wanted was the spotlight to be on her for yet another epic fiasco.

"You think this snow is going to delay our flight out tomorrow?" He asked before she could say anything else.

Forget Ari's issues, she had Gid's real life travel anxiety to contend with and it snapped her back to reality.

"Don't be ridiculous." Ari sandwiched her cellphone against her shoulder as she slid out of the car and bumped the door shut with her hip.

"I'm not," came Gid's matter of fact reply from the other end. "Snow can be a real issue for planes. Like, what if it skids down the runway during takeoff?"

She could barely hear him over the bar noise in the background. Starling Hills came alive around the holidays, everyone going out and celebrating despite the cold and snow. And Salt Cellar Distillery was one of the town's most popular spots.

Tutting into the phone, Ari wrenched open the backseat door and grabbed her dance bag.

"Tomorrow's going to be fine," she repeated for the umpteenth time, gazing up at the sky. Huge snowflakes dropped from black clouds high above. Maybe Gid had a point. *As long as the weather holds off.*

Forget skidding off the runway, she just didn't want to contend with delays. Their trip was one week and planned down to the minute. After the wedding weekend, Ari and Gid were taking the train from Dublin southwest to County Cork for the rest of their trip: staying at a guest-house cottage on a working Christmas tree farm and pygmy goat sanctuary. She couldn't wait for the precious little goats.

"Ari," Gid sighed. "I'm sure it will be but I'm letting you know I'm going to need continued reassurance, okay?"

She could just picture him fidgeting at the bar, perched on a chair and playing with the cardboard coaster.

Colorful Christmas lights crisscrossed the back alley and decorated the trees of the downtown, sparkling like a million tiny jewels. Her small hometown really showed off around the holidays and she freaking loved it. The festive, lit up Main Street was what she missed most about living in Starling Hills. Everdale was only the town over, but she wished she could waltz under these lights anytime she wanted. Distance, and her way-too-busy MBA program, made her little dream impossible. Thank goodness for holiday break.

Gid's travel anxiety was pretty ironic considering how well traveled the guy was. But she supposed it was more the anticipation of the unknown than anything else, worrying about everything lining up just so. She could understand that. That feeling had been creeping up on her more lately, too. But not in regards to her travel plans.

No, their trip was a break from her real life, from worrying about her degree and her future. Whatever support Gid needed, she'd be that for him.

"That's what best friends are for," she said as she yanked open the backdoor of the red, brick building. Warm, yeasty air gust her long, dark brown hair back off her shoulders. "I'm really excited you're coming to Thomas's wedding with me. It's going to be great. Easy."

"Well, I don't need you to outright lie to me."

"I'm not. I *believe* it. I *know* it, Gid," she said as walked down the narrow back hall and into the bar proper, the roar of ugly-sweater clad happy hour goers pelting her in the face.

The abrupt warmth of the bar sent a flush across her cheeks. Ari unwrapped her cashmere scarf as she clacked across the lovingly-restored original hardwood in her knee-high boots.

"That's," Gid said in her ear and, spinning around in his high-back bar chair, to her face, "why you're the optimist in this friendship."

Ari's stomach burned red hot. Her optimism. Something that everyone seemed to love about her, and yet was the very thing that was becoming more and more difficult to access.

She almost let her smile slip. *Almost*. She almost word-vomited everything right then and there. *Almost*. But she refused to let anything ruin the first international trip she'd be taking with Gid. Especially when he was already so worked up about it.

Ending the call, she threw her scarf over the back of the chair and flung herself into the seat next to Gid. "Hey."

"Hey yourself." He nudged a chocolate martini toward her. "It's good to see you. And I'm sorry my travel anxiety is being a jerk."

"Ah yes it's been," she consulted her watchless wrist, "approximately 36 hours since we last convened but, it's good to see you, too. And go fuck yourself, *travel anxiety*."

Ari wrapped her black painted fingernails around the stem of her drink and they toasted. "To a perfect Christmas in Ireland."

Gid made a feeble attempt to stifle his groan before sipping his eggnog martini.

Ari tried her drink, eyeing her friend over the rim. She'd never quite gotten used to seeing him in his work clothes. Pressed chinos, collared button down. A far cry from his nerdy graphic tees and jeans in college.

"Mmm there's cinnamon in this, too," she said. "Cam's a friggin genius. Though your drink seems sus."

"Don't knock it 'til you try it."

Ari wrinkled her nose. "Housemade eggnog? No thanks. I'm morally opposed to drinking eggs."

"You're missing out." Gid shrugged. "Listen, I know I wasn't your first choice for this trip. I know Zahra would have been more fun. Less anxious." He grimaced.

He wasn't wrong: Zahra had been the first to come to mind as her plus one. But Ari had two best friends and no partner to bring. The final decision had been easy, mostly because Zahra couldn't leave Folklore for a week around the holidays.

"I need you to buck up, buttercup. We're going to my darling oldest brother's wedding, and staying at a literal Christmas tree farm, Gideon, for crying out loud!" Ari said. "If you're not excited about that, there's no hope for you."

It was Ari's turn to shrug and look smug. Pretend that her own stomach wouldn't stop fluttering, except her anxiety was about something else entirely.

A holiday wedding would never be her choice for a wedding, if she ever decided to get married (not likely). Since they were coordinating eleven people total including a couple of business owners, a graduate student, and three Contrakale employees, it was the logical choice to have it over Christmas—especially since they wanted to do it abroad. Not that Ari particularly agreed. But it wasn't her wedding. She was just meant to be there for the happy couple.

"Now the Christmas tree farm I *am* excited about. Wedding, too. I'm not a monster," Gid said.

"Good, because you had me worried for a sec."

"It's just the whole getting there that bothers me."

"Well, it'll be fine. Because we'll be together. Alright?" She put her pinky in the air for a promise.

"Ugh, Ari…" Gid moaned, dramatically rolling his eyes before hooking his pinky to hers.

"Gid," she said, staring him down. "I pinky promise I got you, yeah? Like before all our competitions. I'm right at your side."

Ari had started the pinky promise tradition before their first competition as ballroom partners freshman year of college. The guy usually put on a cool as a cucumber front, but when the stakes were high, he couldn't quite shake the nerves.

"Honestly, I'm glad you're coming with me. I don't know if I could do it without you," Ari sighed, swinging her stool toward Gid.

"What are you talking about?" He furrowed his brow. The way he got a deep crease between his eyebrows was very endearing.

"It's just…holidays." Ari bit her cookie straw.

Gid nodded. She knew that he knew what she really meant: she was thinking about her dad.

Ari was happy for Thomas though, really, she was, but something about this one stung. Probably because he was the first of their siblings to officially tie the knot and their dad wasn't here to celebrate. She once thought that grief had been gentle to her, more gentle than it was for her brothers. That she'd already grieved Dad while he was going through his sickness. But in the last year, she learned that grief was a fickle beast that snuck up when least expected.

Gid leaned closer to Ari, putting a hand on her knee and squeezing. "Listen: you're here for me, and I'm here for you. Pinky promise, right?"

"Yes, okay."

He patted her knee once and then pulled his warm palm away.

"What do you want to work on tonight?" Gid asked, sipping his cursed martini. "We could dig up that old *All I Want for Christmas is You* routine?"

Ari laughed. "Oh god, that was...from—"

"The first year we danced together, yep."

"One of our first competitions, right?"

"*And* we came in first place. That easy," Gid said, his voice smooth in the warm bar lighting.

"That easy." Ari shivered, the memory warming her from the inside out.

She considered his question. The week leading up to holiday break had been rough. Finals, papers, presentations, and one horrible meeting with her academic advisor. Ari was barely willing to face up to the repercussions herself, let alone talk about it. Her insides vibrated as she remembered the email that zoomed into her inbox less than half hour ago.

No, she needed to let loose. She didn't need structure

or routine. Ari needed to clear her head before the weekend with her family.

"Mmm…I don't think I really want to work on anything specific. I've been working on school shit all week. Let's just do some improv? Then Mariah."

"Sounds good," he said, sipping his drink. "Got your grades then?"

"Yeah." Ari swallowed, pointedly ignoring his gaze.

Gid frowned when she didn't elaborate. She knew he caught the hesitation behind her words. They'd been so close since they met freshman year of college and now they could read each other like a book. For better or for worse. And he knew when he shouldn't push it—like right now. She wasn't ready to talk about it. She wasn't even ready to think about it.

"Improv it is, then," he said after reading the room and dropping further discussion of Ari's grades.

They finished their drinks just as the live music started up. Loading their arms up with their winter layers and bags, Gid leaned toward Ari's ear.

"You doing okay, pop tart?" He'd called her that since freshman year, when she had a frosted cherry Pop-Tart every day for breakfast.

She considered for a moment admitting out-loud the failure that she'd barely been able to admit to herself… That she likely wouldn't be returning to her business program next semester and graduate with the rest of her cohort, thanks in large part to her grief.

She couldn't believe that her dad was gone. Life just went on without him. He wouldn't be there when Thomas got married this weekend, and he wouldn't be there for any other future milestones in the Callaghan's lives.

Gid had been there through all of it. He supported her through Dad's sickness and death but she didn't want to ruin anything. She didn't want to mar this weekend. It would already be hard enough for her to put it all aside and enjoy.

"I'm fine."

He watched her, waiting for her to say something else, but nothing came out. "You know you can tell me what's going on, right?"

"Of course I do. But there's nothing going on, Gid."

"You know I know when you're lying right?"

"I wish you could take a break from being a perceptive, supportive best friend and let me live in my delusion."

"What would your therapist have to say about that?" He asked, holding the door open to the back stairs that led to the floor up and the dance studio.

"My therapist would say boundaries are healthy." *But, then again, she doesn't know the half of it.*

Admittedly, Ari had been slightly less than open with her therapist since she started going in the spring.

He chuckled warmly. "I'm not sure that applies here, Ari."

She paused halfway up the stairs, turning around to

face him. With Gid two stairs below her, they were nearly the same height.

"I just want Thomas to have a perfect weekend. I want you to have fun. I don't want anyone worrying about me and my fuck ups," she said.

And that right there was the real problem, because everything Ari touched turned to ash. If not at first, at least eventually. She couldn't seem to get around it. She wouldn't mess up this weekend for Thomas and the rest of her family.

Gid furrowed his brow, concern washing over his face.

"That, right there." She circled a finger in the air in front of his face. "None of that."

"Hmph."

"Come on," she groaned. "I need to move."

She stomped up the rest of the stairs and into the studio, finally feeling a sense of peace wash over her after the world's longest week.

FOUR
GID
THEN

THE FRAT HOUSE smelled like sweat and bad decisions. Or, more specifically, too much cologne and stale beer.

Honestly, Gid didn't even really want to be here. His buddy from high school dragged him along to the party, keen to rush the frat, and then promptly ditched him when he got sucked up into some brotastic mingling.

Gid filled his red plastic cup with lukewarm, foamy beer. He took a sip, forcing down the room temperature drink with a grimace. The keg was upstairs, hidden in some guy's room, and the rest of the party got cans of Milwaukee's Best—arguably not the best beer he'd ever tasted. Whatever was in his cup wasn't much better. But, he had to admit, it was doing its job.

Usually a little awkward, the beer was Gid's social lubricant. He moseyed down the stairs to check out the actual party away from the sausage fest upstairs and a squeal of laughter caught his attention over the booming bass of the electronic music.

Across the room, a girl clutched two cans of beer to her chest and howled with her head thrown back. Raven hair cascaded down her back in large, soft curls. A black body con dress hugged all of her curves and Gid instantly wanted to talk to her. But a sea of sweaty bodies separated them and she was beelining it to the dance floor.

Curiosity piqued, he followed her, trying not to lose track of her and her friends as the crowd thickened. His sneakers stuck to the floor, and he couldn't imagine how all of the ladies managed in their sky-high heels.

Gid found her and her gaggle of friends giggling and wiggling to the beat of the music. Taking a sip of his liquid courage, he stepped up to her to introduce himself.

"Hi," he said, bending into her ear.

"Oh my god!" She jumped, turning around and putting a hand to her chest as she laughed. "Jesus, didn't expect someone *right* behind me." She smacked his arm playfully.

Something warm and gooey constricted low in his abdomen at her instantly playful flirtiness.

He swallowed, nervous. While he wasn't great chatting anyone up, he knew if he could get her to dance with him, he might have a chance.

"I'm Gid, what's your name?"

"Ari." She smiled. Her berry painted lips split into a wide smile. "What's up?"

Behind her, he noticed her friends spying on them indiscreetly. One of them, a Black girl with long cornrows, nudged Ari and she stumbled forward. Gid caught her, her hand clutching his forearm.

"Oh my god." She grit her teeth, turning over her shoulder and giving her friends a face that made them all cackle. "Don't mind my friends, they're absurd."

"It's fine," Gid shouted over the music. "I was going to ask you to dance anyway."

"Well in that case…" Ari passed off her extra beer and slid her hand down his arm to lace her fingers with his, immediately twirling herself and leading them away from her friends.

When she picked a spot, she leaned back into him. They swayed a little to the Skrillex remix before Ari pushed up onto her tiptoes to get closer to his ear. "Are you a good dancer, Gid?"

Her warm breath on his neck sent goosebumps down his arms. "I am."

Ari quirked an eyebrow. "How about you show me?"

With one fluid movement, Gid spun her around, pulling her close to him. His palm cradled her lower back and they bounced to the beat. Once they got used to the feel of each other, he slid a hand down her arm and took her hand before spinning her away from him. He registered the look of surprise on her face before curling her body back to his. As much as he wanted to keep her close, now with her backside shaking against him, he wanted to impress her even more. Finally put those years of dance class to a productive use.

He laughed to himself and Ari turned her head over her shoulder before spinning herself quickly away. Now they danced face to face, still connected by their joined hands.

"What are you laughing about?"

He read her lips more than heard the words she said.

Gid dipped to the shell of her ear. "I was just thinking that all those years of dance classes have finally paid off."

"Oh?"

"Yeah." He nodded to her before pulling her closer.

It was hard to have a full conversation while the music was so loud, otherwise he would tell her about the years he spent in his home studio honing his craft. Of the time he invested at the gym, perfecting his tumbling stunts. How he almost followed his dream of studying dance, but ultimately ended up in the College of Agriculture & Natural Resources.

Instead, he held those words back and focused on the music, how her body felt against his. Under his fingertips, Gid could almost sense her movements before she made them. Too soon, the song ended and Ari pulled her warmth away.

"Are you hungry?" she asked, grinning.

Now that she mentioned it, he was. "Starving."

"Come on," she said, before chugging the rest of her

beer, crushing the can, and throwing it on the floor just like the rest of the frat boys did.

Ari gestured in a complicated series of hand motions to her friends and they waved to her, their laughter lost to the music.

Huh.

She led them through the frat house and out onto the sidewalk. Even from outside, the thumping bass of the music vibrated up through his legs.

"Oh my god," Ari laughed, pulling her hair over her shoulder, her perfume wafting toward him. "I'm sweating like a pig."

Her words sounded fuzzy in his ears, still buzzing from the loud speakers. "Feels good out here, though."

It was a gorgeous end of summer night. Cool with a sweet breeze that inexplicably smelled like bonfire.

"Definitely." Ari marched toward Grand River Avenue, clearly on the hunt for drunk food. "I think I hate frats. I don't even know why I let my friends drag me there."

"Free beer?" Gid shrugged, affecting casual. The sandalwood of her perfume still clung to his senses.

She curled her lip up. "But is Milwaukee's Best even worth it if it's free?"

"Fair point."

"Oh, you're not rushing are you?"

"Nah. My friend dragged me along, too."

"You're good people, Gid," she said, swinging her arms wide and spinning as they walked, still dancing. "The

dancing was fun though,"—she shot a finger gun at him—
"and you're cute."

Gid's stomach swooped like a lovesick teenager.
Which, he supposed, he technically still was, despite how
much like an *adult* he felt. Being away at college was kind
of a mindfuck like that.

"What food are you in the mood for?" Gid asked,
veering the subject back to the task at hand.

"Pizza," Ari groaned from somewhere deep within her.
"A huge, greasy, floppy slice of heaven."

They got their slices from the New York-style pizza
place on the corner and decided to walk and eat.

"Where do you live?" Gid asked as they meandered
along the street.

"Brody," Ari said, mouth full of pizza.

"Oh, same." Had he seen her around? Probably not.
Gid would have noticed a girl—woman—like Ari sauntering around the neighborhood. "What hall?"

"Butterfield."

No fucking way. "*I* live in Butterfield."

"No." Ari stopped and spun around, her hair flying
and perfume wafting. "You're fucking with me."

"I'm not."

"We haven't seen each other around?"

"It's only been a week."

"I guess." Ari narrowed her eyes. "Well, this makes
inviting you back to my room a lot easier, then."

Gid gagged on his last bite of pizza. "Sorry?"

"Gid, come on." She fixed him with a disbelieving stare. "What did you think this was? I clocked you coming down those stairs. I practically masterminded you coming up to talk to me."

"You what?" He swallowed as they continued walking.

Ari tapped her temple. "I used my feminine wiles on you."

"Right."

Gid was very confused. He didn't doubt that a woman like Ari had a sixth sense for getting men to do things—he just wasn't usually the target of such schemes. That he'd even gone up to Ari and introduced himself was very out of character for him. Maybe it was the combination of party atmosphere and shitty beer. Or maybe Ari really was onto something and she'd manifested the entire thing.

"You're cute when you're stunned, did you know that?" Ari laughed over her shoulder as she badged them into the dormitory. "Don't worry." She patted him on the chest. "It's all in good fun, my dude. You're cute, I'm cute, it's freshman year welcome week. Just casual."

Just casual. Yeah, he could do casual. Despite that fact that he'd never done anything *casual* in his life.

Raised by scientists, the *scientific method* had been drilled into his brain long ago. Nothing in his life was coincidental which, he supposed, tracked for how this evening turned out. He cleared his throat.

"You're pretty impressive in those heels," Gid said,

jogging a bit to catch up to Ari as she breezed up the stairs.

"That's what nearly a decade of pointe shoes will do to a girl."

"Pointe?"

"Ballerina all the way." She pirouetted in the middle of the lobby.

Gid laughed. This girl never stopped dancing. "I did ballet growing up, too."

He grabbed her around the waist, making her giggle, and lifted her in the air. As if reading each other's mind, he transitioned to drop her down into a fish dive, resting the bulk of her weight on his quad. Two other students sitting on a bench nearby cheered as they held the pose.

Her weight, her body cradled against his, felt good. Better than he wanted to admit.

"Impressive," Ari said as he put her back on her two feet. "You weren't kidding."

"I'm going to miss it. I got accepted into the University of Michigan School of Music for dance but in the end decided to come to MSU for Packaging Science." And a stone still sat in his stomach, wondering if he made the right choice.

"Wow, talk about a 180." Ari held open the door for the stairwell, following her down to her floor.

Gid shrugged, his fingers still tingling where he gripped her around the waist. "Parents," was all he shared by way of explanation.

"Hmm," she considered. "That makes me sad."

"It makes me sad, too."

They turned right out of the stairwell instead of turning left, like Gid would have done. "Huh, I live at the other end of this floor."

Their rooms were at the complete opposite end of a long hallway, which would explain why they hadn't crossed paths yet. There were a lot of people in the hall and everyone was in and out over the Welcome Week trying to figure out books and their schedule and how the cafeteria worked.

She looked back at him over her shoulder. "This night just keeps getting weirder."

Ari swiped her keycard into the slot on her door. "Why did you do it, then? Or, didn't do it I guess?"

"Dance?"

"Mmhm," she said as she flicked on the soft LED lights strung around the room.

"I don't know." He really didn't know now why he made that decision. Something at the time seemed smart and economical about it. Not that his parents were much help. They were just pleased he picked something more *secure* and *certain* than a Bachelor of Fine Arts in Dance. But he didn't want to trauma dump all that on Ari. "Seemed right at the time."

"Hmm," Ari hummed again as she hung her purse on a hook by the door. She pulled her cherry chapstick from the tiny bag, coating her lips over her faded lipstick.

Gid looked around at their setup. "Whoa, y'all got this put together quick."

A set of bunk beds and New York City Ballet poster on one side and a matching set of dressers and desks and Pulp Fiction poster on the other split the space neatly between two people.

"I'm rooming with my best friend, Zahra, the beautiful Black woman that was with me at the party?" Ari sighed, flopping back on her bed—the bottom bunk—her short, high-heeled legs kicking off the end. "We had time to coordinate."

Gid remembered her. "I roomed blind. Our room looks disheveled. Basically as one would expect two eighteen-year-old guys' room to look."

Ari frowned. "I'm sure it's not that bad."

"You haven't seen it yet."

There wasn't really anywhere else for Gid to sit other than a bean bag in the corner, and he didn't want to plop down on that considering what Ari had planned. Or, he assumed she still planned. He'd had sex before but never a random hook up like this. What an introduction to college life.

"Come here," Ari said, seeming to sense his hesitation. She patted the bed next to her.

But he had another idea before getting down on the bed with her.

With one step closer, her heeled shoes brushed his pants leg. With another movement, his hand slid up her calf, feeling the sculpted muscle from years of dance work. Maintaining eye contact, he kneaded into the bulk of the muscle, knowing, despite what she said, that hours in those shoes wouldn't feel great on her legs.

While he worked, his other hand slipped off both shoes, dropping them to the floor one by one. His thumb massaged into her arches. Ari bit her lip and dropped her head back and groaned, a delicious sound that he couldn't wait to hear again later.

As he made his way up her leg, he spotted a tattoo on the inside of her left ankle. "What's this?"

"My Eeyore tattoo." She smiled. "I just got it for my eighteenth birthday."

"Eeyore?" A surprising choice for a tattoo, he thought.

"Eeyore is life," she said very seriously.

He hummed before bending down to kiss the tattoo. Under his lips, her tendons and muscles flexed.

"Get in the bed, you monster," Ari demanded as she scooted up towards the head, making room for Gid.

"Monster?" he laughed, diving right in. Framing her body with his own, Gid held himself upright over her and smiled.

"What?" she asked.

He shook his head, feeling silly and embarrassed and powerful because she wanted *him*, all at the same time.

"Is this real life?" He whispered.

"You betcha," Ari said, arching her chest up toward him as she readjusted her position.

Gid stared down at her, her warm, brown eyes watching him back as her chest rose and fell with each breath.

They'd met just a couple hours ago, but he hadn't had this much fun with someone in a while. Which was pretty sad considering he'd met a ton of new people since moving in and had been partying all week.

But Ari was different, easygoing. He didn't have to put on some macho sports guy facade or pretend he was enjoying the shitty light beer and questionable atmosphere of a frat party. Hell, he didn't even tell most people about dance or how he had been accepted at Michigan and turned it down.

"You can kiss me now," Ari said softly and he imagined that all of those thoughts had just played over his face. She grabbed lightly onto his forearms, running her thumbs up and down, encouraging him.

Gid dipped down, but instead of going right for the kiss, he nuzzled her neck, right under her ear. "God, you smell fantastic, Ari."

And she did. Her scent was immediately addictive; a creamy woodsy smell, like a leather-bound notebook. He envisioned her backstage just before a performance, wearing a tutu and her pointe shoes and smelling exactly like this.

"Mmm," she responded, pushing up into him, asking —almost begging—him for more.

When their lips met, it was soft, the taste of cheese pizza mixed with her cherry chapstick.

Hesitant at first, it didn't take long for Gid to push his tongue into her mouth, meeting hers. As he settled his weight between her legs, her nails dug into his biceps. His insides roared in response.

God, he wanted to know this girl. Not just physically, but actually. He wondered how he got so lucky this evening. How she'd spotted him across the room and picked *him*. Gid wasn't anything special, but here with Ari, he felt significant.

Shifting his position, Gid slipped a hand along Ari's side. Her body curved into his touch until his palm met the bare skin of her thigh. She broke their kiss and a giggle escaped her lips. It was the sweetest sound Gid had heard in a long time. He wanted to bottle that laugh up to take out the next time he had to sit through an awkward dinner with his parents.

"Ticklish," she whispered.

Gid hummed in response, wondering where else she was sensitive.

The dress bunched over his wrist as he continued his exploration higher up to her panty line, kissing her neck and nestling into her hair as he did so.

"Should we—" his voice cracked as he tried to whisper and then cleared his throat, "take off some clothes?"

Ari sighed, her voice still tinged with laughter. "Yes. I'm ready if you are."

Gid thought she could tell exactly how ready he was as his erection rubbed against her thigh, but he appreciated the consent check all the same.

"Yes," he breathed.

Sitting back onto his knees as best as he could on the bottom bunk, he pulled his button down and undershirt off in one motion over his head. Ari reached up, hooking her fingers into his belt loops.

Just as their lips met again, the overhead fluorescent lights blinded Gid and laughter flooded the room.

"Oh my god!" someone squealed. Gid had no idea who. It could have been him.

The next moment, Gid toppled off the bed, sprawling shirtless onto the floor as Ari laughed. "Are you okay?"

"Jesus, Ari, ever heard of using the door chain? Putting a sock on the handle? Anything to warn a girl." A Black girl, who must be Ari's roommate, stood in the door frame.

"Well, I didn't think you'd be back already, Zahra," Ari said as she wiggled her dress down in the bed.

Gid lay, dazed and exposed in the middle of the floor. Zahra picked her way across the room and lent a hand to help him up.

"I'm Zahra, Ari's roommate. You're the frat boy?" she asked.

"Oh, uh." Gid ran a hand through his fluffy, brown hair. "No, not a frat boy. I'm Gid. I actually live in this hall, too. Other end of the floor."

Zahra looked him up and down. "You're cute. He's cute, Ari."

Ari stood and passed him his shirt. "I know right?"

"Wanna watch a movie?" Zahra asked, plopping down onto a bean bag and pulling a burrito from her purse.

Gid pulled on his shirt. *The mood is officially dead.*

Ari looked back and forth between her roommate and Gid. "Umm, sure, hold on let me change."

This night had certainly taken a turn. Gid's mind and body were still in bed, halfway into Ari's panties.

Ari, however, was halfway changed into a pair of flannel Eeyore-patterned pajama pants and a white tank top, putting everything on over her black dress before slipping it off from underneath in an impressive feat.

"Do you want to stay? Watch a movie?" Ari asked as Zahra scrolled Netflix.

Presto chango, Gid thought, as she whipped her hair into an impressively high and large top knot. A perfectly messy bun that only years of ballerina-ing could have perfected.

"I think I'll go," Gid said, still reeling from whiplash. She had invited him to hang out, but in the harsh overhead light, with her roommate unwrapping her burrito, he felt too embarrassed to stay.

"Okay. If you're sure... You know you're more than welcome to stay." Ari raised her eyebrows in a kind of apology as she plucked a pack of cherry Pop-Tarts from a box on her desk.

"Yeah, stay!" Zahra yelled through a mouthful of burrito.

Ari rolled her eyes and shook her head before pulling Gid out the door. She nearly shut it behind her. "I'm sorry about that. Roommates. I guess another thing to get used to living in the dorms."

"Don't worry about it." He swallowed. "I had a good night."

"Me too. Thanks for the pizza."

Gid shoved his hands into his pockets. For a moment he wondered if he'd ever see this girl again—but then he remembered they were practically neighbors. He'd make sure to see her again.

"Anytime," he said, a swell of awkwardness cresting inside his chest. He gave her a small smile.

"You are cute," Ari said, stretching up onto her tiptoes to give him a kiss on the cheek. "See you around."

She went back into her room and shut the door behind her. As he walked back to his empty, undecorated room, Ari and Zahra's giggles carried down the hall after him.

FIVE
GID

GID HINGED over at the hips and stretched toward the floor. His palms rest easily flat against the ground. Bouncing his knees, he woke up the muscles in his lower back, tired from the last week sitting in his desk chair. His body was certainly creakier now than it was eight years ago, when he was limber enough to be accepted into the School of Music, able to do a standing backflip as a party trick and competed in ballroom with Ari multiple times per year.

"You're looking crunchy, old man," Ari said, patting him on the lower back.

"Please, I'm twenty-six and sit at a desk all day. This is damn impressive." Gid stood upright, rotating his hips in a circle. "Not everyone can be a professional like you."

Ari pouted. "Professional? You flatter me, Sims."

"Improv first then tonight, pop tart?" Gid asked.

She looked away at his question, or was it the use of the old nickname? He wasn't sure. Instead of responding, she focused on doing up the strap of her little kitten heels.

Ari had been doing this all night, changing the subject without saying a word. Turning away from what was right in front of her. It put distance in between them.

He'd been noticing these kinds of lost moments more and more over the last couple of months. Gid had chalked it up to her grief about her dad that always seemed close these days.

But maybe it was something else. Something that she couldn't, or didn't want to, share with him. After all, he'd been there for everything with her dad. They'd been through thick and thin in their eight years of friendship.

But after a moment, she snapped out of it. "Improv. Just like the old days."

West Coast Swing was the category the two competed in back in college. Improvisational dance was their comfort place and it sparked something warm inside Gid's chest that she wanted to do it tonight.

He stretched his neck and walked in a circle around the room as Ari queued up the music.

The studio smelled of old, polished wood and faintly of musty velvet, reminding him of being backstage before shows, now a scent so wrapped up in his history with Ari. Just the smell of dance, performance. Combined with her signature creamy sandalwood perfume—Le Labo's Santal 33—the memories transported him... Beyond the dull work week he'd had. Outside of wondering why he hadn't heard from his parents in the days leading up to Christmas (admittedly, they hadn't heard from him either). Away from this lingering feeling of loneliness he just couldn't shake no matter how many Bumble dates he went on.

Ari twirled over to the sound system on her little ballroom heels, the movement looking effortless as always.

"I've been re-watching videos of Taylor Swift's "Willow" set," she said. "I just love how witchy the whole thing is. The vibes are too theatrical for any of my burlesque routines, but I think it would work well for swing."

"Perfect."

Of course, he knew what she was talking about. The two had seen *The Eras Tour* concert film twice together while it was in theaters after, tragically, missing out on tickets to her Detroit shows. The "Willow" performance was a favorite of his, with Taylor whipping around on stage wearing a velvet green cape like she was casting a spell during each show.

Ari set up Bluetooth for the speaker and moved to the middle of the floor. Gid met her there and they aligned their bodies in their imaginary slot to follow backward and forward through the dance. Typically, Gid led their movements, but they were known to take turns, especially when improvising.

As they settled in, Gid's hand resting on her lower back, Ari nestled her right foot just slightly forward, her non-verbal signal that she was ready to follow where Gid took her.

They had danced as partners so many times it was like another way for them to communicate. Underneath his palm, he could sense the tension writhing through Ari's body, but he didn't know why. She hadn't said anything at Salt Cellar, despite the lingering hints of stress when she wasn't talking. Like the way she fiddled with a straw wrapper, twisting it tighter around the tip of her finger until it turned scarlet red.

But she'd always been like this. Not ready to open up until she was *ready*, and he'd just have to be patient with her. Sometimes, it all amounted to nothing. Just the low level of anxiety that she lived with. Other times, it usually was something to do with her dad's illness.

On her phone, Ari hit play before slipping it into the pocket of her stretchy pants, then placed her hand in Gid's open, waiting one. In his head, Gid finished the eight counts to count them in and in sync, he stepped back with his left foot while Ari followed, stepping forward with her right.

There were a couple ways to improvise in swing. In a lot of competitions, the partners only met moments before when they were randomly paired up. Gid had done that a few times, but it didn't feel the same as when he improvised with Ari. There was a certain thrill to dancing with someone he just met, but after years of practicing and knowing Ari, doing improv with her was like a conversation. They went back and forth, molding their performance together. Over time, they'd developed their own voices as ballroom dancers, contributing something different to their partnered movements.

Gid usually established the anchor for their movements, and Ari, ever the sassier dancer of the two, would maintain the stretch and he would counterbalance. But sometimes, like tonight, she would fight against him.

Like molding invisible Silly Putty, Ari whipped further away from their center. With each turn and tuck, Gid tried in vain to sustain their connection, but it became too stretched and slack. They were barely dancing together anymore—Ari moved in her own world, disconnected from Gid and the teamwork of their dance.

So, he let her go. Releasing his hold on her, Gid let Ari spin away from their slot as she moved with the music to her own routine. A strange mix of all the types of dance she'd learned over the years, Ari contracted and released across the floor. Spiraling through the bridge, emotion radiated off her. Gid stepped back and let her work through whatever was on her mind.

As Taylor sang the last words of the song—*wreck my plans, that's my man*—Ari finished, curling in on herself, as if protecting whatever remained inside after her explosive performance.

"That was impressive, Ari," Gid said softly as the next song started up.

Ari pulled her phone out of her pocket, hitting pause.

"Yeah, well," she said, not really acknowledging his praise.

"You doing okay?" he asked again, raising his eyebrows, watching her through the mirror.

She met his gaze there. "I'm fine." Though her creased forehead resolutely implied that she was not, in fact, fine at all. "Just a lot going on."

"Mmhm." Gid nodded. "Wedding stuff, or?"

She sure wasn't making this easy. Then again, Ari wasn't always an easy person to know. Walking across the floor to her bag, Gid caught her frown in the mirror. She crouched down and took her water bottle out, taking a swig before standing up again.

"Yeah. Wedding stuff. I'm not packed yet either," Ari groaned. "I don't know, I'm sorry. I thought this would help, it's just been a long week. You know how dancing always drags up my sad shit. I'm sorry—I know you said you're nervous about the travel tomorrow and I'm being fucking weird. Sorry."

"Stop saying sorry. You have nothing to be sorry about."

"I'm being weird, and I don't want to be weird. I just want to enjoy our trip."

"Christmas tree farm," Gid sang. "How could we be sad and weird on a Christmas tree farm?"

"That's what I'm saying." Ari pouted. "But I *feel* sad and weird."

"That's okay." Gid opened his arms for a hug and Ari

fell into him. "You know you can always be sad and weird with me."

"I want this to be perfect. Can we just pretend it's going to be perfect?"

Gid pulled Ari in closer under his chin. "Well, knowing Thomas and Julia, the wedding is sure to be perfect. And knowing you, the rest of our trip will be amazing, too. There's nothing to worry about, pop tart."

"And here I thought I was the one that was supposed to be comforting you about this whole travel thing."

"We're partners, aren't we?"

And they had been, since freshman year of college. Meeting at the frat party might have been something that cunning, little Ari Callaghan had masterminded, but what had happened afterward had definitely been a twist of fate.

"Come on," Gid said, unfurling their hug but keeping Ari tucked under his shoulder. "Let's call it a night, eh? Mariah can wait. You have to pack, and I need to..."

Well? What did Gid need to do. Truth was, he had his bag packed since last weekend, his suit already pressed and hanging in his grandpa's old leather garment bag, waiting to be hoisted over his shoulder on the way to the airport.

The only thing he had to do at his one-bedroom apartment was sit and be lonely. It really was sad, if he thought too much about it. And that's why he didn't. Most evenings, he hung out with Ari and Zahra, spent time with the Callaghans, or went to after-work happy hour with Susan and Julia. Of course, there were also the nights when he tried his hand at online dating, but that only served to make things feel worse.

"...shave my neck beard," he finished.

Ari bust out a laugh. "Neck beard? Please, you couldn't grow a neck beard if you tried."

"Excuse me!" he gasped in faux offense. "Just because my facial hair doesn't grow in as fast as Danny's or thick as Thomas's, doesn't mean I can't grow it at all," he said.

But he wasn't offended. He didn't care about facial hair, or his inability to grow it. Ari had laughed and that's what mattered. The energy around her shifted again toward *happy*, or at least, *okay for now*. If she didn't want to talk about what was really going on, that was *okay for now*. Tomorrow they were going on their first international trip together and real life could wait.

GID UNLOCKED the door to his apartment and kicked his shoes into the pile near the front door. He hit the light on with an elbow, squinting at the harsh daylight bulb. Changing it out to a softer, warm glow was on his to do list, but seeing as he tried to spend as little time as possible at his place, that never seemed to get done. Just like getting a shoe rack so that he didn't have a trip-hazard pile right in the entryway. Maybe that could be his New

Year's Resolution: go to Target and buy all the things he'd been putting off for months.

Dropping his duffel at the door, he ambled into the kitchen, which was really just a step from the doorway. The living space was a small, open concept floor plan, with a breakfast bar separating the living room from the kitchen. There wasn't a good place, or even space, for a table. Up the stairs was his lofted bedroom and the one bathroom.

It was a pretty cool place, just outside of downtown Starling Hills and closer to his work, but he hated it. He didn't have much furniture and he hadn't bothered to decorate. Even his freshman year dorm had more personality than this place.

Nudging aside a box of cherry Pop-Tarts, he pulled out a bag of kettle cooked potato chips and French onion dip from the fridge and plopped down on the couch before he opened his text messages. Already, there was one from Ari.

Home. Thanks for tonight. I love our weekly dates. Sorry I'm a grump. Excited for tomorrow

He tsked as he read it. Ari, typically boiling over with contagious optimism, was more than allowed her moments of grumpiness. Especially with him, who had seen the woman at her best—like when they got first place in their ballroom competitions—to her very worst —puking on the sidewalk after too many Long Island iced teas. As her best friend, he liked to think he knew every side of her. Yet still she felt the need to hide and apologize.

Don't apologize, he wrote back. *Can't wait to see you tomorrow.*

I'll be bright eyed and bushy tailed. Promise.

That made him frown again. As much as he tried to convince her that she didn't need to perform for him, she still slipped into that role. The fun-loving, constantly twirling, youngest sibling of the Callaghan family.

He ate a couple more handfuls of chips as he looked at his messages.

He had his parents pinned to the top, but it had been a while since they'd texted. It'd been hard to tell exactly how they felt about his decision to spend Christmas with Ari this year. Maybe because he was in denial that they didn't really care if he was there or not.

The whole holiday could only be described as awkward, but then again, that was his entire relationship with his parents especially since he graduated college. It seemed that in his adult years, they didn't pretend with the rest of their siblings like they used to when he was younger: it had been years since he'd seen any of his cousins. Holidays had became a stilted, formal dinner where Mom catered the food in, busted out her special china and Tiffany crystal wine glasses, and they filled the silence with conversation about work and politics.

The whole thing was in stark contrast to the lively Callaghan dinners he'd grown to love.

Sighing, he stood, gathering his snack off the side table, and shuffled back to the kitchen. The stove clock flashed ten PM. Gid needed to get to sleep if *he* was going to be fresh as a daisy tomorrow.

A zip of anxiety shot through him. Usually, his anxiety wasn't so bad, just a passing thing that he could breathe through, thanks to his daily dose of Xanax. But for some reason travel really got to him. His therapist hypothesized it had something to do with his mom and the way she made everything a crisis, especially when traveling. Family vacations were never exactly fun. Really special that he carried that particular neurosis over into adulthood.

By the time he got through his bedtime routine—face washed, teeth brushed, chapter read on his tablet—his eyelids were appropriately heavy. He turned his bedside sound machine-alarm clock on to brown noise and drifted quickly off to sleep.

SIX
ARI

ARI SAT at the airport bar and swirled the ice in her vodka soda.

"Second drink," she said, smiling.

Gid didn't respond. Not even a little smile. He sat slumped over his bloody mary, picking at the piece of peppered bacon, a little pale and a lot exhausted.

At least Ari was feeling more herself this afternoon: the perky and peppy baby sister that her family expected to land in Dublin. Thankfully a melatonin-induced sleep and a morning of pre-trip apartment cleaning had reset her. For now.

"You doing alright?" she asked Gid.

He grunted in response.

"I'll take that as a no?"

Ari and Gid had booked later flights than the rest of the wedding party, making them the last to arrive in

Ireland. Which was fine with her. She wanted the solo time with Gid before she had to play her part around her family, even if Gid was questionable company at the moment. And Ari loved to be fashionably late to everything.

She looked around her, eyeing the bartender. "Do we need another round, or would that make it worse?"

"Another round," he moaned. "But I also need some food. I'm trying to balance out the queasiness and the need to be knocked immediately to sleep when I hit my seat."

"What! No in-flight movies?" Ari pouted.

He narrowed his eyes at her, the bags under his very apparent.

"For one," he said. "Our first flight is too short for that. And for two, do I look like a man who needs eight hours of movies right now, or eight hours of sleep?"

She pretended to consider the question. "Do you want an honest answer?"

Gid snorted softly through his nose. "No. That tells me everything I need to know."

He fiddled with his bag, once more checking that his noise cancelling headphones and ergonomic neck pillow were packed in his absurdly organized, urban-travel-chic carry-on.

"They're still there, Gid," Ari said, laying her head on his shoulder. "And I'm still here, too."

She sipped the last of her drink and flagged down the

bartender to order another round of drinks and a basket of fries.

"Lunch of champions," Gid said, finishing his drink as well.

"Anyway, by the time we're on the Dublin flight, I predict you're going to wake up somewhere over the Atlantic Ocean with a craving for *The Office* and we can sync up and watch together."

Gid groaned. "Please don't remind me of the massive expanse of water we'll be flying over for most of our trip."

Ari whined guiltily. "Sorry, dude. Honestly, I don't know how you've done so much traveling with this level of anxiety."

"Trust me, I am equally as surprised."

"You didn't have to come, you know. You're making me feel awful." She scrunched her nose and frowned. "I'm not worth all this," Ari said, waving her hand in Gid's general vicinity.

"Ari," Gid said, eyes closed and clenching his glass. "You know you're worth it and I wouldn't be here if I didn't want to be, okay?"

Ari's heart did a little somersault as he said the words, *you know you're worth it*. She didn't, in fact, know that. With each passing day she doubted her worth more and more.

But she wouldn't show it.

"You say that, but your pallor suggests otherwise." Ari

swung back and forth on her barstool, fresh drink in hand.

Gid placed a warm, if a little sweaty, palm on her knee. "Christmas. Tree. Farm."

"You're right. And pygmy goats. We need to keep the endgame in mind."

"And please stop your spinning, you're making me dizzy."

The rest of their wait passed in much the same way: Ari feeling guilty and excited, Gid groaning, and both of them downing drinks until their demeanors had shifted.

Ari, if possible, got more bubbly, damn near vibrating out of her seat. "I think the nerves are kicking in."

"What do you have to worry about?" Gid eyed her, now sitting in a fully upright position.

"Pre-*wedding* jitters." She bounced in her chair. "I'm happy for Thomas and Julia, do not get me wrong on that, but holy hell marriage is a permanent thing."

"Marriage is hardly permanent, Ari. Just ask Zahra about her parents. Or Julia about her engagement, for that matter. They both know exactly how fleeting marriage can be."

"You're right, I just... I don't know. I've never really had a proper relationship, I can hardly conceptualize what it would be like to legally bind myself to someone. Feels permanent from where I'm sitting."

"Just because you survive off a steady diet of one-night-stands doesn't mean the rest of us have problems with commitment," Gid said, crunching on a piece of celery from this drink.

"Wooooow, just call me out like that why don't you!"

"I calls 'em like I sees 'em, Miss I-have-an-Eeyore-tattoo-on-my-ankle."

"Okay, Eeyore is life, I don't know what you're talking about." Ari drained her fourth drink and checked the time on her phone. She groaned. "Frick, it's nearly time to board. Vibe check. How you feelin?"

"Bussin."

"I'm...not sure that's how that's used my dude."

"I work with many solidly Gen Z folks and I'm pretty sure I'm using it the right way."

Ari frowned. "Whatever you say, but we need to skedaddle."

Gid slung his leather garment bag over his shoulder, trim hips swaying effortlessly, as if he did this every day.

Maybe the bloody marys did their trick, exactly as Ari had planned. She didn't want her best friend to sleep through their entire first international flight together. She wanted to order shitty plane food and mini bottles of wine and binge watch *The Office* together while staving off jet lag in, what her mother would probably consider, a highly reckless way.

Though, who were they hurting?

"You coming?" Gid turned, further from Ari than she realized.

She'd been following him on a cloud of vodka soda bliss, lagging behind in a daydream.

He walked backward onto the moving sidewalk, his goofy grin and floppy, fluffy, dark hair making her smile. Ari liked seeing his hair without his usual beanie, but also, she loved the navy one that his grandmother had crocheted for him. It suited him and his black puffer coat.

"Don't make me wait all day, pop tart," he said, still grinning, his one free hand flung out to the side.

And—*oh my god*—did her stomach flip?

No...no, those were feelings she hadn't had since that frat party freshman year of college when she brought Gid back to her dorm. What a disaster that had been.

But any romantic feelings had ended the moment they decided to be ballroom partners. Ari knew exactly what kind of trouble she could get into sleeping with her dance partners. Just ask Mitch, her *pas de deux* partner back in high school that she'd hooked up with and it ruined their partnership faster than she could say *grand jeté*.

There were no *feelings* between her and Gideon Sims, thank Christ, and Ari would very much like for it to stay that way.

If only her body could agree with her brain—because her heart stuttered as she caught up to him and he threw an arm around her shoulders.

What the hell?

"Dare I say it, Ari, but I'm feeling excited." Gid flashed her a lopsided grin, a lock of his hair swooping down across his forehead. He brushed it up before speaking again. "I mean, I know my travel anxiety is still there but it's more like white noise than a megaphone roar. Is that the booze talking?"

"Four drinks may have helped, but I like to think it's my calming presence that's doing the trick."

"You always were my lucky charm," Gid sighed and again that little, confusing flutter set off again in her stomach region.

What the fuck?

They approached their gate which was flooded with other travelers in varying stages of relaxation. It was clear some of them had been sitting there for hours—as long as Ari and Gid had been at the bar—with all of their stuff strewn around them like a mini campsite. Meanwhile others weren't relaxed at all, standing clutching their bags with their arms crossed. Ari spied a couple of families with little kids, a bunch of solo travellers, and a scattering of other couples like themselves.

Well, not couples, she supposed, since *they* weren't a couple. But other *duos*.

"What are the chances we're stuck next to a screaming child?" Gid grumbled out of the side of his mouth.

"Mmm..." Ari looked around, calculating. "I'm going with low."

The kids seemed reasonably aged and there weren't all that many of them.

Gid nodded, eyes narrowed, as if contemplating. "I'll take those odds."

"Flight 6446 Detroit Metro to New York Kennedy is now boarding," called the gate agent over the speaker.

"Perfect timing," Ari squealed.

Immediately, the other travelers surged forward to form some kind of line, Gid and Ari among them. She hated this part the most, the clamoring to get on board. They had checked their bigger bags, so she didn't feel the usual rush to get on board and everything in place. But still—she didn't want to be last either. She wanted to be situated and comfy well before take-off.

It didn't take long for them to find their seats. Ari pulled out her AirPods and tablet before tucking her small backpack under the seat in front of her. Gid armed himself with his noise-cancelling headphones and neck pillow and did the same.

"S'not so bad." Gid sniffed as he did up his seat belt.

Ari didn't bother reminding him that this was just the connecting flight and they still probably had at least twenty minutes before his seat belt was necessary. He had calmed down some and she wanted to keep the good vibes going.

"Excuse me," Ari raised a hand at a flight attendant.

"Yes?"

"My friend is a very nervous flier. Could he possibly get a little something," she mimed a drink impression, "before take-off?"

This trick only worked half the time in Ari's experience, but it was worth a shot.

The flight attendant smiled, her bright red lips curling pleasantly. "Let me see what I can do."

She set off with a wink and Ari settled more deeply into her chair.

"You're something else, you know that?" Gid said, and when she turned to look at him, he had that crooked smile again.

"I think you'd know that by now, Gideon," Ari said, her affected confidence shining through.

"You just continually surprise me, that's all."

And goddamn it if that startling spike of heat didn't lick through her insides.

Get it together, Callaghan.

This was Gid, her best friend for the last eight years and not someone she found on Tinder that she wanted to take home for the night. Except, my god, did that sound appealing all of a sudden.

Gid bounced his leg next to her and through her tights she felt his jeans rubbing up and down. Biting her lip, she tried not to imagine how his quad flexed and released under his clothes. A movement she knew all too well *exactly* how it felt from their years dancing together.

Ari adjusted in her seat, crossing her ankles and leaning on the hip closest to him, effectually removing contact between the two. She rested her elbow on the armrest and head in her hand.

"You need to chill, dude." A statement directed at her travel buddy, but also clearly meant for herself.

Because if they were going to get through this week-long trip unscathed, she needed to expunge all thoughts of hooking up. All completely random and totally unexpected thoughts of hooking up with her best friend.

Just then, the flight attendant returned to their aisle, flashing two miniature bottles of wine at them, one white and one red. "Will these do?"

"This is perfect, thank you," Ari sighed, eager for the distraction.

The attendant whisked away, and Ari passed the white to Gid, knowing his preference between the two. "Chug them before take-off?"

"You're on," Gid said, a look of grim determination on his face.

They unscrewed the lids and tapped the tiny glass bottles together.

"To Ireland," Ari said.

"And to traveling internationally for the first time with my best friend." Gid reached over and squeezed her knee, warmth spreading up her thigh from the epicenter of his palm.

She really wished he would stop doing that. Because if he didn't, Ari couldn't help but think they would both be in deep trouble.

SEVEN
GID

GID PULLED his hand back from Ari's knee, acutely aware of the slight way she stiffened under his touch.

The two were intimately in tune which each other's bodies from years of dancing together and this sudden change surprised him. Back in the terminal, he had put his arm around her shoulders and she tensed up then, too. He had chalked it up to the whole family wedding thing but now it seemed more than that.

Had he done something to make her uncomfortable?

He settled back into his seat and tried not to think about it. Not to think about anything—because if he wasn't thinking about Ari next to him, he focused on his anxiety.

It was always a gamble whether alcohol would make things better or worse for him, but the vodka mixed with the heady excitement of being in a foreign country

77

tomorrow morning and he felt *good*. Because while he hated the actual travel part, Gid loved being abroad, and he hadn't traveled since before the pandemic. When Ari asked him to be her plus one, he didn't think twice about accepting.

"Oh," Ari said, rocking forward as the plane started to move. "Taxi time."

Just then, the overhead safety announcements began and Gid's armpits prickled with sweat. He downed the rest of his mini wine and tucked the glass in the pocket in front of him.

Deep breaths, he repeated to himself, breathing in and out through his nose.

"Want to get those headphones on?" Ari asked softly, placing her cool hand on top of his clammy one that gripped the armrest. "It's gonna be okay, Gid. Pinky promise."

He let out a sound disappointingly like a whine.

"Just hold my hand," she said. Ari laced her fingers with his and she didn't flinch at how literally drenched his palm was. "It's all gonna be fine," she murmured, the hesitation Gid sensed moments ago seemingly gone from her body.

His heart beat fast like a bouncing ping-pong ball.

"Okay," he breathed out, giving her hand a squeeze. "You're a lifesaver, you know that?"

"Oh, I know." She smiled, the corners of her berry lips curling up.

Gid leaned back against the headrest, closing his eyes. "Tell me about what we're doing tomorrow."

"In Dublin, you mean?!" The excitement was clear in her voice. "I can't believe we'll be abroad together in a couple hours. And, of course Thomas and Julia have some kind of welcome cocktails planned, but we have the rest of the day to ourselves."

"Hmm?" Gid raised an eyebrow, eyes still shut tight.

"I want to take you ice skating."

"Ice skating? That sounds very festive," he said, both eyebrows jumping up his forehead. "So, what you're saying is: we should keep the alcohol flowing?"

"What else do you think we're going to do during our JFK layover? We *are* in vacation mode, after all. Hey, look at that." Ari pulled back her hand, tucking it under her thigh, and Gid immediately missed her slim fingers between his. The seatbelt light clicked off above them. "Cruising altitude."

"What?" Gid said, sitting up straight to peer around the plane.

"I distracted you through the whole thing. Dazzled you with my wits. It's a special talent of mine." She shrugged, a little laugh tinging her voice.

Gid wiggled his hips back into his seat, his thigh brushing against Ari's tights. A distraction, indeed. One he hadn't expected, or even, honestly, thought about in years. That one night freshman year had been the exception to their otherwise very platonic friendship.

But all of a sudden, he thought, there was something creeping back to the surface between them. That attraction they'd agreed to bury all those years ago in favor of being dance partners.

That was Ari's rule: if they were going to dance together, they were not, under any circumstances, going to sleep together. He understood it, of course, as she explained that she'd been down that road with her *pas de deux* partner in high school with disastrous results. He wasn't about to be that guy; Gid respected Ari and her choices.

Now though, the wicked twinkle in her eye and her body language hinted that he wasn't the only one feeling this *thing* unfurl between them. But what he couldn't decipher was how dangerous it would be to act on it.

Ari, for her part, had always insisted that one-night-stands were her preferred flavor of relationship—and so far she'd stuck to that pattern. She'd had some consistent hook-ups over the years, especially in college, but it never became more serious than a "u up?" text after a night at the bars.

Gid, meanwhile, was strictly a monogamous kind of guy. He had a girlfriend through high school, who broke his heart when they ultimately decided to go to different schools and she refused to do long distance. Which, after a while, he could see was the right decision.

In college, he met and dated his next girlfriend for five years. Since that break-up over a year ago when he was ready for the next step and she wasn't, he'd dated a little bit but was mostly resigned to being single.

This though…this was new.

"Uh oh. You have your thinking face on, Gid." Ari pulled out one of her AirPods, pausing *The Office* episode on her tablet. She was watching the Christmas ones, like she did every year, to get in the holiday spirit.

"It's nothing," he said, shifting in his seat and trying to school his features into something less serious.

Which was more difficult than it should have been. Uncontrollable butterflies swarmed through his abdomen when Ari leaned toward him and her long, dark hair tickled his forearm. A movement that had happened a thousand times before, suddenly charged with electricity.

"Just trying to figure out what to watch," Gid grumbled, fumbling with his headphones.

"Don't think too hard." Ari sat upright, not unlike a prairie dog, scanning the plane. "I want to find that very courteous flight attendant and see if she can sneak us some more wine before this flight is over."

Unbuckling her seat belt, she popped up. "Be right back," she said with a wink.

When she stepped down the aisle, Gid let out a breath, slouching down in the seat. Out of her immediate vicinity, he could breathe and try and untangle this sudden change in dynamic.

He had to blame it on the international travel. In his

experience, it always shook things up inside him that he let lie dormant in his normal, boring life.

But did that mean that he'd harbored feelings for Ari all this time and hadn't realized it? He wasn't sure if that made him pathetic or a good friend.

Admittedly, Gid had to be blind not to notice Ari. She had a soft, lithe dancer's body, long, shiny dark hair, brown eyes that drank up everything in sight, and a beautiful smile that could melt the iciest heart—and had melted his many times over the years.

But it was the way she held herself that struck him most. As if she was always the most important person in the room, whether she believed it at the moment or not.

"Mission accomplished," Ari sang as she plopped back into her seat. "I think the holiday spirit has definitely gotten to that one. She even gave me some Biscoff cookies."

Gid groaned greedily, his appetite was always insatiable when he drank. "What an angel."

"Her or me?" Ari laughed.

Gid considered. "Both."

"That's the right answer. And for that I'll share my wine and cookies."

The rest of the flight passed much the same. Their entire three-and-a-half hour layover, too.

Jokes and *The Office* and, in the end, he lost count of the number of mini bottles of wine—and cookies—they consumed over the Atlantic. They even both got in a little nap. When he opened his eyes, Ari's head had tipped down onto his shoulder. He didn't dare move a muscle for the two more hours she slept, lest he disturb her.

When the announcement to prepare for landing came over the speakers, Gid's anxiety hadn't overwhelmed him once which meant he was in high spirits upon deplaning.

All I Want For Christmas Is You blasted through the Dublin Airport terminal once they made it through customs. Massive, twinkling snowflakes, strings of multi-colored lights, and decorated trees welcomed them to Ireland.

"We're here," Ari breathed. "Can you believe it?"

"Hardly. And in one piece, too."

"Travel anxiety? Don't know her. I give you a solid B for that flight."

"B?! What did you mark me down on?"

"The beginning, before the wine, when you wouldn't settle. Definite demerit on your grade."

"Ouch."

"I calls 'em like I sees 'em, Gid." Ari twirled under the terminal's sparkling lights, her backpack firmly in place. "It's magical."

"It's just the airport, Ari."

"*Just* the airport? Airports are magical," she sighed dreamily. "Imagine what the rest of Dublin is like. The Irish countryside..."

Gid had to laugh. Yes, she was the optimist in this friendship, through and through. But he couldn't forget how she danced the other night, so raw and...pained, if he was being honest about it. He wouldn't, and couldn't, ever force Ari to talk, but there was definitely something brewing under the surface that she was categorically ignoring, either for his sake or her own. He couldn't tell. Maybe both.

"Come on, Gid, you old grump." She looped her arm through his and pulled him along. "Our baggage awaits."

"I am not a grump."

"You're sometimes a grump."

He furrowed his brows.

"That, right there. Grump."

"We can't all be the Sugar Plum Fairy," he said.

But it wasn't the right thing to say. Because that darkness crossed her face then.

"Hey, I'm sorry. Did I say something wrong? You've been—" Gid started.

But Ari cut him off, shaking her head. "It's nothing. Don't worry about it."

"*That's* not very convincing."

"Just drop it, Gid, alright?" Ari stood rigid beside him at the baggage carousel.

He turned to her, but she wouldn't meet his gaze. "You know you can talk to me about anything, right?"

"Yeah," she grumbled, but she didn't elaborate. "All I want is to *not* talk about it for the week, okay? We're in Ireland, Thomas is getting married, *Christmas tree farm...*"

Gid frowned, her caginess setting him on edge. So

where *was* something going on, but if she wanted to ignore it, he would help her.

"Whatever you want," he said.

She nodded. "That's what I want."

The carousel groaned to a start and the people hurried forward, eager for their luggage.

"Wait here," Gid said. "I'll grab our bags and then we'll catch the bus."

Whatever was wrong, it wasn't something casual. The youngest of the Callaghan family—and the only girl—Ari was used to being doted on, paid attention to. Where Gid, more familiar with being forgotten, kept nearly everything close to the chest. Ari had helped to teach him how to share, slowly peeling back the layers of his onion.

But for now, he'd let her have it. Ari would talk when she was ready, and Gid would be there for her when she was.

EIGHT
ARI

GID, bless him, would listen to damn near anything Ari said. She didn't want to talk, so he zipped his lips and kept silent the whole bus ride to Dublin city center.

Which was fine with Ari, since that's what she wanted after all—*not to talk about it*—but he didn't have to take her so dang literally. She knew, though, this was his way of giving her space.

And how was she supposed to just tell people that she was at risk of being kicked out of her MBA program? It was so fucking shameful. Even though it was Gid asking, she couldn't find the words to talk about it.

Like, was she just supposed to be blasé about the whole thing, like she didn't really care what happened? Or was it a tragedy that she brought down upon herself?

In truth, it was a little bit of both.

During her internship in Chicago last summer, she'd gotten a taste of the *real world*. Finally, at twenty-five, she could see a future for herself. She experienced true freedom that summer, making new friends from around the country, earning more money than she knew what to do with. After a lifetime of school, she began to understand what Thomas had chased in New York City.

Staring out the window, Dublin zoomed by. It looked pretty normal, pretty much the same as any American city, but it *felt* different. Knowing she was on foreign soil sent a thrill through her.

Not unlike the little thrills she kept getting every time she looked at Gid. Their flight had been mostly uneventful, except every time their legs brushed, she had to squeeze hers together to temper the fluttering in her core. As a dancer, she was used to controlling her body, honing it to do what she wanted, so this thing it had started doing was confusing.

The bus stuttered to a halt.

"Come on, let's get some cocktails," Gid said, knocking against her shoulder.

Her buzz had all but evaporated since the flight. She consulted her phone, which had automatically switched to Dublin time. They didn't have long until Thomas and Julia's welcome brunch.

"Would it be ridiculous to request a nap right about now?" she sighed the question.

"Yes, because it's ten AM we're only here for six days and you need to adjust to the time change."

"A coffee then?"

"Ah, that we can do, pop tart."

Despite his anxiety peaking on the plane, Gid proved to be an expert travel navigator once on solid ground. With his phone clutched in hand, he steered them to the closest coffee shop. Of course, it was perfectly cute and cozy café and entirely too crowded for their bags.

"Stay out here with our luggage and I'll run in and get our stuff. Your usual?" Gid winked and ducked inside before Ari even had a chance to respond.

Her *usual*. He had ordered coffee for her thousands of times, and always remembered she preferred a whole milk latte extra hot with an extra shot when she could get it. But, for some reason, this time, it made her blush.

Goddamn it, what was going on? Like a freaking switch had flipped inside her brain and she was flooded with dopamine at the mere thought of Gideon Sims. Which was entirely inconvenient at the very beginning of their trip.

Because Ari didn't even know what she wanted. Despite her endless string of one night stands, she found herself wanting someone to stay. It was fun, of course, but at some point, she started to get tired of it. Ari wouldn't have minded some of them sticking around, but it always got too messy.

She didn't want to complicate things with Gid and risk losing him forever.

"Piping hot, just like you like it," Gid said, popping back out of the shop.

She took the drink and Gid lead the way over the cobblestones.

"We aren't too far from the hotel, actually," he said.

"Perfect because I need a shower. I stink."

"Nonsense," Gid said, leaning over to bury his nose in her hair. "You smell the same as always. Santal 33."

Ari snorted a little laugh, trying to conceal that missing-a-step feeling that echoed inside her.

Now *that* she didn't realize that Gid knew. When she went off to college, she decided she needed a more adult-level fragrance. Her mom never understood why Ari spent over two hundred dollars on a bottle of perfume, but Ari thought it was worth every penny.

Especially now, as Gid's breath tickled her neck, a soft moan of approval escaping his throat.

As he pulled away, Ari caught a glimpse of his eyes, dark with...was that desire? A look he hadn't directed at her in years. Occasionally, in those first couple years of their friendship, she'd sense it on the dance floor, as he pulled her close or their bodies passed each other with just the right amount of friction. Not that West Coast Swing was a particularly sexy dance, but sometimes the vibes just hit that way.

Ari cleared her throat, inhaling the cold Dublin air, and took a sip of her steaming hot coffee. She needed to get a grip if she was going to survive this trip unscathed.

* * *

AFTER THANKFULLY SECURING EARLY CHECK-IN, Ari stepped out of the fancy hotel shower, wrapping the ultra-plush towel tight around her body. The thing was blessedly cozy from the towel warmer. Steam curled the short little hairs around her forehead, the rest of her long hair clipped on top of her head with a massive claw.

She turned up the Ed Sheeran on her phone, remembering the time over the summer when she, Zahra, and Gid saw him play an acoustic set the night before his sold-out stadium show in Detroit. It was one of the most magical nights of her life, all thanks to Gid who orchestrated the logistics of the whole thing.

Humming along to the music, Ari slathered her entire body with moisturizer, which made her feel excellent after the long hours of travel. As she walked out of the bathroom, she pointedly ignored the extremely lush looking bed literally screaming her name. The temptation to lay down was so great, but Gid was right, they couldn't mess up their jet lag. Staying awake until tonight would be the best way to try and normalize for their trip.

Just as she sat on the edge of the bed, the siren song of

it too strong, there was a knock on the door. Ari jumped to her feet, still cocooned in her towel.

"Uh, one sec," she shouted to whoever was on the other side.

"It's me! I heard you're here!"

Me was Julia, Ari recognized her voice right away and tore open the door.

"Eeeee!" the two both screamed, laughing, jumping, and hugging until Ari's towel started to slip.

"Oh shit, sorry hold on let me get dressed real quick. Come in, come in." Ari left the door wide open, grabbed her long red sweater dress and stepped into the bathroom.

"You're gonna be married in two days!" Ari squealed from the bathroom.

"I know, I can hardly believe it," Julia said.

From around the corner, Ari heard the soft whoosh of the duvet and knew that Julia had laid down on the bed. Jealousy had never come on so strong or so quickly.

"Oh my god, you look fantastic in red," Julia said, turning sideways on the bed as Ari came out of the bathroom.

The oversized sweater dress was the perfect mix of comfort and fashion. She unclipped her hair as she bent to pull on sheer tights.

"Thank you, but the focus should be on you, darling Bride. And I have to say this peachy, creamy silk number is absolutely your color." As Ari said it, Julia's cheeks flushed peach to match, and she pulled her oversized cardigan tight over her slip dress.

"Thank you," she mused, suddenly a little shy.

"Everything all set for the weekend, then?" Ari asked as she pulled out her make up bag and plopped down in front of the full-length mirror.

"Yep," Julia said, twisting her sweater around her finger. "The wedding planner has been fantastic and handled literally everything. Thomas is still a nervous wreck but now that everyone's here, I think he'll calm down."

"He just needs a drink or two," Ari laughed, smudging her smokey eye makeup.

"How'd your semester end?" Julia asked, sitting up on the bed.

Ari's stomach dropped and she nearly lost dropped her eye brush.

She didn't want to talk about school. She didn't want to think about school. Of course, everyone was going to ask her about it. Her semester *did* just end. She should be going into her last semester of her business program, getting ready to graduate in the spring.

And now she was spiraling, so she just closed her eyes for a moment. Letting out a breath, she refocused, just like she did before going on stage for a performance.

"Fine, nothing to report." Ari shrugged, the lie slipping out easily.

"And how was the flight? I didn't see Gid, just heard you were here from T."

"Oh." Ari coughed and tried to swallow at the same time which made her choke on the word. "Uh yeah, good."

Julia watched Ari in the mirror and raised her eyebrows. Ari refused to meet her gaze, afraid of what truths might be written on her face.

"Same old, ya know. Gid and his travel anxiety, too much wine, not enough sleep." She shrugged.

"Why do I feel like something happened that you're not telling me about?"

"Nothing *happened*, Julia."

"If you say that again I might be convinced."

Ari grabbed the throw pillow from the accent chair and tossed it behind her head at her future sister-in-law. Julia rolled and dodged it.

"Watch it! I'm wearing silk!" she shrieked and hopped off the bed.

"You're the one that laid down on the bed, not me."

"Fine, well, finish getting ready and meet us downstairs. Brunch starts in fifteen, yeah?"

"Open bar—don't worry I'll be there. And on time!"

"For once," Julia laughed as she tucked out the door.

Ari finished her sparkly, smoky eye forgoing her usual full face of makeup out of sheer exhaustion.

"This'll have to do," she told her reflection, before slipping into her platform ankle boots. She grabbed her clutch and yanked open her door, only to find Gid standing there, fist raised and ready to knock.

"Fancy seeing you here," Ari joked, raising her eyebrows. She hoped that she sounded less flirty and more sarcastic, but her brain was mush. Between the jet lag, and lack of sleep and real food, Ari could barely tell up from down anymore.

Gid laughed and tucked his hands into his pockets. God, he looked fabulous. Good enough to eat.

Ari shook her head, clearly delirious if her thoughts had ventured down that line of thinking. But—he did look good. A grey suit with a black shirt underneath—that he seemingly had found time to iron?—with the top two buttons undone. His hair looked artfully messy, unlike her's which she was sure was frizzing more by the second.

"So," Gid said, and Ari jumped, realizing they were just standing in her doorway.

"Right, let's get some cocktails." She brushed past him, letting the heavy hotel door fall shut behind her.

As if she hadn't been close enough to him in the last twenty hours, the tiny hotel elevator put them nearly on top of each other. They'd ridden up separately, as it would have been near impossible with their luggage, and it was damn near impossible now with just the two of them.

Well, impossible if the goal was to not rub against Gid at all—which it *was*—and not to smell his absolutely intoxicating aftershave, a combination of eucalyptus and patchouli.

Ari leaned against the miniature handrail and tried not to look Gid in the eye. Which left her staring at the floor since the damn elevator was covered in mirrored surfaces.

She couldn't look up because then she'd see her best friend staring at her from a million directions. The mirrors were meant to make the space feel bigger but Ari had never felt so claustrophobic.

NINE
GID

"I'M DEAD ON MY FEET," Ari said, breaking their silence as she leaned against the handrail, her feet crossed at the ankles.

The elevator inched slowly to its destination.

"Well, you look stunning," Gid adjusted the cuffs of his shirt under his suit coat, appraising her from head to foot.

"Thank you." Ari pulled her long, dark hair over her shoulder.

But she still refused to look at him. His stomach hardened, part anticipation and part confusion. *What the hell is going on here?*

He wanted to reach out and touch her, he wanted to pull her against his chest. Something they'd done a million times as friends and dance partners, but now there was something else.

He wanted to run his hands through that gorgeous

mane of hers, he wanted to claim her, have her as his own. Pull her close to his side and show the entire world that she was his.

Clearing his throat, he pushed those thoughts away. Whatever flirtation had happened on the plane had clearly jarred her. And the last thing Gid wanted was to make Ari uncomfortable. He would follow her lead, and for now, that meant the silence was so tense he could slice it with a knife.

After what felt like an eternity, the elevator doors slid open, and he pulled back the grate.

Gid, refreshed from a shower, looked around the hotel lobby. It really was *a vibe* as Ari would say. Beautiful parquet flooring aged from years of use, stretched out in front of them. His dress shoes clapped softly on the wood, reminding him of the sounds of the dance studio. All the walls were red brick, with intricate sconce lighting hanging at regular intervals.

"Wow," Ari breathed, apparently thinking the same thing that he was. "What a freaking vibe."

Gid smiled to himself and tucked a fist into his pocket, putting a damper on the desire to pull her into his side. But he didn't have to, because she bumped against him and looped her arm through his elbow as if it were the most natural thing in the world.

Ari had always been hot and cold, prone to extremes of her emotions, but she really had thrown him for a loop in the last twenty hours or so. Gid could only assume it had something to do with what she didn't want to share with him, what she refused to talk about. And he would play along. He would be anything that she needed him to be. And if she wanted him as arm candy, he was happy to take up the role.

"You don't look too bad yourself, Gid." Ari squeezed his elbow, returning the earlier compliment.

"You don't have to tell me," Gid laughed.

Ari reached to slap him on the shoulder. "A little humility never hurt anyone."

"Hey, I paid good money to get this suit tailored. I know it looks good."

They wound their way through tiny hallways off the lobby to the back, private bar that Thomas and Julia had booked for brunch. The hotel had a classic, vintage feel, and as Gid pushed open the swinging porthole door to the back room, he couldn't help but feel they were walking into a speakeasy. With a hand on her lower back, Gid guided Ari through the doorway. The moment she saw her mom, she took off like a rocket.

"Oh Ari, honey." Her mom smiled, arms wide for a hug. A tall and soft woman, Molly favored billowing outfits and gave the most sincere hugs—the picture of warmth.

After she had appropriately smothered her daughter, she pulled Gid in for his own hug. Her salt and pepper curls tickled his nose.

"It's so good to see you, Gid," she said, even though he had just been at the Callaghan dinner last month.

"It's good to see you too, Molly."

"And all of us in Ireland," she sniffed, pulling one of Sean's old hankies from her pocket. She had one more often than not and was prone to tears since her husband's death. Understandably so.

Ari squeezed her mom's hand. "If only Dad were here."

"If only," Mrs. Callaghan said wistfully, her eyes filling with tears. "He always did want to come here with you all as grown kids."

"We know, Mom. We got this," Danny, Ari's middle brother, said, strolling over while he sipped an espresso martini.

For once, he was without his trademark backward baseball cap. He nodded a greeting at Gid before giving his mom a quick side hug. "And Ari's finally shown up! How was the flight?"

Ari took a deep breath, her shoulders rising, and sighed it out. "Fine."

"That good, eh?"

"Just long and this guy," she bumped Gid with her hip, "insisted I can't take a nap in order to sync with the time zone or something."

"Don't worry," Lacey, Danny's girlfriend, said joining their conversation. "Keep the buzz going and you only need to make it until, like, five PM and you'll pass out 'til the morning. Perfect."

"I like your thinking," Ari grinned. "Gid, what can I get you?"

"No, no, you stay here and catch up with your family. I'll get the drinks. Vodka soda?"

Ari nodded in response, that same pretty little flush creeping up her cheeks as when he ordered her coffee hours before. God, what he would do to see that flush again and again. He could think of a few decidedly inappropriate ways that he'd like to make that blush flood her cheeks.

The party passed by in a blur. Thomas made a welcome speech—looking dapper but nervous—and Julia shone brighter than the sun, as any bride should so close to her wedding day. He knew their whole backstory, and he was so happy that after Julia's failed engagement she'd found real love with Thomas.

Ari never left Gid's side. Her soft, cashmere sweater dress was never far from his fingertips. He couldn't tell if he was imagining it, or if she was slowly, achingly slowly, inching closer to him as the late morning turned into early afternoon.

By the time brunch was over, he could be sure that he wasn't making it up. Ari stood in front of him, her backside rubbing ever so gently onto his front. They said their goodbyes to Danny and Lacey, who were going to continue the party at a pub around the corner with

Heather, Julia's younger sister, and Reagan, her date. Everyone else had their own sightseeing plans.

Gid knew the way Ari's body moved and she often brushed by him as they danced, but in this context, it was intoxicating. Alone now at the hotel bar, he grasped onto her hip, his fingertips digging into her soft strength there, and she responded by changing the angle against him.

The next second, she turned towards him, both of them clutching their drinks, sipping down the second drink dregs.

"Suddenly I don't feel so tired," Ari purred, her smokey eye makeup sparkling.

"No?" Gid raised an eyebrow. "Do you want to go out with Danny and them?"

"Uh-uh." Ari looked up at him with big eyes.

That look was danger. That look stirred things up in Gid he didn't expect. He swallowed them back down, not knowing Ari's intentions. They had this little dance they were skirting around, a lot of things they weren't saying but their bodies communicated. A little touch here, a look there...but he needed to know what she wanted with her words before he would let himself get carried away.

"What are you thinking then, pop tart?" The words were heavy on his tongue.

He didn't expect her reply.

"Ice skating."

* * *

THE SPARKLING DECORATIONS really made the ice rink glitter like a holiday wonderland. It had been easy enough to get to the harbor just outside of Dublin proper via public transit, though Gid would have suffered much worse to see the smile that lit up Ari's face. His fingers itched for his phone to capture the way the purple lights made Ari's hair glow. Slipping his phone from his pocket, he took a stealthy photo of her as she looked up and all around, wonder palpable on her face.

Once the two got fitted into skates, they tottered onto the ice, which wasn't as smooth as he wished it was. But with all the people looping around in circles, that was bound to be the case.

"Maybe this wasn't the best idea," Gid said as he worked out his balance.

"Don't be silly, this is amazing." She stretched a hand toward him, her black fingernails glinting under the lights. "Take my hand."

Her slight palm against his was so warm and soft. So inviting. He wondered how the rest of her body would feel under his palm, roving over her curves.

With a flick of his wrist, Gid pulled her around, close to him, and caught her on the waist.

"These lights make you glow, Ari," he said into her hair. He caught a whiff of her scent again, spicy and floral, woodsy and wild. All he wanted was to smell it again and again, with her hair draped around him and her scent lingering on his pillow for days.

She laughed into his chest, light and fresh as Christmas morning snow.

God, how was he suddenly so into his best friend? Maybe the jet lag had really knocked some screws loose.

"Come on, Gid, let me show you some moves."

Ari pulled ahead of him, their hands still clasped, as she pumped her legs and pulled him along. For a dancer, he was as awkward as a baby deer in the skates. He laughed at her joy but also wondered why he thought this would be a good idea when he hadn't skated in years. Did he want to embarrass the shit out of himself? Apparently.

Eventually, she let go of his hand as he found his legs and trailed along behind her. Her loose hair blew back as she gathered speed and attempted little twirls on the ice. Her core strength and dancer gusto propelled her around.

With the holiday music and laughter floating around them, the smile on her face, and the easy way between them, Gid could fool himself into believing that Ari's thoughts mirrored his own.

Always with her, he didn't feel the low-level anxiety that burned under his skin, causing him to second guess every word he said or move he made. Somehow it seemed natural for her to skate back around him and lace her arm through the crook of his elbow. Somehow, he never wanted to let go.

He dipped down to her ear, nosing his way through her curtain of hair. "You're good on skates."

"I'm even better off them." Her eyes glinted wickedly up at him, a jolt of desire piercing through him.

She skated away then, leaving Gid standing stock still in her wake. If he didn't know any better, he would say that was a pick-up line.

Was Ari Callaghan trying to pick him up? There was no way. It had been years since anything sexual had crackled between then but holy hell, he swore there was something there now.

After a while, she looped back around, the two skating around in circles, laughing and joking and forgetting about the real life they left behind in Starling Hills. Here in Dublin, it felt a million miles away. Like they could be totally different people if they wanted to.

Eventually, Ari swung in front of him and stopped him on his skate-tracks. She took both of his large hands in his.

"Listen. It's been a long day for us. My jet lag is making my head pound. Do you want to go back to the hotel? Maybe get a last drink at the bar before passing out?"

His heart pulsed in his ears. Somehow, he knew that she wasn't really asking for a drink. Somehow, he knew exactly what was on her mind, and it was the same on his. Somehow, he knew she felt this wild thing developing between them.

Gid didn't respond with words, he just took Ari's hand and led her through the crowds and off the ice.

Their transit trip passed by in the blink of an eye—

probably because Gid's mind was already back at the hotel, wondering what exactly would happen next. He had his own wishes, but he wouldn't say anything until she did.

At the hotel, they paused outside the bar, Ari halting him with a tug of his hand.

"I want to feel good tonight, Gid." Her cheeks flushed with the statement. "Can you do that for me?"

It must be the jet lag. It must be the intoxicating newness of being abroad. It must be...a dream. He was dreaming, that was it.

Gid cleared his throat, gazing down at her. "Well, this is a new one for me."

"Too much?" Ari ducked her head.

Something roared inside Gid. He never wanted Ari to feel ashamed of asking for what she wanted. He lifted her chin lightly with his finger, holding her eyes, taking them all in.

"Not at all," he breathed. "You can tell me exactly what you want tonight, yeah?"

With his finger still on her chin, she nodded, wide eyed. "Yes."

"What would make you feel good right now?" Gid licked his lips, eager to hear exactly what she wanted.

"Take me back to my room." Half demand, half a question. "Do you want to come back to my room?" she asked, her eyes widening even more.

"So, you've felt it, too?" Gid whispered as Ari stepped

closer to him and he forgot where he was, what they were meant to be doing.

"This shift between us? Yes." She nodded and her dark hair flashed with the movement.

Gid pushed his messy flop of hair back off his forehead. "And then what happens after the week?"

Ari shrugged, her eye contact searing. "Back to normal, I guess."

He clenched his jaw, breaking away from her gaze. "You could do that?"

Could *he* do that? He'd done it once, but that was years ago. Their friendship had never been weird because of it, their dance routines never faltered. The two were always in lockstep.

But this? Well, even though he felt it too, he hadn't expected this turn of events.

"If it's okay with you, it's okay with me." She laced her fingers into his and gave a squeeze.

With his other arm, he wrapped it around her waist and pulled her close. An ache bloomed behind his ribs, something forgotten that was put there long ago. By her, by this girl. By Ari Callaghan. They never asked each other for anything, but now she was asking him for this.

"You want to be mine?" He asked, nosing into her hair. Gid swallowed. "For the week?" He tacked on, immediately feeling too exposed and vulnerable.

Ari latched her hands around his neck, pulling his forehead down to meet hers.

"Yes," she gasped.

This could be dangerous. This could be awful. But for Ari, he would do anything, be anything, that she wanted. And so, he let her lead him to the elevator, the tiny one that was so claustrophobic on the way down now seemed like the perfect size.

All alone and hidden from view, Ari pushed him up against the mirrored wall. She was small, but damn she was strong.

In the next second, Gid ran a hand over the curve of her waist, exploring the planes and dips that he knew so well. Somehow, they felt different now, new. The soft cashmere of her sweater dress tickled his palm.

"I can't wait to get you upstairs," he groaned into her neck.

They hadn't crossed the threshold of their lips touching, but they were close, so close. He peppered small touches along her long neck: his nose, then his cheeks, his chin, his lips, testing out how it all felt.

"Oh yeah?" Ari pushed her hips against him, rocking her weight.

Gid growled, overcome with raw hunger. It had been a long time since he felt this close to someone. He was lonely, yeah, but he didn't know what he wanted anyway.

But he knew now exactly what he wanted.

The elevator finally lurched to a stop, and they unlatched the grate, tumbling out into the hallway. The sconce lighting illuminated the way to her room.

The lock clicked under her fingers. Gid could barely handle it anymore. He cradled Ari around the waist, swung the door open, and flipped her around inside.

The door clanged shut behind them, and he braced her against the full-length mirror. One hand still circled her waist, the other palm flat on the cool glass beside her head.

This was the final moment, the last moment they could turn back. And Gid wanted to be sure.

"You're good with this?" he whispered, staring down at her.

This close, all she had to do was tip her chin up to his and they would be kissing.

"I want to be yours," she said. "For the week."

His stomach squeezed at the expiration date, but he'd been the one to say it first. It was safer that way, not to expect anything from each other.

They were playing roles now, forcing intimacy into their empty spaces. Why was that suddenly so scary?

TEN

ARI

INSTEAD OF KISSING, instead of getting any closer, they just stared at each other.

As the festive lights from outside the window bounced around in the wind, their sparkles moving up and down over Gid's face in the dark hotel room, Ari silently dared him to close the gap between them. She willed him with all her might. The sensual power of the moment before that first contact rushed over her.

Was he waiting for her to ask for what she wanted? For a kiss?

She didn't want to. Ari could be patient bordering on stubborn, though. She could wait, the tension between them pulling more taut with each passing second.

"Hmm," Gid murmured. His eyes roved her face, as if coming to some conclusion.

Then without warning he picked her up and hauled her over his shoulder.

Ari's stomach did a pleasant little flip as she squealed in shock and, surprisingly, delight. "Gideon!"

"You're being intentionally difficult," he grunted as he marched over to the bed.

"Put me down!" She giggled and wiggled her legs.

Gid clamped a free arm over her legs. "Not a chance."

He held her over his shoulder as he kicked off his shoes then unzipped her boots and let them fall to the floor. He grabbed her foot, pressing his thumb into the arch of one, then the other. His fingers brushed ankle, lingering for a moment over the Eeyore tattoo on her left one. She remembered, with sudden clarity, Gid doing the same thing that very first night in her dorm room all those years ago.

When she invited Gid to her room, she didn't know what to expect. But this confidence from Gid surprised her, in a very, very good way.

"You haven't told me what you want yet," Gid said, a steely edge to his voice. And with a flat hand, he gave her a playful slap on the ass through the layers of her cashmere and tights.

"Oh." She jumped a little from his touch, pleased with the control he'd taken.

"I'm waiting, Ari," he said, his words full of icy heat.

Gid stood at the foot of the bed in the dark with Ari firmly in place over his shoulder. She knew he was strong, but it seemed like he could do this all day. Her heart raced, feeling everything all at the same time, leaving her breathless.

Gid's hand moved slowly over her tights, caressing her calf, tickling the back of her knee, and settled in the inside of her thigh, right at the base. The thin barrier between their skin seemed to heighten the sensation.

She swallowed. "Put me down."

Even though she didn't really want that. Somehow, she liked being tossed over his shoulder like this.

Gid kneaded the soft muscle of her thigh, ghosting his fingers higher. "Where?"

Her mouth was dry. "On the bed."

Not that there was much else to choose from, but she supposed the accent chair could provide a change of scenery.

He murmured his agreement. Sauntering around the edge of the bed, he flicked the bedside switches, and a warm day-glow blossomed around them. Gid paused, pulling his phone out of his pocket and swiping through screens. A soft, jazzy Christmas playlist came to life.

The next moment, he flipped her off his shoulder and onto the edge of the bed.

One entire wall of the room was windows overlooking the roof next door and alleyway below. The colorful glow from the lamps and Christmas lights on the cobblestone street reflected across Gid's face. He gazed down at her, a hungry, shadowed look on his face. Ari's stomach flipped.

"How do you like my room?" she asked, leaning back on her elbows and looking up at him from this new angle.

"It smells like you. And your stuff is everywhere." He laughed with a half-smile.

"Hurricane Ari."

They were stalling with small talk and they both knew it.

Gid took off his suit jacket and tossed it neatly over the chair. Looking down at Ari, he pulled at his belt to adjust his pants. She licked her lips and he followed the movement.

"What do you want, Ari?" His voice was edged with a command.

A loaded question. She couldn't think what she wanted first. Her hands tingled, grabby and eager, but they weren't quite there yet. They hadn't even kissed. Maybe that was the place to start.

"Kiss me." Her words were soft, barely above a whisper.

Gid knelt before her, using his own knee to nudge her legs open, making space for him to crouch before her. Her sweater dress rode up, bunching just where her hips bent, exposing her to him. But he wasn't focused between her legs. Gid stared at her lips. One hand floated around her neck and the other to her waist as he cradled her, and their lips met.

Heat showered over her and pooled in her belly as he covered her lips with his. A gentle kiss that fit together like two warm puzzle pieces, softly exploring. With him holding her up, Ari moved her arms, sneaking her hands to untuck his shirt, roaming to find skin underneath.

With contact, he jumped, tensing his muscles. "Your hands are freezing," he said into her lips.

"Warm me up." Another request.

"Gladly," he laughed darkly.

Releasing where he'd had a hold of her, Gid reached for her hands, taking them in his own. Ari fell back flat onto the bed as he pushed her arms over her head. When he flattened on top of her, she felt his hard length against her thigh, and she moaned into his mouth.

Gid pulled back slightly. "Felt that, did you?"

Oh, she felt it alright. Ari bit her lower lip and nodded. His hardness, even through her tights, sent a shiver down her spine. She needed more. "Undress me."

She didn't have to ask him twice. Sliding his palms flat along the sides of her thighs, he dipped underneath the edge of her dress again. The thin, nylon barrier between them somehow increased the depth of his touch and sparks raced over Ari's body. Gid lifted the soft cashmere away from her stomach and her nipples pebbled from arousal and sudden chill. Ari's arms were still over her head and Gid slid the dress the rest of the way off, tossing it over his shoulder.

Ari lay on the bed in only her tights and black mesh bralette. Gid groaned and she wiggled under his direct attention.

"You are stunning," he whispered, diving for her clavicle, nibbling from her shoulder to her neck.

Ari wrapped her arms around his neck. "Roll over."

Some light pressure on his shoulder was enough to get him to flip on his back. She mounted him and with only her tights separating her pussy from his pants, Ari rubbed herself against him, enjoying the disparity of her being nearly naked and Gid still fully clothed.

She felt fully in control in this moment. Tempting and teasing him, as he was still fully dressed. Nothing else mattered except this, right here, right now. This was exactly how she wanted to feel tonight. Not worried about school, stressed about Thomas's wedding, or missing her dad.

Just chasing something that felt really fucking good. She knew she could count on Gid to give it to her. She only had to ask.

His hands gripped her waist, his fingers squeezing into her soft belly. Arousal swelled low in her pelvis as she stabilized herself with her hands flat on Gid's chest and her clit rubbed against him.

"You like this, Ari?" he rasped, his grip tightening on her.

"Yes," she whimpered. "Touch me."

Gid shoved one hand down the waistband of her tights, finding her center immediately and rubbing as she ground down. It didn't take much, and she lost her will to stay upright. He cradled her back, and flipped her over, wrenching her tights down around her ankles. Her legs flopped open wide and before she knew what was happening, Gid crawled between her legs, plunging a finger into her pussy and his tongue lapping at her clit.

"Oh my god." She fisted the comforter and her toes curled as the sensation built within her, wound tight as a top. All she could think about was the release, desperate to see stars.

But her orgasm was an elusive thing. The more she thought about it, the more it seemed to hide from her. She whined her frustration. Gid, unaware of the thoughts buzzing in her brain, added another finger inside her, alternating rubbing her clit with his tongue and thumb.

"You're close, Ari, I know it," he said into her cunt.

He had no idea what was going on inside her head. Goddamn, he was a champion, eager to please her and willing to bring her to completion, but her body just wouldn't listen.

This was becoming futile. Try though he might to get her there, it wasn't going to happen this way.

She sat up, looking down at him between her legs and, Christ, he was so sexy down there. The way he looked up at her with hungry eyes—dear lord.

"I want to fuck you," she said, eager to distract him from the fact that she wasn't going to get there that way. Maybe if she got on top, she could come. That was always her favorite position.

"Whatever you want." Gid pulled back from between

her legs, standing at the side of the bed with his erection bulging in his pants.

"Let me help you." She pulled her tights off her ankles and scooted to the edge of the bed. With wide eyes, she looked up at him. Gid raked his fingers through her hair, petting her as she reached for his belt buckle. Once she got his pants undone, she pulled them down as he braced himself on her shoulder and stepped out of the pants. Then she unbuttoned his shirt, pushing it off him and lifted his undershirt over his head.

Ari took a moment to enjoy his silhouette in his tight, black boxer briefs, which left nothing to the imagination.

"Condom?" She asked, before they went any further.

Gid bent for his wallet and pulled one out. Ari peeled the waistband of his briefs down and his cock bounced out. She licked her lips at the sight. With one hand, he rolled the condom on and with the other, Gid teased at Ari's nipple through the mesh of her bralette.

"How do you want it?" he asked.

"Me on top."

"Mmm," he murmured before laying down on the bed.

Her pussy throbbed between her legs, but the sensation of orgasm had all but receded. She needed the release and hoped riding him would bring her there. Bracing herself with her hands on his chest, she rocked over his cock, spreading her wetness over the condom.

Slowly, Ari dropped down on top of him, moving up and down as she coated his length. Gid's fingers stabilized her at the hips, grasping tight. Inch by inch, she lowered, until finally she sat flush on top of him. She breathed around him, adjusting to the feel of him inside.

Her heart raced, realizing it was her Gid, one of her best friends, full sheathed inside her. Somehow, in this particular moment, it felt so freaking right, and she marveled how it had never happened before.

"You feel good, Gideon." Her hair fell around her in a curtain as she leaned over him.

"You feel amazing, pop tart." He squeezed tighter at her hips.

After a moment, she began rocking back and forth, grinding herself against him in the motion she knew most guaranteed her to orgasm. Ari closed her eyes, focusing on herself... her core... her pleasure... The heat between her legs built, but unwelcome thoughts swarmed her mind, obtrusive and loud, taking over her concentration.

School. *You'll never be smart enough.*

Dad. *Dead.*

Her siblings. *Partnered up, and you'll always be alone.*

Stop being so hysterical. Stop being so much. Too much. Too loud.

Tears prickled the corner of her eyes as her frustration built, overpowering her orgasm.

She didn't stop moving though, and the sensation became more grating and painful than enjoyable.

"Hey," Gid said, his voice so far away. "Ari."

She wasn't paying attention, barely in the room

anymore. He let go of her hips, dropping his hands to her thighs and squeezing there instead.

Ari furrowed her brow down at him. "What?"

"Are you okay?"

Once she stopped moving, she realized his erection was no longer rock hard inside her.

"You went away," he said, gazing up at her from the pillow. Concern lit up behind his eyes in the warm, fuzzy light.

Instead of saying anything, she just rolled off him. Her bare feet hit the cool floor.

"What?..." he rolled onto his side.

"You need to leave," Ari said, bending to pick up her tights. She found the toe and balanced on one foot to pull the stocking up one leg and then switched to do the other. "I'm sorry."

This was a mistake. It was supposed to make her forget the rest of her shitty, stressful life. The one she had waiting for her back home. So much for that plan.

"Did I do something? I thought we were having fun. Just for the week, remember?" Gid sat up and moved to the edge of the bed.

Ari was already over this conversation, she couldn't have it, not with him. She just wanted to pretend this had never happened.

"We were, Gid, okay? It was great. But this was a mistake." Her words were flat and Gid bristled. "Blame it on the jet leg delirium or me making bad choices like usual, but this shouldn't have happened. I'm sorry."

"Okay." He leaned on his thighs and folded his hands, still stark naked.

Stomping around the room as much as she could in tights, Ari picked up her sweater dress and dropped it over her head.

"Don't worry about it," she muttered. "We'll be fine tomorrow."

She hoped. Maybe that was a lie. Something to make herself feel better for this stupid, rash decision she'd made to hop into bed with him.

"Wait," Gid jumped to his feet when it was clear she wasn't calming down. "I mean, should we talk about this?"

Ari placed her hands on his chest. "I don't think we have to. We can just pretend like it never happened."

But that felt like a lie, too.

He grabbed her wrist as she tried to turn away. "Talk to me."

"Gid? What do you think this is?" She drew a finger in the air, momentum building behind her words. The chaotic kind. The not good kind. The more he wanted her to talk, the more likely she was to say something really stupid. "You don't owe me anything. We don't have to talk about it or whatever. I just wanted a fuck, okay? An orgasm, a release. A little shot of bliss to forget my stupid freaking life. It just didn't happen. And now you're going to leave."

With each word, his eyes widened, hurt etching itself across his face. Ari knew she was saying some hurtful things, but they were also true. What did it all matter anyway?

"That's it?" Gid stood with his arms at his side, his palms open.

"Yeah, this is it." She gathered her hair over her shoulder and shrugged.

Gid dressed hastily and shoved his feet in his shoes. He looked at her one last time, as if he wanted to say something. But she didn't want to hear it. She couldn't hear anything else, anymore words they couldn't take back.

He really was cute and sweet, her Gid. He'd been the perfect gentleman. And if she hadn't been so messed up in the head, maybe they would have had a nice, long night. A nice, long week.

But here they were, facing off in front of her door, and Gid was about to leave.

"I'll see you tomorrow at breakfast, okay? It'll be like nothing ever happened." She pulled the door open, and he stepped through.

When the door clicked shut, Ari finally let out a cry that she muffled against her palm. One sob, and that was it.

ELEVEN

ARI

AT EIGHT-THIRTY IN THE MORNING, so said her phone, someone knocked sharply on her hotel room door.

"Ari!" It was her mom yelling on the other side of the door. "You're supposed to be up already! Are you up?"

When Ari didn't immediately respond, her mom kept going. "The Wards are all up and dressed, and Lacey and Julia are downstairs, and even the boys are ready for brunch but...I haven't seen you yet!"

Ari groaned, not loud enough that her mom could hear...or so she thought.

"I can hear you moaning in there! Are you still in bed?"

"God, Mom," she yelled, still warm and curled up in the duvet, "I'm up! I'm not a damn child."

Though she certainly felt like one. She hadn't fallen asleep until well after two in the morning. She'd undressed again just after Gid left, slipped naked into her bed, and prayed for sleep that never came. Even reading her Kindle didn't make her sleepy.

Her brain wouldn't stop reminding her of the ridiculous decisions she'd made to bring her up to this point. Always, always, always ruining things with her rash choices.

She'd wanted to be held, she wanted a release. And Gid—she knew he would jump to give it to her. Even if these feelings were something unearthed from years ago, he always said yes to her.

At some point, the hamster wheel of her brain lulled her into sleep because it was now, apparently, morning and she'd overslept because she'd forgotten to set an alarm.

Of course. Add it to the list of things she couldn't help but mess up.

Today was the big day-before-wedding brunch at the hotel restaurant. For a micro-wedding, Thomas and Julia really had gone all out. It was impressive, if annoying, if she was being honest. Ari had this whole itinerary in her email which she'd tried as hard as she could to ignore. They had a combo elopement planner/photographer coordinator whose specific job it was to hustle them all around Dublin and forty-five minutes out to the coast to the elopement site so Ari figured she didn't really need to commit the thing to memory.

But she probably should have at least remembered to

set her alarm this morning. Her mom would not let her forget this faux pas.

And then after Sunday brunch, Ari would be free of familial obligations as they all went their separate ways and Ari and Gid took the train to their Christmas tree farm wonderland.

Now, her stomach curdled at the inherent romantic implications of the whole thing. How stupid she was last night. Combine day-drinking and a little jet lag and, bam, Ari was making *great* decisions.

Was the rest of their trip doomed for failure?

Mom knocked at her door again. "Come on, Ari. Up."

Ari frowned at the door before stumbling out of bed. Frick it was freezing—she grabbed the robe and wrapped it around her. She caught her reflection in the mirror and holy hell, her hair was a rat's nest. Apparently, she hadn't slept soundly. Beauty sleep—don't know her. There's no way she'd be able to fool her mom into thinking she had already been up.

Unlatching the door with one hand and smoothing her hair with the other, Ari prayed this would be over quickly. "See, I'm up," she said, holding open the door and shrugging her shoulders.

"Uh huh." Her mom crossed her arms over her chest. "Slept in a bit, I see?"

"Forgot to set an alarm."

"Ari, that's—" she started into a lecture and then sucked in a breath, "Jesus, Mary, and Joseph—is that a hickey?" Mom's voice reached a supersonic pitch. "How the hell did you get a hickey, Ari?"

Oh my god. Ari slapped a palm to her neck, remembering the exact spot Gid had sucked on last night. But, a hickey? Was it a hickey? He gave her a motherfricking hickey? What was he, fifteen, and never kissed a girl's neck before?

"It's not a hickey."

"Then why are you covering it up?"

"I don't even know what you're talking about." But Ari didn't move an inch.

"You better cover that thing up, missy, and be downstairs in ten minutes. We're going to start without you." Her eyelids fluttered closed. "I don't even want to know where *that* came from."

"Fine, fine. I'll be right down." She shut the door in her mom's face and ran to the mirror.

Yep, right there, clear as day was a little lip-shaped mark on her neck. "Jesus, Mary, and Joseph," she muttered, echoing her mom's sentiments.

As if last night wasn't humiliating enough, worming its way into her brain, now she had to have this badge of dishonor to remind herself exactly what a mess she was last night.

Embarrassment flared alive inside her gut, threatening to consume her. But today wasn't about her. She needed to figure her shit out and put it aside so that Thomas and

Julia could have the beautiful wedding weekend they deserved.

She turned away from the mirror. Bright winter sunlight streamed through the gauzy hotel curtains, lightening the moody colors of the space. Ten minutes. Spinning around, it looked like a bomb had gone off in her tiny little hotel room. Her shit was everywhere, even though she'd only been in Dublin less than twenty-four hours.

Ari didn't want it to be morning. She didn't want to see her mistakes in the bright morning light.

"Fuck," she cursed, closing her eyes.

If she pretended as hard as she could, maybe last night hadn't happened. Maybe she didn't have a little breakdown mere seconds away from orgasm. Maybe Gid, one of her best friends, wasn't in her bed last night, and was just a figment of her imagination after jet lag delirium.

Yeah, she'd go with that.

If it weren't for the physical evidence on her neck, she almost believed it, too.

Ari raked a brush through her hair, pulled it back in a high slicked ponytail, washed up, did her makeup as quick as she could, and pulled on the outfit she'd had planned for this pre-wedding breakfast for months: long, wide legged, Christmas-red silk pants, and creamy white silk blouse with a bow tied loose at the neck. She bent to do up her heels and with some gold rings and a chunky, clear plastic bracelet, she was basically ready to go.

Except for the hickey. She narrowed her eyes at the mirror just as there was another knock on the door.

"Ari!" It was Lacey, and she was breathlessly whispering through the door. "Your mom said to come check on you."

With a groan, Ari yanked open the door. "Come in."

Unlike her mom just a couple minutes ago, Lacey was a more welcome guest. She wore a camel brown turtleneck sweater dress that hugged her ample curves and had a high slit up the side. Her long, blonde hair fell over her shoulder in natural waves.

"God, you look great." Ari wrinkled her nose, feeling very under slept.

"What's that look for? You look amazing." Lacey booped her on the elbow, and then latched on, pulling her closer. "But, my god, your mom wasn't joking: you do have a hickey. What the hell, Ari! Is this...is this from Gid? Poor, unsuspecting Gideon Sims?"

Lacey frowned, but her eyes sparkled with devilish merriment.

Ari yanked her elbow away making a frustrated sound. "I would appreciate if y'all started focusing on the soon-to-be-wedded couple and *not* me, thank you very much."

Lacey whistled. "Did the man even know what hit him?"

Ignoring the question, Ari turned to the mirror and started delicately applying makeup to her neck so that it didn't stain her cream-white shirt.

"We're just worried about you is all," Lacey said, suddenly serious over Ari's shoulder.

Ari's stomach dropped. *Worried about you.* That was literally the last thing she wanted. She didn't want anyone to worry about her. Think twice about her. Have to be concerned with what was going on in her life. And yet, she couldn't quit keeping herself from messing up so that she warranted such a fuss.

"It's nothing," she mumbled, stretching her neck long to one side and applying concealer.

"It's not just this, ya know?" Lacey continued. "I know it's not really my place but...your family is noticing things. You're coming to dinner less, your mom says you barely call anymore, your brothers miss you, you haven't talked about school or your job hunt in ages. They say you're drinking a lot. And I get it, I was a party girl, too, so I think they're being a little ridiculous but I know Danny is watching, you know?"

Ari froze, latching eyes with Lacey in the mirror. Her hazel eyes were so full of concern that it made Ari sick to her stomach.

Drinking a lot. What did that even mean? She was young, still in college, *and* she knew some of the shit her brothers got up to when they were her age. Not like they were angels.

But that wasn't even the tip of the iceberg when it came to Ari's problems. No one even knew that she was *this* close to academic suspension.

"It's..." Ari's insides lurched at just the thought of spilling everything right here, right now.

Wouldn't it be easier if she just told someone? If this secret wasn't just hers to bear? As quick as the thought came to her, her internal shutters snapped shut. "It's nothing, like I said."

Lacey searched Ari's gaze in the mirror, clearly not believing her. But after a moment, she let it lie.

"Alright," she said with a sigh. "Come on, you look gorgeous. Let's go. There's Bellinis downstairs."

The boutique hotel was a refurbished red-brick Georgian-era building and damn was it gorgeous. Her brother really did his research before picking this place. Or maybe it was Julia. Ari's heels clicked on the wood floor—such a satisfying, comforting sound, just like being back in the dance studio. Emerald green and mustard yellow velvet chairs and bold, statement tables caught her eye all around as they walked into the private dining room. Modern, dramatic chandeliers hung over the space, scattering soft light.

Yes, Ari could see herself getting very tipsy in one of those comfy looking chairs.

"There she is," Danny essentially hollered over the low hum of conversation. He turned sideways to slide between the small clusters of people chatting with his own as-promised Bellini clutched in hand. "Slept in, didya?"

Ari narrowed her eyes playfully up at him. "Yes," she said, with a sassy wiggle of her head.

Despite the storm clouds gathering in her chest, she had a role to play here, and she was determined to nail her part this weekend. For Thomas and Julia. This was their wedding and Ari wasn't about to ruin it.

Lacey looped her arm through Ari's. "Let's get you a drink," she whispered in her ear with a little squeeze at the crook of her elbow.

Maybe Ari could fool her brothers who—god love them—were great but easily distracted, but Lacey was another story.

Fresh cocktail in hand, Ari and Lacey found Julia, who looked fantastic in a white jumpsuit. Her brown hair fell loose around her shoulders. Happiness radiated from her as she introduced Ari and Lacey to her parents and Thomas smiled goofily down at her. His puppy dog eyes were so smitten.

Ari knocked him with a hip. "That's gonna be your wife."

"Can you believe it?" He played with the sleeves of his grey sports coat.

God her brother looked so freaking happy. And, her own thoughts on marriage aside, she was happy for him too. Julia was his perfect counterpoint—they'd lived in bliss ever since he moved back from New York City.

With a drink to her lips and the bubbles in her stomach, Ari could almost forget last night's disaster. The heady mixture of Prosecco and true love gave her a reprieve from thinking about school and life back home. She smiled over her glass and easily made small talk before brunch was served.

It was only once she'd relaxed a bit that she thought to look for Gid. What an awful wedding date she was. But he was a grown boy, he could handle himself. Her eyes landed on him in conversation with her mom, but he was staring right at her.

Ari choked on her beverage. That laser-focused gaze honed right into her core, warmth spreading from the center of her chest. What she would give to know exactly what he was thinking right now. And if things weren't so awkward all of a sudden, she'd march right up to him and demand to know.

She grit her back teeth together and froze.

As if reading her thoughts, Gid's cheeks flushed in a way that Ari should not find attractive at all, but my god she did. She wouldn't mind taking him up to her room right now and getting on her knees for him, if he didn't trigger something inside that she definitely didn't want to examine. The humiliation from the night before trickled down her back like hot needles all the way to the base of her spine. By all rights, last night shouldn't have happened. She shouldn't feel this way about him.

And yet...

Gid stared, long enough that Ari forgot where she was for a moment. Dublin? With her family? For her brother's wedding? Maybe. She couldn't be sure anymore.

Lacey whipped around ready to cajole Ari back into conversation with her siblings.

"Uh?" she said, immediately clocking the awkwardness between Ari and Gid. "Whoa," she whispered.

Goddamnit Gid looked handsome wearing all black. His crewneck sweater fit him like a glove. The memory of his fingers ghosting over her skin made Ari's nipples pebble right there. As if Gid sensed her reaction, his knuckles blanched on his champagne flute. She cleared her throat.

"So, it *was* Gid?" Lacey whispered to Ari.

Gid's throat bobbed, and Ari clutched her champagne flute.

"Shut up, Lace," Ari said out of the corner of her mouth. She wet her lips, wondering if Gid felt as parched and starved as she did.

This feeling was confusing. Hadn't she kicked him out in the middle of the night after their failed night of pleasure? Why did she crave his body again so badly?

Gid combed his dark, floppy hair back. He looked nervous, just like he did before their competitions. Before the flight yesterday.

They could get past this. They had to if they intended to survive the week. Ari shrugged her shoulders, the silk of her top gliding smoothly over her skin.

Lacey scrunched her nose, confused. Rightfully so.

Now Danny noticed the awkwardness, too, and her mom. Thomas remained locked in his own awkward conversation with Julia's dad, which was mostly one-sided toward Thomas.

Ari rolled her eyes and shook the tension from her shoulders. She was here to enjoy her brother's pre-wedding brunch. And at least six more Bellinis.

Just then Julia turned around, too. "Gid! Oh my god this hotel is gorgeous. Thank you so much for recommending it."

Now Ari raised an eyebrow.

"No problem." Gid forced a charming smile onto his face. "Glad you love it. I know the owners. Met them when I was studying abroad in college."

His eyes flicked to hers when he said it. Hmm, this was news to her. Ari's cheeks burned remembering how his gaze bore into hers last night.

Ari crossed an arm over her stomach and rested her opposite elbow on top. She downed her drink and placed it on a passing tray, grabbing a new one in one swift movement.

"I need to pee," she mumbled, and she marched off in search of the bathroom.

This was going to be one hell of a week.

TWELVE
GID

LACEY ARCHED one particularly questioning eyebrow at him. Suddenly, the airy dining room wasn't so spacious. A kernel of dread stuck itself in his throat and he desperately wanted to pull at the neck of his sweater to dislodge it.

God, he was overreacting yet every bone in his body wanted to follow Ari and—*I don't know*—see if she was okay?

Last night replayed over and over in his head. The way Ari had absolutely zoned out in the middle of riding him. How, when he grabbed onto her thighs, she blinked and seemed to be coming back from a million miles away. It had scared him and he'd been worried about her ever since.

Now, his ridiculously strong desire to follow her

scared him, too. Because obviously she didn't want to be around him.

But this was a mistake. Her words from the night before echoed in his ears.

He shouldn't follow her, and yet, his body seemed to work of its own volition. He put his drink on the table and muttered, "I'll be right back."

Lacey, apparently the only person still interested in their charade, followed him with her quizzical gaze. Somehow, he thought she might be enjoying this. But as he left the dining room, Ari was already out of sight.

Shit. Should he follow her into the bathroom? That wasn't really the best idea: she'd stormed out, clearly needing some space. He had no idea what to say anyway. God what an idiot he was.

So instead of choosing anything, he paced in front of the bathroom door, working off his nervous energy. He stared at the pattern of the wood floor, parquet arrows pointing this way and that, as he walked one way and then the other. Maybe he could divine a direction, some kind of answer, if he focused there hard enough.

Last night had been a mistake she'd said. So, why did it absolutely feel like there was something still there, unanswered? He didn't regret it. Only that he didn't insist on staying to hold her through whatever she was clearly going through.

Typical of him to insert himself where he wasn't

wanted. It happened all the time with his parents. It made it hard for him to make friends when he was younger and their family moved around a lot for their research. Which is how he learned it was easiest to be alone, more often than not.

The bathroom door creaked open.

"Gid?" Ari's dark nails dug into her hip, elbow popped out to the side.

He hesitated, looking into her face. What would he find there? Her voice didn't give anything away.

"Didn't expect you to follow me," she said.

Still, he couldn't discern what her words might imply. *Just look at her.*

He lifted his eyes to hers, his eyebrows raised in question.

"What do you want me to say?" She sounded defeated, exhausted. "Last night was...well, like I said, a mistake. You're my friend, Gid. My best friend. I don't know what I was thinking. I'm sorry."

She stepped up to him, a couple inches taller in her heels than last night, and closer to eye height. Kissing height.

"Can we be adults about this?" she asked.

Gid's tongue darted out and wet his lips, traitor that it was. Ari didn't miss the movement and a laugh so low it was almost a growl rumbled in her chest. That sound did things to his insides. He didn't feel exactly like a friend or an adult right now. He shoved his fists in his pockets so that he wouldn't reach out and touch her.

Ari tracked the movement and frowned, just a little, before her unreadable mask snapped back into place.

"That's what I thought," she said, before downing the rest of her Bellini and walking away.

"Do you want to talk about this?" Gid said to her back, with an edge of desperation that he couldn't keep from his voice.

"Not really." Ari didn't turn around when she responded.

It was going to be a long day.

* * *

THOMAS AND JULIA had their wedding weekend planned down to a tee. And now that everyone was in Dublin, the festivities could truly begin.

Since Gid hurdled over his travel anxiety, he could focus on the fun, too.

Except a new anxiety had taken its place.

If only he'd accommodated for the tiniest hiccup of Ari, who clung to her champagne flute, part of, but separate from, everyone around her. She had her shields up. That much was obvious to him. And of course he'd been the reason why.

What kind of friend was he, who fell into bed with her at the first suggestion? Why didn't he stop and reconsider?

There was no going back now, clearly. He would honor her wishes and pretend that it didn't happen, but it would be hard to forget the way she tasted.

Ari grabbed a fresh drink and narrowed her eyes at Gid across the room as if she could read his thoughts. How her scent lifted off his skin when he stepped in the shower that morning, evaporating into the mist. How soft her long, dark hair felt between his fingers. How wet her pussy was when he finally dipped into her tights.

He cut that last thought short; that was definitely too distracting.

Even though Gid tried to ignore her, her silhouette in the warm, slanted winter light called to him. Her olive toned skin popped against the cream of her shirt. God, she was truly gorgeous. How had he been able to ignore that fact for years?

A clattering on the table jolted him out of his daydream.

"Ari!" her mother hissed as a couple people gasped.

Julia stepped back from the table and stood. She held her arms out to the side, looking down at her silk jumpsuit.

"It's fine," she said breezily, dabbing at her outfit with a linen napkin.

But Ari's mom stared daggers at her daughter. "What's gotten into you?"

Gid watched, his insides doused in ice, seeing the scene as an outsider to the family. There were a lot of people frowning all of a sudden and Ari jumped to her feet too, knocking into the table as she did.

"Oh my god, Julia," she whined, "I'm so sorry."

Gid searched the table and quickly spotted the knocked over champagne flute. His stomach tightened. Such things happened at weddings, but for the drink to land in the bride's lap specifically was far from ideal.

"It's fine," Julia repeated in an attempt at grace, despite the tension etched on her face.

But Ari reached toward her with her own napkin. Gid saw the next couple moments in slow motion. The end of Ari's napkin caught on Julia's glass and when Ari stretched just a bit further, the second glass toppled over, dousing Julia's camel leather flats in Bellini.

The entire table groaned as Julia froze, staring at her feet. "These are my wedding shoes."

"Alright." Gid stood, breaking the deafening silence. He put out fires at work every day, and this was just another scenario to manage.

Except that when he spoke, eight pairs of eyes turned to him, their expressions ranging from shocked to enraged. Only Ari and Julia didn't look his way. His stomach twisted like a knotted rope, but he kept his cool. "We can get this sorted."

"And I think you need to stop drinking," Thomas muttered at his sister.

Oh no. This was the kind of conversation Gid usually tried to avoid. His family was strictly non-confrontational, burying their heads in the sand when it came to anything *messy* to discuss. But Gid knew the Callaghans weren't like that. They tended to air their grievances.

He really wished they wouldn't do so right now. Not after the night, and morning, Ari had.

"I'm sorry," Ari responded, standing up straight and lifting her chin in a hint of defiance. "I already said so, it was an accident."

"Would it have happened if you hadn't already drank —what—six Bellinis all to yourself?"

"That's not fair. Everyone's drinking."

"No one's drinking like you."

Julia put a hand on Thomas's forearm. "It's alright."

"Hardly." Thomas threw his napkin onto his chair. "First, you show up late this morning. And now you're drunk and spilling drinks on my bride?"

"It was an accident." Ari wrung her fingers in front of her, her eyes glassy but desperate.

"It's not always the fucking Ari show."

The table cringed at that.

Something feral growled inside Gid's gut. He liked Thomas, but he could be a dick. And the deer in headlights look on Ari's face made Gid want to pounce on him.

Instead, he fisted his hands at his side and tried to shrink away from the scene.

"Come on, T," Danny said, barely loud enough for Gid to hear, his eyes wide and meaningful. "You don't want to ruin your wedding, man."

"I don't have to." He gestured across the table, his palm open like he was serving a platter. "Ari's already seen to that."

Thomas stalked out of the room leaving silence in his wake. Ari stared after him, her mouth open and her hands shaking.

"It's fine, Ari. We'll figure it out." Julia squeezed her future sister-in-law's shoulder. "I'll go talk to him, alright?"

Julia pulled off her soaked flats and waltzed from the room barefoot, surprisingly poised for the drama that just erupted over her brunch table. Heather followed behind her and then Julia's mom did too, both avoiding eye contact with Ari. Julia's dad remained at the table, munching on a strip of bacon.

At least someone still had their appetite.

There was nothing Gid could do, not now in front of the rest of Ari's family. They were just friends, but goddamn, did he want to curl Ari into his chest, smooth her hair down her back, and comfort her.

"Really, Ari." Her mom tutted at her daughter and sipped her cocktail. "You're supposed to be an adult now. Between the hickey this morning and now this, I swear you're still a child."

Ari's shoulders stiffened with the chastising as icy dread dropped into Gid's stomach.

Hickey? Oh god, was that from him? What a stupid question, who else could it be from? He knew he'd gotten a little carried away last night, but he never meant to mark her. Gid shifted his weight, hoping that no one could sense that *he* had been the one to give her the bruise.

Slowly, Ari raised her head, her spine ramrod straight. "Yep, let's all pile it on Ari. It's fine she can take it." She grabbed the closest champagne flute and downed its contents.

Her mom gasped.

Danny's jaw hardened. "That's probably not a good idea, Ari."

"Don't you all get it yet? I don't care! I don't care what you all think of me, I don't care what I do, what I look like when I do it, or what you think when I do it. It's *my* life. I'll do with it what I choose." Ari stormed out of the room.

"I'm really sorry about all this," her mom said, clearly speaking to Julia's dad, gesturing around the table. "We're not usually so dramatic."

He grunted in response.

"Weddings. Am I right?" Gid tried to be cool, but his brain had left the room with Ari, still focused on the hickey from last night. "I'll just step out and let things cool off."

For the second time today, he followed in Ari's wake. Like a specter, the faint scent of her perfume wafted behind her. A weight settled in Gid's chest when he caught sight of Ari pacing in the hotel's courtyard.

"Hey." He pushed the door open and stepped through in a swirl of freezing air. "Come back inside."

Her sharp gaze cut right through to his heart. "What are you doing out here, Gid?"

He shrugged. "Trying to get you to come back inside."

Ari stopped pacing and watched him. "I don't know why you even care."

The ice in her voice sent a shiver down his spine. He desperately wanted to know what was going on with her. There was clearly something more that was bothering her, sending her into this spiral. Why she was so closed off, and to him of all people? He clenched his molars together with a click.

"Ari..." he sighed out her name, loaded with a lot of the things that he couldn't untangle in his own brain.

His gaze drifted to her neck, searching for the hickey that he'd left there. Though he remembered the exact spot where his lips caressed her skin, he saw nothing. She'd done a good job with the makeup. None of it had even gotten on her cream top. "I'm sorry about the..." he gestured to his own neck instead of saying the word.

For a moment, he swore that her pupils grew, but in the next second, they were back to her usual sparkling brown.

"Listen, Gid, we don't owe each other anything, okay? This is kinda messed up but," she pursed her lips and shook her head, "I'd just rather we pretend nothing ever happened between us, alright? It'll be easier that way."

We don't owe each other anything. She kept saying that.

For some reason, her words hurt more than he

expected. Gid looked toward the sky, covered in a layer of snow-white clouds and rubbed his hand on the back of his head. When he looked back down at her, she lifted her eyebrows, waiting for his response.

"Yeah, sure, you got it." But inside, his entire body screamed that wasn't what he wanted at all.

THIRTEEN

ARI

THE VIBES of the brunch were officially dead. Hell, most of the day was shot. It was meant to be a day of pampering for the gals: Julia, Ari, Lacey, Heather, and their moms had scheduled massages, manicures and pedicures, and an early dinner without the guys who were touring the Guinness Storehouse followed by a mid-afternoon Dublin pub crawl that Thomas had curated specifically to their tastes.

Except that try though she might to relax, Ari absolutely couldn't. She apologized to Julia, who laughed the whole thing off, bless her, but things with her mom and Thomas were more fraught.

The Callaghans had a rough go of it for the last year and a half. Between her dad's long fight with cancer, death last fall, and the transitional phase of Callaghan's Coney Island to Thomas's leadership when he moved back to

Michigan, this wedding was meant to ground them back into some kind of normal.

But of course, Ari had to go and fuck it all up.

Typical.

She stayed in her own little bubble of stewing thoughts, begrudgingly thinking of Gid's touch on her naked skin as she got her massage.

Gid. Another thing she'd royally messed up.

God, he was so sweet the way he looked at her with concern, with those steady brown eyes that could very nearly see into her soul. The only way she knew to get him to stop looking was to be mean to him, but that didn't seem to deter him either.

Oh, the way he'd let her take control in the bedroom until things fell apart. It was a conundrum, the way he commanded her to take the lead. The juxtaposition made her toes curl.

With the lavender aromatherapy and the message therapist's fingers working her feet, she started to drift into a slightly-less-stressed state. Her poor feet had taken a beating over the last half a year as she kept them stuffed in high heels chasing corporate success. Some good that had done her.

The room was dark, with the other ladies in their own room getting their own massage, and ambient music floated around Ari, transporting her. Her eyes drifted closed as the massage therapist worked up her legs, undoing knots in her calves and hamstrings.

Ari smiled to herself as her body tingled, almost entering another plane of being. She sighed, and imagined it was Gid's hands working along her body—up her back, neck, and into her scalp. Despite the disaster of their one night together, she couldn't help thinking of how his belt buckle felt as she undid it. The way he tossed her over his shoulder like she weighed nothing. How he joked with her and smirked at her over their airplane drinks.

The massage therapist held up the sheet, having finished on Ari's back side. "Time to flip over."

She tucked the sheet around Ari's chest after she rotated and then repeated the process, working up Ari's body from her feet.

This was what she'd been missing for the last year. The tension from her dad's death, school stress, and grief that always seemed to lurk around the corner. With a shock, she realized that she never felt truly safe for the last year, always on the edge of some kind of disaster.

Disaster had found her alright. Especially if she was about to be required to take a semester off school.

Ari sighed, attempting to focus on relaxation.

And then the massage therapist got to her knees and quads. She pushed deeply into a couple knots on the outer side of her thigh—where Ari's iliotibial band was always tight from dancing. Pain that bordered on pleasure washed over Ari as the therapist worked out the knots. Melting into the massage table, Ari let herself be carried away. When the massage therapist worked even deeper into the tight spots, Ari's pelvic floor tightened, and her stomach lurched. Then with the therapist's next touch, an orgasm ripped through her.

"Oh," she barely breathed before pulling her lips between her teeth to hide the intense pleasure radiating from her pelvis. She wiggled her hips, repositioning just slightly, completely stunned by the waves pulsing through her core. Her chest heaved with the effort to keep the feeling secret, her lungs full of air and burning.

As the sensation subsided, Ari hazarded a glance as the massage therapist, who faced Ari's feet with her elbow still cranking through Ari's tight IT band. She seemed to be none the wiser at the orgasm that had just steamrolled through Ari.

Shit, well, that was awkward. She'd heard of exercise induced orgasms before, but never knew a massage could bring one on. *Jesus, Mary, and Joseph.*

And yet... the bundle of nerves that had haunted her since the night before was finally released. This was exactly what she'd been chasing yesterday when she propositioned Gid.

Too soon, the massage was over, and the therapist left Ari to get dressed in privacy. She pulled her hair over her shoulder, sitting at the edge of the bed. What the hell just happened?

* * *

THOMAS WAS STILL IGNORING Ari at the rehearsal dinner that evening.

"I'll talk to him," Julia whispered. "Don't worry."

Not that Ari cared. Thomas could be a little shit and, hey, it was his day. Or weekend. Whatever. Usually, she would have given him his attitude right back, but that would have just dug her into a deeper hole.

"Ari." Gid put a hand on her lower back. A move that, one week ago, wouldn't have meant much to her, but now it sent sparks of heat flaring through her body. God, it was confusing to have sexual attraction to her best friend all of a sudden. "Can I get you a drink?"

"I'm not drinking," Ari mumbled.

Gid laughed. "Oh, come on, it's a wedding."

Ari stared daggers at him. "I'm not trying to have a repeat of this morning."

"Drunk Ari is always a little clumsy." He looked down at her and smiled, as if drunk Ari was his favorite thing in the world.

And, honestly, sometimes it felt like she was. The two of them definitely had some fantastic drunk times in college. Dancing down the sidewalk at two in the morning. Eating a whole pizza between the two of them. Stealing pint glasses from local bars every other night.

"You weren't even that bad this morning. Don't worry."

"Please, Gid. Don't try and make me feel better. Thomas seemed to find it pretty traumatic."

"Ah by the third bar today, he forgot all about it."

They both looked in Thomas's direction who stared back at them with a clenched jaw and a heavy brow.

"Okay, maybe he's still a little upset," Gid muttered, looking back down at Ari. "How was the massage?"

Ari cleared her throat and she flushed. She hoped that he wouldn't see her blush in the restaurant's low lighting. "Umm, it was good."

Gid raised an eyebrow. "You don't seem convinced."

"No, well, it was very relaxing, exactly what I needed." Which wasn't a lie.

"Glad to hear it."

And ever since the massage, her sex drive hummed with a low purr. All afternoon she was tied up in knots. Confusing thoughts of the massage therapist's hands on her skin and Gid's long, sure fingers between her legs. She squeezed her thighs together now at the thought.

Considering how things ended with Gid, it was definitely a mistake, but damn would she like to try again. Just two friends having fun.

Or would it be just more self-sabotage?

Ari licked her lips. "Yeah, thanks."

They sat down at the long table, Thomas and Julia at one end, parents at the other, and siblings dotted in between. The velvet of the emerald green chair felt good under Ari's hand. She kept rubbing her fingers on the seat even when she sat down with Gid on her right. When he scooted his chair in, his foot landed right beside hers, their legs touching from thigh all the way down to calf. Her body crackled alive from the contact. Did anyone else at the table notice the way her body sparked with Gid's touch?

Ari chanced a glance at Gid, and he smiled back, innocent as a cherry Pop-Tart, before focusing on Thomas who stood at the head of the table.

Her brother held a glass of Prosecco in the air and Ari picked up her water. God, she felt like a child. But after this morning, she wasn't going to risk another drunk mistake at this wedding. She'd already ruined Julia's shoes, she didn't need to ruin anything else.

Gid's warm stable hand reached under the table and clasped her knee. Another jolt of surprise. A splash of water sloshed over the edge of her glass.

"Relax." His soft whisper tickled her neck. "You're shaking the whole table."

Ari hadn't even realized that she was bouncing her leg. Now that she was still, Gid didn't move his hand. Instead, he squeezed with a light amount of pressure.

"I want to thank you all for coming," Thomas began. "It means so much to Julia and me that you're here, at Christmas, celebrating with us in our unconventional kind of way."

He sniffed, and Ari knew what was coming next. Her heart thumped in her chest. If Thomas was going to cry, her mom was going to cry, and then Ari was going to cry, and Danny—who never cried—would start crying. The

Callaghans would be a blubbering mess. A fitting way to round out these last thirteen months.

"It's been just over year since my dad died." His voice broke on the word died.

Heat raced down Ari's arms, watching her brother, his eyes already glassy with tears. God, her brother could be a pain, but she loved him. After his speech, she would march right up to his stubborn ass and hug him and properly apologize for this morning. From the other end of the table, Mom sniffed. Ari frowned against the tightness in her chest that always came before tears.

Thomas's voice was thick with emotion when he started speaking again. "I just wish he was here to see how things ended up between Julia and I—this long, strange story we've had. Dad always loved Julia, even back in high school. He wasn't the only one."

His little joke broke some of the tension. And yet, when Ari laughed, her tears finally spilled over.

"Somehow, I think he always knew we would end up here. Tomorrow, we'll spread some of his ashes as part of our ceremony, so I like to think he'll be there in spirit."

Streams of tears ran down his cheeks. "So, cheers to Dad, and to everyone for being here with us."

Ari smiled, raising her glass a little higher in toast, crying now in earnest.

She clinked glasses with Lacey on her left and then turned to Gid on her right. His eyes roved her face, taking her all in, her entirety. The hand that was on her knee moved to her chin, his thumb caught one tear, and he smiled his crooked grin, so soft and sweet. His eyebrows furrowed and he opened his mouth as if he was going to say something. Julia popped up at the head of the table, interrupting their moment.

"Not that there's anything else to say following my fiancé's perfect speech, but I wanted to thank you all for being here, too. It really means a lot to us."

The table toasted again, and Ari pushed to her feet, weaving around Danny and Lacey to get to Thomas. He was seated, but stood up when she reached his elbow, looking down at her with red-rimmed eyes.

"Can I have a hug?" Ari asked, arms open wide. She was going to get a hug whether he accepted her apology or not. After that speech, the Callaghans were all a little fragile.

"I'm sorry," she huffed as Thomas pulled her against him. "For this morning. For being stupid. I should have been more careful. And I already apologized to Julia," she said, her voice muffled against his chest as she squeezed her brother around the middle. It really had been a while since the two had properly hugged.

"Listen. *I'm* sorry," he said, pulling back. "I was an ass— "

"Yes," she cut in and he frowned. "Sorry, sorry keep going."

"And you're right: it was an accident. Even if you were Bellini wasted before noon."

"It was brunch. And I'm on vacation. It's Christmas for Pete's sake! And the drinks just kept coming. What was I supposed to do?"

Thomas raised an eyebrow.

"Right, right. I know. Yes. I'm sorry, you're sorry. Everyone's sorry." Ari craned her neck around Thomas. "And I'm especially sorry to you and your shoes, Julia."

Julia waved her future sister-in-law off. "It's fine. Heather and Reagan worked some magic, so we're all set."

"Cheers to Heather and her girlfriend then," Ari said across the table, and Heather raised her drink in appreciation.

"We're good?" she asked Thomas.

"All good. Love you," Thomas said, his eyes pulling down at the corners as he gave a flat non-smile smile. One of his trademarks since his moody teenage years.

"Love you, too, T."

Feeling pounds lighter, Ari waltzed back to her seat. She huffed as she dropped into her chair next to Gid, who seemed happy to have her back.

"Well, if that wasn't just the sweetest thing," Gid said, leaning closer to Ari, keeping their conversation between them.

"Sibling love is pure and complicated, Gid, and I'm sorry you don't have a sibling to share it with. I love and hate my brothers, literally at all times, but I would cut a bitch for them in two seconds flat."

"That's what I love about you," Gid said, his hand again suddenly warming her knee.

Oh. Ari clamped down on her outward expression of what Gid's words did to her.

What the hell? They always said they love each other —they're best friends after all—but after what happened last night...well, the words took on a different kind of meaning.

Even though Ari definitely did not have a crush on Gid. Imagine—Gideon Sims... The guy who she met freshman year, who raced cardboard boxes down the hallway with his roommate. Who she ran next to on the treadmill for hours at the university gym. Who's seen her literally projectile vomit her drunken two-in-the-morning burrito onto the sidewalk and gave her a piggy back ride home after it.

Yeah, no.

She loved him, absolutely. But she wasn't *in* love with him.

Though the way his hand curled around the inside of her knee, into the crook of her upper thigh made her shift her hips in her seat.

"Tell me to stop, and I will," Gid whispered into her ear, and she took a sip of water, casual as ever.

She made a strangled, approving sound in response.

As if he had no idea whatsoever that his touch drove her bonkers, Gid turned his focus across the table, softening the hard stone exterior that was Julia's dad by talking to him about deer hunting.

Deer hunting. Literally Gid had zero clue what bow hunting entailed but my god was he good at pretending. It was one of the things that Ari loved about her best friend that, despite his anxiety, he could have a conversation with anyone at any time and do so sincerely. He had a rabid curiosity about the world and everyone in it.

This charade was new, though. The way he kept his focus entirely on Julia's dad while slowly, criminally slowly, inching his hand up Ari's thigh. It was almost as if he didn't realize he was doing it, that his hand worked completely independent of his body.

Somehow, she knew exactly what his touch meant: *I'm not talking to you right now, Ari Callaghan, but you're all I'm thinking about.*

"Ready for your trip?" Lacey turned to Ari, interrupting her thoughts.

"Oh." Ari's hand slipped and knocked her knife into her plate. The servers were just bringing out their salads. "Yeah, for sure."

"Where are y'all going exactly?" Lacey's eyes lit up, eager for details.

"Well," Ari took a shuddering breath, trying with all her might to focus on some ever-loving detail of her and Gid's little Christmas trip, "we're taking the train out to this little village in County Cork that's basically made up of this Christmas tree farm and staying at their cozy guest house."

Gid's hand reached the edge of Ari's skirt, a border to cross. She held her breath as Lacey asked a question about their route, and wondered what Gid would do next. Wondered what she wanted him to do. Wondered if anyone would notice. Between the tablecloth and the napkin in her lap, she prayed no one would.

Because her body was alive and sparkling and, mistake or not, she desperately wanted his exploration to continue.

FOURTEEN
GID

IF YOU ASKED Gideon Sims forty-eight hours ago when he and Ari Callaghan boarded their first flight what he would be doing at Friday's rehearsal dinner, he most assuredly would not have answered teasing the shit out of her with his hand halfway up her thigh and plunging under the edge of her skirt. But holy hell was he enjoying it.

"Saw a 6-point, an 8-point, and a doe just last week," the man across from him grunted, his grey-brown mustache wiggling as he smiled, apparently pleased with whatever the hell that meant. "Shot the 8-point and should be done processing by the time we get home."

Processing. That sounded dreadful.

"Congrats." Gid tilted his head across the table toward the man.

"What do you do with the meat?" Molly chimed in on the conversation.

Of course a bunch of Michigan folk wouldn't have an issue with talking about hunting deer over a nice, plated dinner. Gid stabbed at a forkful of salad with his free hand as Molly carried the conversation.

"Gid," Ari hissed, an unspoken warning, as she gripped the wrist of his hand nestled pleasantly between her strong dancer thighs. "What are you doing?"

An excellent question. One he didn't exactly have an answer for other than something had awakened between the two of them, something that he couldn't ignore as she sat next to him, all emotional, and smelling of that cursed Santal 33. She always smelled great, but now, something about that sandalwood wafting off her skin drove him absolutely bonkers.

Maybe because he knew now how it smelled on his skin the morning after.

"I can stop." He lifted the pressure off her warm skin.

She squeaked in protest. A little whine that he wanted to record and play over and over in private.

"I..." she exhaled, inching her hips forward, pushed her legs further under the table and giving Gid more access to the space between her legs. "No, that's not what I want."

Her brown eyes blew wide, her pupils dark and pushing the golden brown color to the edge of her iris.

She *liked* this.

Servers walked around the room, clearing their salad plates, and Gid swallowed.

Don't get carried away, buddy, his little internal voice whispered. Yes, he knew that he had a tendency to go all freaking in on everything in his life, eagerly and obsessively chasing whatever carrot dangled in front of him. But this was Ari. She wasn't a carrot. And they were in front of her family. He couldn't embarrass her, not after what happened this morning.

But oh the way her silky skin tickled the pads of his fingers. He wanted more.

His appetite for the woman beside him shocked him. Ari Callaghan. The girl he'd met freshman year of college who walked up and down their hallway in Eeyore pajama pants and clay face masks. Who pulled all-nighters in the undergrad library with him, cramming for exams and finishing papers. Who took warm vodka shots out of red solo cups with him at eight in the morning before Saturday football games.

What they say about traveling abroad really was true. It sure did open your eyes.

"Gid," she whispered his name like she'd done a million times before, but somehow, that one syllable word hit different. Her fingers dug into his wrist as his fingers dared to inch higher.

He hazarded a glance around the table. No one was paying them any attention. Heather was deep in conversation with Julia. Danny and Lacey were grilling Thomas.

Reagan chatted with Julia's mom, and Molly and Julia's dad still talked about hunting.

Gid inched his hand further up her thigh, staring down at her lap, heat climbing his neck. "I can stop whenever you want." His lips barely moved with the words.

"Mmm." She nodded and pulled her lips between her teeth.

"But I really don't want to."

Ari exhaled, melting into the chair.

The main plates came around—filet mignon and fingerling potatoes—and Ari put both hands on the table. She scooted her chair forward, closer to the food, which resulted in Gid's hand slipping even higher. A little, painful moan rumbled in his chest as his pointer finger grazed the edge of her panties.

What color were they today? He imagined sliding them off her hips, down around her ankles. Maybe leaving them there while he spread her legs.

What the hell had gotten into him?

"Right, Gid?" Julia said, from across the table.

Both Ari and Gid jumped apart, knocking the table. Their drinks jostled. His hand suddenly chilled in the absence of her warm body. It screamed out again for the contact of Ari's skin, but instead he fisted it and rested it on the table.

A couple eyes darted in their direction, but Gid tried as hard as he could to play it cool. He picked up his water glass, suddenly parched, as Ari reached for her silverware, ready to dig into her food.

"Right, I'm sure, but I missed the question?" He flashed his most charming, shit-eating smile to take the attention off Ari.

"I was just explaining to Heather how funny it is that you actually went to high school in Everdale but only met Ari freshman year of college. And now Ari lives in Everdale and you live in Starling Hills." Julia cut into her steak, her expression giving nothing away if she knew the illicit games Gid and Ari had just been playing under the table.

"Yes, that's right," he said, leaning forward onto his elbows. Ari still hadn't completely regained her composure. "We lived in the same dorm. And on the same floor. Butterfield Hall."

"What a small world." Heather laughed, grabbing her wine glass.

"We had a blast. Remember when your buddies snuck a keg into their room and invited everyone in the hall to a party?" Ari chimed in, no longer breathless and ready to dig into her meal.

"It was a mess. I think half of the hall got a Minor in Possession ticket that night." Gid put a piece of steak into his mouth.

"But you snuck me out." Ari smirked at him.

"I snuck you out."

"Honestly, I kind of forgot about that."

Their conversation was personal sized again, just between the two of them. They'd begun their own volleying conversation of reminiscing, the rest of the table falling away. As often happened between them, their rapid dialogue, full of memories and inside jokes. It didn't make it easy for others to keep up.

"How could you forget? We had to walk around the entire dorm, from the back entrance to the front, without our winter jackets and it was basically blizzarding. Then we had to wait in the front common room, miles away from our floor, until the cops cleared out. It was a certifiable disaster," Gid said.

"Oh god." Ari covered her mouth as she laughed. "You're right. Then we huddled under fuzzy blankets watching *The Office* until we warmed up."

"And there was hot cocoa."

"Buttershots hot cocoa."

"Your specialty! How could I have forgotten your little pint of butterscotch schnapps."

Gid never forgot those little details, seared like a trail of sugary-sweet breadcrumbs through his neural pathways. "I'm never without my Buttershots," he said, very seriously.

Ari shook her head into her meal. "Those were some good times."

"The best."

She smiled up at him and her crisp brown eyes sparkled with fondness and...something more.

Something that mirrored the crazed heartbeat galloping in his chest.

* * *

AFTER DINNER, their party moved into the even lower lit hotel bar. Open bar all night, courtesy of Thomas and Julia. Dangerous. It didn't take long for their already intimate party of eleven to become eight, when the parents went to bed.

"Let's play a drinking game," Heather squealed, her eyes sparkling as she looked around the group.

"That is an excellent idea." Ari sidled up to Julia's sister. "I like your style."

Heather placed a hand on Ari's forearm and pouted endearingly before they both broke out into peals of laughter.

"I'll play, but this bride will *not* be hungover for her wedding day, so I'm switching to soda water and lime." Julia said, strolling to the bar for a drink.

"Never Have I Ever," Heather said, as if the game was already decided.

"What are we, eighteen again?" Thomas grumbled, taking a sip of his neat whiskey.

Which was funny, considering Gid hadn't felt more like his carefree younger self in years. But the guys all kind of looked at each other in mutual agreement that they would endure this for the ladies, who were already excited.

"Get in here, Juju." Ari bit the straw of her gin and tonic, the drink she ordered once she had a full stomach of food, and scooted over on the bench. "My soon to be sister."

"Just because you're little, and cute, *and* soon to be my sister, you're allowed to call me that. For now." Julia narrowed her eyes at Ari but laughed as she hopped onto the bench.

"Phew, Ari, you're lucky she didn't cut you. I tried calling her Juju once and she screamed at me," Heather said, settling on her side of the massive booth.

Julia rolled her eyes. "Shut up."

Gid laughed at all of the siblings—blood and soon to be in-laws—and the easy way they seemed to get along. He missed the camaraderie of college, having friends ready to hang out at the drop of a hat. Being an only child with parents who were too busy to cultivate a relationship with him was in stark contract to the Callaghan clan. He moved to Starling Hills and found a job at Contrakale to stay near Ari. His stomach clenched and the water-bellied sensation that he associated with his anxiety washed over him.

It'll pass, he told himself. Clutching his drink, he took a sip straight from the rim, having left the straw behind at the bar.

He slid into the booth on the open side next to Ari and

his fingers burned. The sensation ebbed in his stomach and before he could think twice, he snaked his arm around Ari's waist, feeling her curves underneath her blouse.

She turned to him, inching her upper body back to keep the requisite space between them. But she caught his gaze, and Gid's blazed down into hers. Her eyes bounced around seeking for a second before perhaps finding what they were looking for and she smiled.

"Hey." Ari settled against his side, nestling her shoulder under his.

"Hey yourself." Gid caught a whiff of her perfume and it nearly stopped his heart.

Seriously, what the hell was going on with him?

"Alright!" Heather called, raising both arms in the hair. Reagan grinned up at her date's hands in the air, cradling her chin and then shaking her head. "You animals know the rules. Ten fingers in the air and each person says some shit they've never done and everyone puts a finger down who has done that nasty shit. Every finger down is a drink."

"Buckle up bitches," Danny crooned, proudly displaying his ten fingers in the air. Lacey gave him a self-deprecating smirk. "What?" He shouldered her. "We're adventurous."

Lacey guffawed. "Don't flatter yourself."

"I'm going first," Thomas said, looking like he was absolutely not enjoying this.

Julia couldn't contain her heart eyes in his direction if she tried.

"Never have I ever taken ecstasy," Thomas started.

"Boo you're so boring," Ari snorted, putting down one finger.

And Gid did too, because they took X together their senior year of college spring break in Mexico. Definitely a questionable life choice that he wouldn't dare repeat again. He bumped his hips into hers at the memory and she smiled.

Heather, Reagan, and Lacey put their fingers down, too. Danny looked offended.

"Sorry babe," Lacey said.

Everyone with nine fingers still standing took a drink.

Julia cleared her throat. "Never have I ever...stolen something from work."

Gid chuckled at his co-worker trying to imagine her sneaking around Contrakale and looking for things to steal. That was definitely more Susan's kind of behavior, taking something just because she could.

"Okay," Heather moaned, "number one that's a lame never have I ever and number two not even a stack of post it notes?"

"Nope." Julia wiggled in her seat looking a little holier than thou and Heather scoffed in response.

"Okay, you're boring too, just like your future husband," Heather said.

"Hear, hear," Ari laughed and raised her drink across the table to cheers her soon-to-be co-sister-in-law.

"Please make this next one a good one," Heather said to Ari.

"Don't worry, I will," Ari said, tilting her head in concentration.

Gid's fingers itched to still be circled around her waist. He wanted to tease her with little touches dusting along her skin. But, being true to the rules, he had to keep his eight remaining fingers in the air.

"Never have I ever been in public with a butt plug in." Ari twisted her lips in a fierce grin.

Gid's stomach flipped when she said it. His brain conjured up the absolutely deranged image of Ari kneeling with a pretty pink crystal butt plug winking between her cheeks, her dark hair cascading down her back. The fantasy sent him into a spiral.

"Jesus Christ, Ari," Thomas cursed, shaking his head at his little sister.

"I said I never have!" Ari said, flicking her pointer finger in the air at her brother.

Meanwhile, Lacey theatrically put a finger down and took a drink.

"Okay now I need details," Heather said, staring open-mouthed.

"Nuh-uh, not around family," Danny said as Lacey opened her mouth to answer. Even in the low light, his cheeks flared plainly magenta.

Gid sucked air between his teeth as everyone stared at him, ready for his turn. "Well, I'm not sure how to follow that."

"This is just the beginning, buddy," Heather said and her eyes flickered with a wicked light.

He racked his brain. What was something that would be just naughty enough to keep the game fun, but not too over the edge? Not that he'd done anything too wild himself. Hooking up with Ari last night was about the most reckless thing that he'd done in years.

Shit. Again, he thought of the hickey he'd left behind and how careless he'd been to do it. Clenching he jaw for just a moment, he let the anxiety wash through him and he shoved it away.

"Never have I ever had sex in the back of a car." Innocent enough, yet a fantasy he'd never fulfilled himself.

Thomas and Julia caught each other's gaze and swallowed a mutual giggle, then put a finger down and took a drink.

The game passed in a haze of naughty never-have-I-evers, random ones, or some that were downright awkward, until each person had two or three fingers remaining. The group had definitely been targeting the soon-to-be-wed couple, with questions like "never have I ever lived in New York City," which got Thomas to put a finger down, or "never have I ever written smut," which was specifically for Julia.

"We are so close to getting one of you blissful souls to

lose the game." Ari scrunched her lips to one side, focused on her brother and Julia, who each had one finger left.

"Not that it matters, since you've been drinking a non-alcoholic drink, *JuJu*." Heather booped her sister's nose across Thomas.

Gid sighed and weighed down into his seat, his bones aching with a deep sense of melancholy. How he freaking yearned to be part of something as close as this mixed sibling group.

Ari leaned her head back against his shoulder as if in response to something that she sensed within him. Gid desperately wanted to know what was running through her mind, what his best friend was thinking about him, about them, right at that moment.

"Alright," Heather's eyes flashed deviously. "I have the perfect question to get you both out."

"Oh lord." Julia braced herself, sitting up straighter.

"Don't worry it's not that bad." Heather laughed. "Now I'm talking it up so much it's going to be kind of lame."

"Let's have it," Thomas said, eyeing Heather.

"Okay, okay. I'm surprised it's taken us this long to get here, but... Never have I ever had sex with my best friend."

Shit. Gid choked on his drink, sending it up the back of his nose. He started coughing, eyes watering, and Ari gave him major stink eye. Now he could definitely hear her thoughts: *Smooth much? Chill the fuck out, Gid.*

Yep, he definitely had sex with his best friend, just last night. And it had been a very confusing day because of it.

But their little horizontal dance was a secret, while these two old high school best friends, Thomas and Julia, were about to tie the knot.

"You okay there, Gid?" Danny asked.

"Yeah, fine. Sorry." He put his three remaining fingers in the air.

Ari still stared at him. He heard her say, *don't you dare put a finger down for that, Gideon Sims.*

So, he didn't, and Heather clapped and squealed. "Ha ha! The lovebirds lost."

"Yeah, yeah," Thomas said and he bent down to kiss his fiancée on the cheek, his lips moving against her cheek, close to her ear. "Good game."

"You, too, babe." Julia patted his hand on the table.

Seeing their casual affection made Gid's heart ache. For the first time in a long while he admitted to himself that that was exactly what he wanted, too.

FIFTEEN
ARI

SLOWLY, everyone drifted from the table back up to their hotel rooms. It was getting late and the ladies had an early morning for hair and make-up.

For a small, casual wedding, Julia was pulling out all the stops, that was for sure. Not that Ari minded getting absolutely pampered but it was all a little exhausting. Especially on top of her inner turmoil and complicated by this *thing* with Gid.

Sure, over the years of their friendship she'd wondered how the guy was in bed. He had an easy way with women that suggested he knew exactly how to please one.

Of course, their night had ended in disaster. And agreeing to forget that it ever happened wasn't exactly going to plan.

She'd had plenty of casual sex over the years, with

friends, co-workers, people who she never intended to be in a relationship with. She had practice in things just being same old same old between two people, despite the sex. There was only her one rule: no sex between dance partners. And this was exactly why.

Because status quo didn't seem to be returning with Gid. Already they were so intimate on the dance floor, adding the intimacy of the bedroom made things confusing. Lord was she confused.

First, his little hand game on her leg at dinner. God that was...hot. Completely inappropriate and downright distracting, but it turned her on a crazy amount and left her with no outlet other than her tiny vibrator that night in her hotel bed.

The moon peeked through the clouds, casting a blue glow through the gauzy curtains of her room. The Christmas lights twinkled faintly outside her window. And Ari lay naked in her bed with her hand between her legs.

It seemed that one orgasm—albeit one she hadn't been prepared for—wasn't enough for Ari Callaghan. Nope, today her body was greedy as hell, apparently desperate to make up for the orgasm she missed with Gid.

If she thought about that too much right now, she'd lose this one too.

Ari circled her clit with the softly buzzing toy, lips pulled between her teeth, chasing the wild sensation of

Gid's hand inching higher and higher at dinner. Her toes had tingled, for Pete's sake.

Now, they curled, working out a frustration knotted deep in her belly. She dipped her fingers down into her pussy, catching the wetness there, pushing and stretching her channel, as she circled her clit with the cool plastic clutched in her fist.

Her nerves tingled at the base of her spine and her pelvic floor tightened. The orgasm was right there, she was just about to crest that hill when—

Someone knocked softly on her door.

Ari jumped. "Fuck," she cursed under her breath as she clicked off her vibrator.

Who the hell would be knocking on her door this late at night? Of course she had a guess and, if she was being honest with herself, a wish of who it was.

She grabbed the hotel's big, white robe before dropping her toy in the pocket and padding across the room. She looked through the peep hole, and there was Gid, in fisheye relief, hands shoved in his pants pockets, still dressed from dinner.

Ari unlatched the door and pulled it open, stepping back to welcome him in without words. He didn't say anything either and passed by her, one hand clutching the nape of his neck.

When she shut the door, she turned. "What are you doing here, Gid? It's late."

"I couldn't sleep," he said, meeting her gaze with his

own wild, glassy eyes. The top two buttons of his dress shirt were undone and she watched his Adam's apple bob as he swallowed.

Ari knew the feeling she saw there. The same sensation pulsed through her veins. It wasn't desire, it was something more, something stronger. *Longing.*

"I think we need to talk," he said.

Ari swung on the spot, frozen. "We've already talked, Gid. There's nothing else to say. Last night was just a mistake."

Even as she said it, she didn't really believe it.

Gid stepped toward her, so that they stood toe-to-toe. "And tonight at dinner? Was that also a mistake?"

His words were hot lava seeping into her bones, threatening to make her combust. Warmth spread over her cheeks as she floundered for an answer. But standing this close to him, with that heat radiating from him, all logic failed her.

"Yes," she squeaked out the word, "it was."

Ari laced her fingers behind her back, as if he could sense the evidence of her aroused frustration on her fingertips.

Gid narrowed his eyes. A laugh rumbled through his chest and echoed in Ari's core.

"I don't believe you," he said, as if he knew Ari was lying through her teeth.

Ari didn't believe herself.

"I don't know what to tell you, Gid." Her lips barely moved as she said the words.

"Tell me you want this, pop tart."

She did. She wanted him to touch her so badly. But she was too afraid to destroy this too.

When she didn't respond, Gid stepped back. "I'm sorry, Ari. I can leave if you want."

"No," Ari said too quickly, closing the gap between them. "No. That's not what I want. I want you this."

"Hmm, good." He just reached up and twirled a lock of her dark hair around his pointer finger. "Because I think I figured out a way to not violate the terms of yesterday's agreement."

"Oh?" she whispered, unmoving, barely daring to breathe for fear of making a false move.

Gid drew her lock of hair wrapped tight around his finger to his nose. He let it unravel there, still holding on to the end. Tingles raced down her neck, starting where the ends of those hairs inserted into her scalp.

Nothing good happened after two AM, and yet, Ari stepped closer to him. He wrapped his palm around her neck, laced his fingers into her hair. Ari shivered, unable to hide her reaction to his touch and Gid put pressure on his thumb, right behind her ear.

"Never have I ever,"—he started, and Ari put up five fingers—"wanted something so badly that I shouldn't."

Ari put a finger down.

"Never have I ever," she said, "cared less about what I *shouldn't* want."

This was a dangerous game. And Ari didn't care. She didn't care that it was the middle of the night, that she'd insisted the other night was a mistake. She wanted to chase this feeling, consequences be damned.

"So, we have that in common," Gid said, pulling Ari closer by the neck and tilting her face up to him.

As he looked down at her, Ari heated under his devilish stare. Lord, she wanted to know what was going through his mind right now. She had the sense that it was something naughty. Something she'd love.

"Never have I ever," Gid started, his voice low and rough, "done mutual masturbation."

Heat seared through her core at the suggestion. She shook her head, looking up at him, eyes wide. "Me neither," Ari whispered.

"Can I watch you masturbate, Ari? While I sit in that chair," he pointed over her shoulder, "and touch myself, too?"

Ari nodded, her pulse racing. Technically, this didn't cross the line between them.

But actually it crossed so many lines. Lines that Ari absolutely did not care about after what happened at dinner, now that it was after two in the morning and she was still amped up from her missed orgasm when Gid knocked on her door.

Gid took her chin in his hands, his gaze locked in on

hers. "And I want you to think of me while you do it, okay, pop tart?"

He didn't wait for an answer before he let go of her and stepped over to the chair.

"Did you bring one of your toys, Ari?" The way he asked implied that he already knew the answer.

Gid had been exposed to many conversations between Ari and Zahra about their vibrator collections, so of course he knew that it was likely that Ari traveled with one. That he asked her with such authority made her knees weak.

This time, he waited for a response as he unbuttoned the top of his shirt, then his sleeves and rolled up the cuffs. Her stomach clenched at his exposed forearms.

"I did," she said, before pulling the little bullet out of her pocket.

"Good girl," he murmured, a knowing grin on his face. "Are you ready?"

It was clear who was in control here and—*holy shit*— Ari was ready to obey. "Yes."

"Get on the bed." Gid flicked his chin to the king-sized thing, the sheets rumpled from her restless movements moments before he showed up. "Take off your robe. I want to see everything."

Ari walked up to the bed and slipped off her robe, exposing her backside to him. She heard Gid adjust in his seat, humming his approval at the sight of her. Crawling up on to the bed, Ari continued the show until she slowly flipped around to face him and her legs fell wide open.

A thrill shot through her limbs, completely naked and exposed, while Gid was still dressed. It felt good to let go, for someone else call the shots for once. Because she explicitly trusted Gid, she relaxed knowing that she didn't have to worry about making the wrong move.

"Look at you, Ari. So very pretty against those white sheets," he praised her, rubbing himself lazily through the outside of his pants. "Your bare cunt is everything."

Ari gasped, his words winding her tighter. Slowly, she traced her fingers along her waist and down between her legs, over her soft lips. Goosebumps chased over her skin at the delicate touch. She wasn't embarrassed to be so laid out like this. Instead, her body lit up like a Christmas tree.

"That's it," Gid encouraged her as she continued her gentle exploration. "I want to see how you come, baby. Show me how you pleasure yourself."

Ari reached back for a pillow and propped herself up. With one tentative finger, she touched her clit, already electrified. She didn't have to check to know that she leaked wetness down between her cheeks.

"It won't take long," she told Gid, her voice tight.

"You were already masturbating before I got here, weren't you, pop tart?"

A tight whine was the only response she could give.

From across the room, Gid undid his leather belt. The thick slap and drag of it along the buckle made her press harder onto her clit. Once he undid his zipper, Ari tipped her head up as she watched him pull out his cock, stiff and begging for attention. Her mouth watered, eager to be filled, and she ground her hips down into her hand.

"So eager," Gid murmured as he fisted himself. "Use your toy, Ari."

He spit into his hand and then continued his own pleasure.

"I'll come apart in seconds," she said, even as she clicked the button to turn on the little thing. She selected her favorite rhythm. The vibrations in her hand notched her desire higher.

"Then let's see if you can come twice before I come once."

"Never have I ever come twice in a row," Ari gasped as she moved the toy to just above her clitoris.

"Oh, pop tart, then tonight's the night," Gid said darkly.

As Ari spiraled the vibrator closer to her epicenter, her core coiled tighter. She didn't dare close her eyes. The sight of Gid, clothed, gripping himself and staring at her amplified every single little sensation rippling through her body. Her hips rolled over the luxurious cotton sheets, syncing with the alternating rhythm of the toy. Ari moaned, the sound escaping from some place she usually kept locked away.

"That's it. I want to hear you," Gid said. "I want to see you come apart, Ari."

Had it been twenty seconds? Or twenty years? The pleasure surging through her sent her into another plane where time simply didn't exist.

Finally—or was it too soon?—Ari touched her sensitive bud with the vibrator and her orgasm tore through her. She dropped her head back as another wave of wetness trickled from her core onto the sheets under her. As she made sounds she never heard before, Ari kept the toy against her, wringing out every sparking feeling she could from the orgasm.

Distantly, she heard Gid move across the room. He came closer and she tilted her head up to look at him before trying to close her legs.

Gid knelt before her and rested a hand on her knee, keeping her legs open. "Can I touch you?"

"Uh-huh," she whined, the aftershocks from her orgasm still burning in her veins.

"You look so stunning when you come. I'm going to get you to come again." He took the buzzing toy from her and touched the inside of her leg.

"What about you?" she whispered.

"Trust me, this is everything I want right now." He kissed the inside of her thigh, right in her crease. "Relax."

Gid clicked the vibrator to the most punishing setting: full blast, continuous pulsing. Ari whimpered, slightly concerned.

"Let go, pop tart. I've got you."

His touch dragged up her thigh and over her outer lips

before thrusting one finger inside her. "Fuck you're wet, Ari," he said, his voice wound up and pained. "I think you can take another."

Ari stretched, impaled on his fingers. As if on their own, her hips picked up the same grinding motion as before. She chased more depth, more sensation. She wanted his palm flush against her.

And then the vibrator touched her clit. "Oh my god."

"That's right," Gid chuckled.

Ari had closed her eyes, but she could feel his focused gaze on her. He sensed every single little motion of her body, just like when they danced together. But it was hard to tell who led now. Was Gid commanding her pleasure? Or was he following her writhing movements?

"Fuck, Gid," she ground out.

"Yes baby," he said, pinching her bud between the toy and his fingers. "Are you going to come a second time for me?"

Ari could barely take it anymore, but there was something stopping her from that next crest.

As if sensing it, too, Gid leaned forward and put his tongue on her.

"Jesus," Ari screamed. With one final grinding movement of her hips, she exploded. Bucking against him, she chased every sensation that she could.

When it was done, she lay back, exhausted. "Oh my god," she laughed. "Holy shit."

"Holy shit is right. That was..."

"That takes care of a couple 'never have I evers.'"

They laughed as Gid stood up and leaned over her. His lips almost landed on hers before he stopped.

"Can I kiss you?" he whispered, brow furrowed almost as if he was pleading.

"Mmhm," she murmured, nodding.

The kiss was gentle, quick, his lips warm from being between her legs.

"Thank you," she said, as he stood up and turned away.

Ari quickly covered up with her robe, feeling like the spell was broken. Well past two in the morning now, Ari wondered if what they'd just done had been a mistake. Another mistake. But her blood sang with satisfaction suggesting this was exactly right.

"Umm," she said. "Do you want to stay, or?"

She didn't really know what would be best. At least offering couldn't hurt.

"No," Gid sighed, all tucked away and running a hand through his fluffed-up hair. "I think I should go. I'll see you tomorrow?"

The sinking in her gut told her she actually did want him to stay. And he refused. What did that mean?

Nothing. It didn't mean anything. Because this meant nothing, too. Like they had agreed.

With one last look behind him, Gid slipped out the door.

* * *

ARI SET six alarms for the next morning, determined not to sleep in again. But holy shit was it early. After Gid left her hotel room, Ari tossed and turned in a restless sleep all night. Damn him.

She arrived in Julia's suite, where they were doing hair and makeup all morning, eating breakfast and drinking Bellinis before driving forty-five minutes in a party bus to the coast. There was a little inn-turned-wedding venue at the cliffs that would serve as their base for their ceremony.

The morning passed in a blur of color palettes and make-up brushes and by the end of it, Ari had a long, intricate plait that lay over her shoulder, an understated smoky eye, and deep red lips to match her emerald green velvet long sleeve dress.

Despite the flurry of activity in the bridal suite, Ari's thoughts kept drifting back to Gid. Soon, they'd be celebrating Christmas by themselves on the Christmas tree farm surrounded by fir trees and pygmy goats. She'd definitely be lying if she said she wasn't looking forward to some alone time with her best friend. And after last night...she had no idea what to expect.

But that's what he was: her best friend. And best friends didn't have unexpected sexual encounters. Especially around weddings when everyone was already feeling so vulnerable. It was just like Ari to mess up something as straightforward as her friendship with Gid. Her best friend. She wanted to keep him that way.

Right?

"Earth to Ari." Julia waved a hand in front of Ari's face.

"You look perfect, Juju," Ari said, focusing on the bride.

She really did. Even as Julia rolled her eyes at the nickname, her cheeks flushed peach, highlighted by softly glowing makeup. Everything about her look screamed effortless, minimal beauty, from her low, knotted bun to her silk chiffon dress. The floor length gown had the same peach undertones as her skin and was topped with sheer, beaded long sleeves that ended in silk bows mid-forearm. Her magically clean leather flats peeked out from underneath.

"Thank you." She handed Ari a cocktail. "Here, drink with me."

"Are you sure?" Ari laughed.

"Yes, I'm sure." Julia waved a hand between them as if to say, *I'm so over your drunk ass spilling two Bellinis on me at brunch the other day.* "I'm really happy you're here."

"Of course I am. Where else would I be?"

"I just know with school and your career and everything you have a lot on your plate." Julia gave Ari a small smile.

Ari's stomach plunged. School. Career. Say either word three times fast to summon a stomach ache. Except that no one, not even Gid, knew the trouble that she was in back at Everdale College.

"Ha," Ari laughed, tossing her head ironically to one side, "yep they sure do keep us busy over there."

Julia sighed and turned toward the window, pulling aside the curtain. "I know it was risky for us to plan a seaside elopement for the dead of winter, but the weather turned out more perfect than I could have imagined."

She wasn't wrong. Somehow, despite being two days before Christmas, the weather was ideal for Thomas and Julia's brief outdoor ceremony. Bright sunlight streamed through the window and it looked far warmer than Ari knew it was.

"We'll need our sunglasses for the ceremony," Ari's mom laughed, joining the two women. "There's supposed to be snow tomorrow, I heard. Hopefully that doesn't mess up anyone's travel plans."

"Oh god, don't tell Gid," Ari groaned. "His travel anxiety was a bear on the way here."

"It'll be great," Mom said, squeezing Ari's elbow. "I'm just so happy to have my family all together." She twisted her wedding band around her ring finger.

"If only Sean could be here, too," Julia said softly, leaning into her mother-in-law.

"He is," Mom said with a sad smile, "in here." She rubbed a hand on her chest.

Standing on the Irish coast an hour later, everyone

bundled in their winter coats and with sunglasses on, Ari thought, *Dad really would have loved this.*

She sighed, and under her teddy bear trench, she stayed warm. With Gid standing at her side, she was even warmer.

She couldn't deny the way his presence buoyed her spirits. He always had, ever since they first met. Making her laugh in the dorm cafeteria over questionable chilis and bowls of soft serve ice cream. Laying on the floor of her dorm room and helping her understand chemistry formulas. Unlimited pinky promises to always be there for each other. Would that change now?

Seeing Thomas and Julia, holding hands in front of their officiant with the backdrop of the Irish Sea stretching behind them, tears prickled Ari's eyes. It wasn't just them and their love, but it was the last thirteen months washing over her in waves.

She knew all her siblings and her mom were thinking the same thing: Dad should be here. The mantra repeated in her head to the cadence of her drumbeat heart, syncing up with the waves washing over the rocks below, until the rest of the world dropped away. She wasn't even paying attention to the ceremony anymore.

But when Thomas picked up the small box of Dad's ashes, another hand tucked into Ari's pocket.

Gid. She turned to him, her face wet with tears she didn't even realize had spilled over. He locked his pinky with hers. Solid and sure, always there.

Fuck. If only Ari didn't destroy everything she ever touched, this might be something she could keep.

"Ari," Thomas said, gesturing the box toward her.

It was her turn to spread a bit of his ashes. Both her brothers already had, then Mom would spread the rest. Gid squeezed her hand from inside her pocket and then withdrew his warmth. Ari walked past Danny, squeezing his shoulder. The wind sucked little bits of hair from her plait, tickling her cheeks as they danced wildly around her. She took the box from Thomas, who gave her a side hug, and Ari stepped closer to the barrier at the cliff's edge.

God this land was wild. The sea crashed violently below, churning up white foam. Deep sadness washed over her that Dad had never gotten to see Ireland with them. He always wanted to. Somehow there was just never time. Which seems ridiculous now, considering.

She shook the box, loosening some ashes onto the wind, and they were gone. Some little piece of her dad was gone. Gone forever. The finality of the moment hit her square in the chest and she let out one sob, which the wind took away too.

Ari handed over the box to her mom, who emptied the rest without shedding a tear. Instead, she smiled into the sun.

Gid looped his arm around Ari's waist, holding her in the moment. The ceremony ended with the officiant binding Thomas and Julia's hands together with rope in a series of intricate loops and knots. They stared into each other's eyes during the handfasting and Ari wondered if she'd ever find a love as pure and true as theirs.

Just as the thought raced through her brain, Gid pulled her closer, in front of his tall, lanky frame, and curled his other arm around her, cradling her back against his chest. It felt so right, so perfect, but...it was a mistake. They agreed it was a mistake. They were friends, best friends. Not lovers, not some random people that they could risk fucking around with. If things went wrong between them, Ari would never forgive herself.

And yet, as Ari melted against Gid, his belt buckle rubbing against the small of her back, she thought it was a mistake she really wouldn't mind making again.

THEY HAD dinner at a little pub in town. The place glittered with colorful Christmas baubles, a Charlie Brown-eqsue tree, and a roaring fire in the hearth. After the meal, Ari sat next to the flames, Guinness in hand, while everyone mingled and chatted. The whole thing was a warm hug after the strong winds of the cliffside.

It was the beginning of the next chapter of her brother's life, but it was the closing of the mourning period of her dad's passing. Not that anyone could really put a timestamp on that. Ari swallowed thickly, staring in the popping fire.

"What are you thinking about?" Gid asked, sliding into the chair next to her with two fresh Guinness.

Ari sighed. "Dad."

Gid didn't say anything, just nodded.

"He would have seriously loved all this, Gid." Her mouth tightened involuntarily to the side as her sinuses pinched. She already cried for him so many times, she wasn't sure there'd be a day when the tears dried up.

"He would have," he said, putting a hand on hers. "Listen, I know there's something going on, Ari, something you haven't told me. And you don't have to, but I'll be here for you whenever you're ready, alright?"

Her stomach twisted into knots as she held his gaze.

"But, if you want," he continued, "we can just take a break from everything for the next couple days. Live in our own winter wonderland."

It sounded so appealing. Could she do it? Could she leave behind all of her stresses and worries? The things that haunt her in the middle of the night?

Gid's eyes searched her face. "You can do it."

Ari bit a corner of her lip. "It's like you can read my thoughts."

"Mmm. Something like that." He squeezed the nape of his neck. "So, what do you say, pop tart?"

Her lip pulled free as she grinned wide. "I can do it."

"Thatta girl," he said, swilling his pint.

And damn if those two little words didn't send a shock of warmth straight to her core, reminding her of everything they did last night in that middle of the night haze.

"It's gonna be a good rest of the week."

She couldn't help but think that he might be right.

SIXTEEN
ARI
THEN

ARI SAT on the closed toilet seat, inhaling from her vape. She ran a hand down her black sweater dress, pulling her ponytail over her shoulder. Fuzzy white noise filled her ears. She breathed...in...and out...attempting to clear her mind like her YouTube yoga instructors taught.

It wasn't working. The roar in her ears grew louder, but it wouldn't drown out her thoughts, which only became more insistent the longer she sat alone here.

Everyone was downstairs, mingling, talking about Dad, *celebrating* him, like he wanted. But it didn't feel like a celebration at all. It was a wake, a funeral, the end of an era. And holy hell did it hurt.

God, she thought she was ready for this. After the years of his lung cancer treatment, and all the highs and lows that came with it, and then his decision to stop treatment this fall. Ari thought she was ready to say goodbye.

She could put on a strong face for her brothers, her mom. She could help them, be the positive little dancing fairy they expected her to be. But after the long day of recounting memories of her dad and hearing stories about him, she was spent.

Ari put the vape to her lips again, inhaling until her lungs burned.

A soft knock interrupted her thoughts. "Ari?"

She crossed her ankles, tucking one arm under the other next to her tummy.

Without waiting for a response, the door swung slowly open. Gid stuck his heard around the door. Even from her view across the bathroom, she noticed his freshly shaven cheeks. It made her heart clench for some reason.

"Hmm?" She said, when she saw it was just her friend. Her best friend.

"There you are, pop tart," he said, leaning back against the counter. He looked great in a classic black suit and white shirt. "Doing okay?"

Ari shrugged. She didn't feel the pressure to give Gid a fabricated answer. With everyone else downstairs, she had a role to play.

He pulled a flask out of his inside jacket pocket and shook it in Ari's direction. Without a moment's hesitation, she reached her hand out and took a sip.

"You're so reliable," she laughed.

"Never without my Buttershots." Gid ran a hand

through his fluffy hair. "I'll be here for the rest of the day, you know?"

"I know." She truly did. Never for one second did she doubt Gideon Sims, on the dance floor or off.

"Let me know what you need, eh?" Gid sipped the schnapps then rubbed his lips together.

"I will."

But she didn't have to. Gid moved around the room, talking to her relatives and Dad's friends. He made easy small-talk regardless of who it was. He always could, despite his anxiety. It was impressive.

Anytime Ari's hands were empty, he filled them with a vodka soda or tiny plate of appetizers. Cheese cubes and sausage chunks—her favorites—and some grapes.

"For balance," he winked when she wrinkled her nose at the fruit. "You can't survive on cheese and meat alone."

"Oh yeah?" she laughed, her shoulders relaxing down her back. "Try me."

"No, please," he said, covering his mouth with his hand to hide his laugh. "Let the record show that I did not challenge you to that—you did that to yourself."

Ari swatted at him as he continued past, moving on to greet some other relative who had shown up. God it felt good to know he was there.

Later, he helped the older folks out the door and made Irish coffees for the aunts who stayed behind to keep Mom company.

"Gideon!" the loudest one hollered. "You are *too* much."

Even from upstairs where she was changing, Ari knew he must have told one of his dirty jokes. Somehow he always had the best ones. She rolled her gray sweatpants until they were slung low on her hips and dropped an oversized Michigan State tee over her head.

Coming down the last stairs, Gid looked her up and down before smiling. It warmed her insides after such a long day.

"Nice shirt," he said.

Ari looked at her chest and realized the shirt was one of his old ones.

"Forgot you stole that one." Gid stuffed his hands in his pockets.

"I don't know if that's entirely accurate," Ari said, plopping down on the stairs. "I seem to recall you leaving it here."

Snorting a laugh, Gid jiggled his keys in his pocket. "Should I go get my stuff?"

"Stuff?" Ari wrapped a finger in the soft t-shirt.

"Yeah, change of clothes. Thought I might stay a while."

Ari smiled. "That sounds great."

She stayed seated on the stairs, where she caught Thomas talking to Mom then giving her a peck on the cheek. Looked like he was going out. When he walked back into the kitchen, the door swinging behind him, Ari saw Julia waiting in there. He gave her a kiss before pulling her out the back door.

Ari laughed at the sight of them. *Fucking finally.*

The front door opened and Gid hopped back inside, worn high school sports bag cradled in his hands.

"Oh my god, I always forget you were your high school's, like, star basketball player." How he had time for dance, gymnastics, and basketball in high school would forever be a mystery to Ari.

"Hardly," he laughed. "We never won, but I do consider myself the best player on that team—despite my clear delineation as the team's benchwarmer."

"Yeah right," Ari said, standing up.

Gid shrugged, raising the bag. "I'm just gonna change."

"And then meet me downstairs?" Ari crossed her arms around her stomach. She needed some darkness and de-stimulation. Maybe just watch one of their comfort films.

"You betcha."

She twirled, her stockinged feet slipping smoothly on the fake vinyl hardwood. In the basement, she nested, moving pillows and blankets around for maximum of coziness. She switched the soft blue LED lights on behind the TV and grabbed the remotes.

"Okay," Gid said as he sauntered down the stairs in a grey Henley, tight over his soft biceps, and blue flannel pajama pants. He even had slippers on. "I'm actually thinking *Below Deck*?"

"Oh hell yes." Ari clicked on the TV as she nestled into her blankets. "Excellent suggestion."

The super yacht crew reality show was their favorite particularly mindless thing to watch together. She inhaled on her vape, the smoke singeing the back of her throat. She really should change to gummies, but hadn't been able to give up the sensation of smoking, the way just that little act calmed her nerves.

"Can I have some?" Gid asked, snuggled in his own blanket palace, eyeing her vape.

"Oh yeah, of course. Sorry," she said, passing him the stick.

"All good, I know I, like, never smoke."

Ari clicked right to their favorite season.

"Pop-Tarts?" Gid lifted up a box that Ari previously missed. "Cherry, of course."

"Oh my god I love you," Ari said. Words she'd said a million times before, but somehow in that moment they felt heavier. More texture than before.

Maybe that was just the heady combination of grief and weed talking.

"Thanks for being here." She stretched out, reaching an arm across to rest on his forearm.

"Of course, pop tart."

It wasn't long before Ari drifted off into a contented sleep to the dulcet tones of super yacht crew drama.

When she woke the next morning, she was so freaking comfortable, wrapped in all the pillows and blankets on the old, sagging couch. But she immediately sensed she was alone. He often did that—left after Ari had fallen asleep. At her apartment in Everdale, he'd lock up from the outside, driving the twenty minutes back to his place in Starling Hills. Last night was just like any other night.

She hadn't expected Gid to stay, but she found herself wishing he had.

SEVENTEEN
GID

GID COULDN'T HIDE the spring in his step as he walked with Ari through Dublin city center to the Connolly train station, their rolling luggage bouncing along over the stone street beside them.

They were really doing it, taking the trip they talked about for years. But between their chaotic school and work schedules, it just never happened. When she had invited him as her plus one to her brother's wedding, it didn't take long for them to figure out it was the perfect opportunity for them to explore some of the country. With the wedding behind them, the rest of the week was theirs.

Gid couldn't help but think what they'd get up to. When he went to Ari's room the night before the wedding, he didn't really have a plan. All he knew was that he couldn't settle his mind and he needed to see her.

What unfolded happened naturally after she

answered the door with mussed hair and rosy cheeks, her chest heaving and wrapped up in that blessed robe. He'd known exactly what she'd been up to. And damn did it make his blood run hot in his veins.

Their agreement, their truce, whatever it was, be damned. He couldn't stand that they'd agreed their hooking up had been a mistake. And after how they had behaved at dinner...well, Gid had been still wound tight from that.

At two AM, the thought of touching Ari Callaghan felt like anything *but* a mistake. When he got her to come a second time, well, that was fucking exquisite.

"This is it, Gid," Ari said, clutching the handle of her luggage. "We're taking the trip."

He smiled to himself, struck again at how their thoughts seemed completely aligned at all times. Maybe they were just that much in sync. He wondered if she was also thinking about what they might do to *pass time* over the next couple of days...

And yet, she was the one who insisted what they'd done was a mistake. Though she willingly, happily, participated in their late-night tryst before the wedding.

Somehow, it felt so freaking right. But Ari always lived a little too much in her own head, overthinking and rethinking everything until none of it made sense anymore.

"Yes, we are," he said. And it made something possessive awaken inside him that he didn't have the courage to fully explore right now.

Ari practically skipped down the street. "Does Ireland have police boxes?"

"You mean the ones that look like the TARDIS?" Gid laughed, remembering all of their college *Doctor Who* marathons.

"Yes exactly."

"I don't think those exist anymore. If there are any, they're decorative."

She hummed, considering. "Imagine getting whisked away by the Doctor."

A frown darkened Ari's brow as she slowed the spring in her step.

There it was: that something that had been lurking behind her typically sunny outward disposition. Gid didn't know what it was, and he didn't want to know...yet. He wanted to keep her distracted and happy for the time he had with her before she went back to school and he had to go back to his work life. If he could just keep her entertained enough maybe it would be okay. Maybe he could make whatever was hurting her go away.

"I would run away, for sure. Take a break from real life." Ari frowned down the street.

"Isn't that what we're doing?" Gid knocked her shoulder.

She laughed flatly through her nose. "I guess. But I actually have to go back to that dumpster fire."

Now Gid frowned. He wasn't doing a very good job of keeping her distracted from whatever dark cloud had her down. They were almost to the train station. He needed her to be out of this funk before they got on the train—that was his goal.

"Just think about roast Christmas dinner at the tree farm," he said. Their hosts had messaged them a few days ago, inviting them to their main house if they wanted to celebrate with them. "I wonder if they make Yorkshire puddings here in Ireland?"

"What's a Yorkshire pudding? Dessert?" Her eyes lit up, probably thinking that 'pudding' meant something drenched in caramel syrup or sprinkled with cinnamon sugar. Food always did work as a good distraction for Ari.

"Far from it." Gid grabbed on to the straps of his backpack, warming with the memories of the year he spent abroad in England. "It's...well, it's hard to describe. It's like a pastry but also like a roll? It puffs up real big and is amazing with gravy. I had it at Christmastime when I was studying at Oxford. Big English thing. Not sure about Irish though."

"God I want one. I hope they make them for Christmas."

She wrapped her hands around Gid's biceps, clinging to him as they walked. A move that wouldn't have meant much to him before they started up this *thing*, but now sent a warmth searing through Gid's belly.

But Ari didn't seem to notice. "I missed you so much

that semester. That subletter you found just wasn't the same."

"Trust me, it pained me to see all the house party pictures on Facebook when I wasn't there."

"As if you weren't having the time of your life over here."

She was right, of course. Though he had missed his friends and the house that the six of them—including Ari—had shared junior year, he wouldn't trade his semester studying abroad for anything. He traveled all over Europe and met so many people he never would have otherwise. He still considered it some of the best time of his life. Being abroad again now made all the nostalgia of then wash over him like the waves crashing on the rocky cliffside.

"Let's get a coffee," he said, nodding at the little sandwich shop at the entrance to the train station, and interrupting their conversation. Mostly he needed a distraction, a moment to breathe and gather his thoughts as they shuffled into the line.

"I missed you when I was gone, too." Gid looked down at her, continuing the conversation from before.

"Yeah?" Her cheeks flushed rosy red, maybe from the sudden switch of cold into warm, or maybe from the same memories that Gid had conjured up in his mind.

That summer after junior year... Gid was back stateside and a couple of their housemates left for the summer but four of them stayed behind, Ari and Gid among them. They took classes and worked their random jobs—Ari as a bartender and Gid at the library —and went to house parties all over town. Drinking every night of the week was normal, when their bodies could better handle the Jägermeister shots and shitty beer. They'd play beer pong, kicking everyone's butt until the sunrise, and then walk the sidewalks home in the blue-dawn summer. They ate dinner together on the couch and watched old episodes of *Doctor Who* on a loop.

It was the only time since that very first night, Gid thought, that maybe they were more than friends.

It wasn't really a crush exactly. It was like a thing that kind of almost happened between them.

Everyone else thought they were sleeping together. And they laughed their asses off about it, letting the rumor flourish and playing it up when they had a chance. Hanging off each other and giving each other big messy smooches after too many beers. Because what did it even matter? They knew they weren't sleeping together and it was kind of funny that everyone else thought they were. Their friendship never changed because of it.

And it didn't change their friendship now. Or, it couldn't. He wouldn't let it.

But still that *possibility* that they were so close to hooking up in college (again) left a mark on his soul.

Just like Ari's big, brown eyes burning into him. There was more in her gaze than he wanted to examine right now. More of his own emotions reflected back at him. More than he was ready to admit.

"Yeah," he laughed, still holding her gaze but playing it off. "They don't make beer pong partners over here quite like you."

She rolled her eyes and turned away. Though not before he caught the little corner of her lip that she pulled into her mouth, hiding a smile.

"It's the height." He mimed tossing a ping-pong ball through the air toward an imaginary red solo cup at the end of a long table. "No one expects such a short beer pong shark."

"Oh, shut up." But now she was truly smiling. Incandescent and pure.

They got their drinks—him a flat white and her a hot chocolate—and walked back outside to a light snow. Snowflakes caught in Ari's dark eyelashes, making her look dipped in sugar. Gid licked his lips. The desire to kiss the cold from her eyelashes washed over him so strongly that he had to take a minuscule step back. He clutched his drink with both hands to stop himself from touching her.

God was this...was he...falling for Ari? After all these years? *Now?*

He cleared his throat. "We should go in the station and check the train times."

Ari nodded and they walked in side-by-side, people hustling and bustling around them. The overhead speaker blared an announcement, but the Irish accent combined with the echo of the station made it hard to tell what was said. Looming above the tracks, the giant schedule flipped erratically and the growing crowd underneath let out a collective groan.

"That can't be good," Gid muttered.

"Hmm?" Ari asked, looking around the station with wide eyes, and—unfamiliar as she was with international train travel—apparently oblivious to what was actually going on around her.

He pushed away from her with a couple long strides and looked up at the board. There was their route— Dublin to Cork at 1120—with a glaring all capital designation: CANCELLED. His heart plummeted into his toes.

"Do you know what's going on?" Gid hazarded asking another grumpy looking traveler next to him.

"Trains are all cancelled."

Thank you for stating the obvious. "Do you know why?"

"Didn't ya hear the announcement? Some track issue with all the snow." And the other person stomped away.

All the snow? Gid looked back outside and nothing about the weather seemed particularly remarkable.

Finally Ari looked up at the board. "Oh. That doesn't look good."

Gid grabbed the base of his skull, just giving a little pressure in an attempt to relieve some of the tension. "No this isn't good at all."

Of course something like this had to kick off their little trip. They only had four more days together in Ireland. He knew planning it like this in the first place could potentially be an issue, with the tight timeline and unpredictable weather. But they'd wanted to take a trip like this for years, and the stars only aligned so often for something like this. He wasn't about to pass it up.

"Well," he said, his brain flipping maniacally between options like a rolodex. They needed to get to County Cork for their reservation at the tree farm, where they'd spend the next couple days. And he wanted them to be perfect days, just the two of them. Reading books and doing crosswords in front of the electric fireplace in the little guesthouse then going outside to visit with the pygmy goats and walk the rows of fir trees.

They didn't really have a ton of options. There was a bus, but maybe the bus system would have the same issues with the snow. And bus travel in snowy weather didn't sound great.

Which really only left renting a car. Something they planned to avoid in favor of seeing the country via rail. And, of course, made their train tickets completely useless. Still, that seemed like the best option.

"I think we'll have to rent a car."

"I can't drive on the left side of the road." Ari looked at him with wide eyes. "In the snow. Are you going to drive us?"

Gid masked his anxiety. This was another reason they had avoided car rental in the first place: neither of them was keen on driving on the opposite side of road.

But he'd do it. For her and for this vacation.

"Yeah," he shrugged, aiming for casual. "It'll be fine."

Thankfully, there was a car rental about a ten-minute walk from the station and they were able to get the last all-wheel drive vehicle—a Suzuki hatchback—with minimal pain. They sent off a message to their host letting them know their arrival would be well later than planned. How much later was impossible to tell.

"This feels weird," Ari said as she settled into the passenger seat on the left side.

"You're telling me." Gid sat in the driver's seat, adjusting his seat and mirrors to the appropriate angles.

"Doesn't really look like enough snow to cancel all the trains." Ari leaned forward and looked out the windshield. "Hopefully it doesn't get any worse."

"Thank you for stating the obvious."

"What!" She turned to look at him, and he gave her a bit of a frown. "Oh I'm sorry aren't we supposed to like, go with the flow or whatever on trips? Don't get all grumpy on me Mr. Experienced Traveler."

"Easy for you to say, you're not in the driver's seat."

"Is this your first time renting a car abroad?"

"Yes. And my first time driving on the *wrong* side of the road."

"It won't be so bad once we get out of Dublin?"

"It won't be so bad if it stops snowing."

It wasn't lost on Gid that their mood flipped back and forth depending on who needed to be the grump at the moment. His usual golden retriever demeanor was a bit lost under all the travel stress, though.

"Oh, come on. It's an adventure, right? That's what you've been telling me all these years about going abroad and stuff?" Ari squeezed his hand that rested on the shifter—because of course this was a manual transmission, too.

At least he'd learned to drive his dad's old manual Mustang when he was in high school.

Ari's long, raven dark hair cascaded over her shoulder as she leaned toward Gid over the center console.

"Right?" she grinned up at him, her eyes sparkling with some of the excitement that she was talking about. That he'd told her about so many times.

"You're right." He nodded, turning the car on and shifting into gear.

The speed bumps were all just part of the journey.

EIGHTEEN
ARI

INSIDE, she was freaking out.

But outside, she was supportive best friend extraordinaire.

Plans were plans for a reason and she'd hoped that at least one thing in her life over the last thirteen months could be routine.

Apparently not.

The rail technology and snow had conspired against them, sling-shotting them into these alternate plans. She sat in the passenger seat re-calibrating her expectations for the trip. Instead of them sitting and joking on the train, relaxing as the scenery zoomed by, now they were in a rental car. One of them slightly more stressed than the other.

Ari bent toward the windshield, peering at roadsigns

as the GPS guided them on the car's display screen. Dublin was set up like a maze apparently. Not like the straight, grid-like streets of suburbia that she was familiar with back in Michigan. Gid's knuckles whitened over the curve of the wheel, switching back and forth between that and the shifter.

"Take a right here?" The direction came out like a question.

"Here?"

"Here." She reinforced it with some authority as her Google Maps swiveled around and adjusted her view of their route.

Gid's eyebrows pulled low, a frown playing at the corners of his lips. His concentration face. The kind he got back in college when he was lining up the perfect beer pong shot or studying for his physics final.

Thanks to traffic, it took double the estimated time to get out of Dublin. And, because it seemed that Ari had, in fact, jinxed their entire trip, the snow got so much worse as they left the city. Gid definitely drove more cautiously than she'd ever seen him.

"God I'm starved, Gid. We're never going to make it at this rate?" Ari had her feet up on the dash and her arms crossed over her stomach. It had been a long time since their brunch this morning.

His frown etched deeper. This trip had barely started and it was a disaster.

"I'll stop at the next gas station. We can get some snacks."

When they stopped, Gid hopped out of the car. "I'm going to fill up the tank. Not sure what'll happen in this weather. Then we can go in there and check out the food situation."

Ari nodded and twisted a lock of hair around her finger, trying to pretend like she wasn't miserable. According to the Google Maps, they were barely halfway there and it was nearly four o'clock. With the cloud cover from the storm, it was basically dusk already.

Gid opened the car door a crack, and with it came a gust of wind and a swirl of snowflakes. His dark brown hair was dusted with them.

Now Ari frowned. "You need your beanie."

He laughed. "I'll get it when we're back in the car. Come on, let's get snacks."

Ari pulled her teddy bear coat around her—somehow also woefully under-equipped for a blizzard despite traveling by choice in the winter. They really messed up their packing list.

Or Ireland really messed up its damn weather.

Maybe both.

They braced against the wind that seemed to only be picking up and Gid wrenched the shop door open for her. A little bell tinkled over their heads, and when Ari looked up, there was a spring of mistletoe over the door. How festive.

Her cheeks flamed, remembering what the two had done the other night. Holy hell it had been hot. When would they do anything like that again? Since that second orgasm ripped through her, they'd been basically chaste. Which was probably for the better anyway. It was a mistake. That they made twice. A mistake they could still move past.

"Oh, you must be needing to get somewhere tonight driving out in this weather!" The clerk called to them with a cheery wave.

"It's not too bad," Gid said, bunching his shoulders up in the warmth of the gas station.

"Haven't seen snow like this since Emma back in 2018." The clerk frowned. "It'll get worse before it stops. Not supposed to stop until after midnight."

Just what they needed to hear as they browsed the snack aisle.

"I've never seen any of these snacks in my life, but I would eat just about anything at this point," Ari grumbled.

"Let's divide and conquer, and then I'll grab us some Cokes."

"Got it."

Gid surveyed the crunchy snacks, grabbing a bag of Tayto cheese and onion chips and Meanies—something which looked distinctly unlike an American bag of potato chips. Ari, naturally, gravitated to the sweet things, picking up two Cadbury Snack bars and a package of some pretty cookies called Mikado, whatever those were.

"I found Pop-Tarts!" Ari squealed, grabbing two packages of the cherry flavor, her favorite.

Gid made a beeline for the drinks while Ari went to the counter.

Thankfully, the clerk didn't have any more unhelpful commentary.

Ari settled in the passenger seat and Gid dumped his snacks into the driver seat before heading back around to the trunk for his bag.

"Oh, there's a whole emergency kit back here," he called, half-shouting over the wind. "Some of those crunchy space blankets in case we need to camp out."

"Don't you even say that, Gideon Sims," Ari hollered over her shoulder.

In a minute, he slammed the trunk and ran around to the driver side, his navy beanie firmly in place on his head. He looked really cute in that hat. Ari's heart stuttered as she realized she'd just thought that.

She was distinctly not supposed to have such thoughts.

But then Gid showed up in her room. The way his dark voice had told her exactly what to do to herself... It felt like a fever dream now. Especially since they hadn't said a word about it between them. Probably for the best.

So then why couldn't she get the feeling of his fingertips on her naked skin out of her brain? Why couldn't she forget how it felt when Gid had skimmed her panty line under the table at the rehearsal dinner? *How* could she forget the dangerous look in his eye as he sat across the room from her, cock in hand, and watched her pleasure herself? The thought now sent chills down her spine, distinctly unrelated to the snowy weather.

Even the way that he grasped the steering wheel in this situation was extremely attractive. She now knew just how strong those fingers were.

Apparently years of travel experience made such kinds of mishaps par for the course. But driving in a blizzard? She knew he didn't anticipate that. And despite his clenched jaw and permanent frown, he handled it with grace.

"Turn right to get out of here," Ari said, looking down at the Google Maps still guiding them on her lap. She opened the package of cookies as he used his turn indicator to signal getting back into the road. "These are pretty little cookies." She turned it over and sniffed at it, unsure what to expect from the flavor.

"Mmm," Gid grunted from the driver's seat, back to business.

"You want anything?"

"I need to keep my eyes on the road and both hands on the wheel, Ari. No time for snacks."

"I can feed you," she said.

His gaze flicked to hers and her cheeks heated. She

hadn't intended for that to be filled with such innuendo, but apparently they were both wound tight enough that it was absolutely suggestive.

Gid cleared his throat. "I'm good, thanks, pop tart."

"Right," she mumbled, and shoved the cookie in her mouth before she said anything else ridiculous.

She immediately regretted it. "Oh my god this cookie is disgusting."

Gid snorted out of his nose. "What does it taste like?"

"Like a freaking Grandma cookie. Don't ask me to explain that, but it just tastes like something Grandma Callaghan would have served, rest in peace." She frowned as she chewed it and forced herself to swallow, washing the taste down with a sip of Coke. "It's like bubblegum or cotton candy. Something distinctly un-cookie-like." She picked up the package and inspected it. "Tricky little thing, wouldn't have expected something so disgusting from them."

"Okay, I'm gonna have to try one of those," Gid said, as he inched along the road at a criminally slow speed. Keeping his eyes forward, he leaned over to her side of the car. "Feed me."

The way his absolutely innocent request came out like a command she had to obey sent chills racing down her arms. For one second, his eyes flit in her direction, before snapping back to the road, and she wondered if he felt the energy crackling between them, too.

She swallowed, suddenly parched. "Alright," she exhaled, reaching a cookie toward him.

His lips closed around the cookie and all she could think about was the way his lips had taken her nipple into his mouth. The way his tongue swirled around its peak, using his teeth to push the sensation just slightly over the edge into pleasurable pain.

Get it together, Ari, she chided herself. She must be really worked up if she was getting this turned on just by him eating a disgusting Grandma cookie literally from the palm of her hand.

Finally, Gid swallowed, his Adam's apple bobbing, and *oh, yeah*, she was still stupidly turned on.

"You know, I kinda like it." Gid laughed a little as he chewed and Ari felt momentarily lighter.

"Weirdo," she snorted back.

Gid readjusted in his seat, pushing his hips back and hunching over the steering wheel, immediately back in serious mode. "This weather really isn't letting up. Roads are getting worse."

All-wheel vehicle or not, they were driving slower and slower, especially as the roads got more narrow.

Ari's heart fluttered, this time out of nerves and not because of how much she wanted Gid to slip his hand between her thighs again. The man needed to concentrate on the road, after all. She wasn't driving, but she couldn't see much further beyond the hazy sphere of their head-lights reflecting off the spectral white flurries.

"Are you good to keep going?" Ari asked, shoving another nasty cookie in her mouth just because of the nerves that sparked under her skin.

Gid paused, then nodded. "Yeah. Yeah I should be good."

Ari blinked and then from the wall of white in front of them flashed two red brake lights like the eyes of a demon from hell.

"Gideon!"

There was a hollow sound, like an empty gallon of milk being run over and exploding—the car in front of them colliding with another, unseen vehicle—and his arm shot out across Ari's chest, pinning her shoulders back against the seat as he pumped the brakes. Like a pro, he turned the wheel, not too fast to spin them out but just enough to avoid the accident in front of them.

He skidded into the other lane, breezing by the two cars, and slid back onto the correct side of the road.

Hyperventilating, he released Ari's shoulders and clutched the wheel with both hands once more.

"Are you alright?" He breathed, teeth grit against the blizzard outside.

"I'm fine," Ari said, her arms braced at her sides. "Are you?"

"Not really." He shook his head at the open road. Or what he could see of it at least. "This is bonkers. How far do we still have to go?"

Ari consulted her maps, her stomach still in knots. Not

only were her nerves frayed from being in such close proximity of the man she had an increasingly stronger attraction to, but now also a near death experience. Basically.

"Well, it refreshed and...yep, my phone can't get signal now." She moved it around the car as if two feet to the left or right would boost it.

"Shit." Gid slammed a palm against the steering wheel.

"It's fine," Ari said, laying a hand on his thigh. It was a reflexive move, something she'd done a million times before, but now her hand tingled with the touch.

Gid reached down and cupped his hand around hers, slightly shaking.

"You're not okay, Gid," she whispered.

He shook his head. "No, I'm not. We need to stop. Wait out the storm."

"You heard the person at the gas station—it's not forecasted to stop until after midnight."

Gid's molars snapped together and he put his second hand back on the wheel. "Then we overnight in the car."

That really didn't sound ideal, not at all, but Ari wasn't about to argue with the guy who had already driven them halfway across Ireland in this ridiculous weather.

"Alright." She shrugged. There was nothing else to say. Maybe they could just lean their seats back and get some sleep.

Gid breathed audibly through his nose, clearly not

happy with this idea either. But they were quickly running out of options. Unless they happened to come across some kind of motel in this whiteout. Which didn't seem very likely. They were clearly in the middle of nowhere, considering Ari's lack of phone signal.

"I'm just going to stop at the next gas station or restaurant or whatever kind of parking lot I see."

"Okay."

Ari's chest hurt from holding her breath. From holding it still. She'd never seen Gid so serious and upset. The muscles of his jaw worked as he stayed hunched over the wheel, squinting into the white, shadowy, growing darkness.

"There." He pointed with one finger over the wheel. "It looks like a gas station, shut down for the night. It's Christmas Eve after all, I guess they'll all be closing up shop? Most of these kind of middle-of-nowhere places do."

Ari murmured her agreement, stunned that she'd forgotten it was Christmas Eve. But considering the chaos of the day, it wasn't entirely shocking.

The soft click of the turn indicator broke the silence between them as Gid pulled into the parking lot. He put the car in park, the wind howling outside.

"I guess this is it." Gid finally let go of the steering wheel and frowned down at his hands in his lap. "This is a disaster."

"It's not," Ari said, even though she was just thinking

the same damn thing. She waved the bag of Meanies—whatever those were—in the air. "We have Meanies."

"Ha," Gid laughed, defeated. "This just wasn't really what I envisioned our trip to be like. Our first trip abroad together."

She dropped the snacks and pulled his shoulders toward her chest, his head lolling into her. "I highly doubt this is what anyone would have imagined, Gid, but here we are. At least we're safe."

"At least we're safe." He sat up and looked into the back seat. "Not sure how we're going to keep warm, though."

"Didn't you say there were those emergency blankets in the back? I'll put down the back seats and we can hunker down back there."

"You are not going outside in this weather," Gid said, undoing his seatbelt and about to jump out to navigate the back seats down.

"No one has to get out. I'm small enough to crawl back there and wiggle the seats down from the inside." She looked him up and down. "You might have a little bit of a hard time getting back there, but I have faith in you. We can do this without opening any doors and letting out any heat."

"Whatever you say, pop tart."

"Watch me."

She unclipped her seatbelt and dove between the front seats into the back. First, she pushed their luggage to the side and then unhooked the seatbelts before unclipping the backseat and pushing the two pieces flat. Finally, she pulled out the two silver blankets in a racket of crinkles.

"It's basically luxurious back here." She smiled up at Gid from all fours.

Gid's face softened slightly watching her from the front. "Alright, but I'm about to take off my shoes and I can't be blamed from the smell that fills this car afterward."

"Gross, but fine." She flipped her fingers toward her palms in a grabby gesture. "Get back here."

He turned off the car and kicked his shoes off before pretzeling his body in an impressive shape to flip into the makeshift bed Ari had made. Sitting with crossed legs on top of the folded down seat, Gid fully hunched over in order to fit.

"See, it's not so bad." Ari grimaced.

"I wouldn't call it comfortable." He looked around. "Let's try laying down."

Ari's stomach flipped, completely of its own volition. The last time she was horizontal with Gid, they were distinctly naked and having sex.

"Okay." The word came out smaller than she meant it to.

"It'll be fine," Gid said, a softness creeping into his eyes.

Her body was betraying her of things that Ari kept

telling her body it shouldn't want. Being this close and being intimate with Gid was a bad idea, considering their agreement, the lines of which were becoming increasingly blurry.

But maybe...maybe it wasn't so bad. The way he'd cared for her today, over the last few hours in particular, keeping her safe. With everything in her life being so unstable over the last thirteen months, safety was special. Rare. Holy.

"We'll just lay here," Gid added, searching her face.

Maybe her thoughts were too obvious on her face. They both lay on their sides, facing each other, because there wasn't much room for anything else. Gid pulled the safety blankets over both of them.

"Wait a sec," Gid said, twisting and somehow digging into his bag at this awkward angle. He pulled out a sweatshirt and laid it down under both of their heads. "Pillow."

His scent, a soft patchouli musk, bloomed in the car. It took everything in Ari not to nestle her nose into the sweatshirt. But as she laid her head on it, she didn't need to. She was close enough. And damn if the scent itself was enough to make her feel safe.

"Gid," she said, her voice soft. Their hands found each other between them, their fingers lacing together. He bent his arm and brought their hands, clutched together, to rest on the sweatshirt between them.

"Ari," he breathed, as he rubbed his thumb along her pointer finger, back and forth.

The back of his hand brushed across her lips. She closed her eyes against the friction.

"Maybe I was wrong." The words tumbled out before she could second guess them.

"Hmm?"

"About...this."

To his credit, he didn't say anything. He waited for her to go on, to fill the silence.

"It's a bad idea, right?" Her heart thudded under her sweatshirt.

"I..." Gid licked his lips.

"Maybe we could just do it and get it out of our systems and when we go home after the week, things will just be normal."

For a moment, Ari could have sworn she saw his shoulders slump, but then he smiled. "Did you just say do it?"

"Shut up." She broke their clasped hands to push against his shoulder. "And yes, I did."

"I think," he started, lacing an arm under her sweater, quickly finding skin, "if we *did it*, it would definitely keep us warm."

"Mmm," she agreed, her own arm looping around his waist. "Never have I ever *done it* in the back of a car..."

Gid laughed, somehow both sweet and dark. The next moment, he pulled her closer, and his erection rubbed against her stomach.

She quirked an eyebrow. "Oh?"

He growled and nuzzled his nose under her ear. "I've been thinking about being this close to you since that night before the wedding. Just waiting for you to give me permission to touch you again."

Gid's hot breath whispering in her ear sent sparks pulsing down to the base of her spine. Him mentioning *that night* that he watched her before finally touching her, forcing another orgasm out of her, made it real again.

"Yeah?"

"Fuck yeah." He nipped at her earlobe. "I've been desperate for you."

Ari liked the sound of that. Running her nails up and down his back, she asked. "How desperate? Tell me everything."

He pushed his hips into her, grinding jeans on jeans. "Last night, just before I drifted off into sleep, I thought about how soft your bare pussy is. How good my fingers feel inside you. I remembered your sweet taste, Ari, and how hungry I am to give you the orgasms that you deserve."

Her core squeezed at his words. "Oh," she squeaked.

Gid pinched the soft skin at her hip. "Too much?"

Ari cleared her throat before going on. "No. I want more."

Gid slid his flat palm up the soft plane of her stomach, goosebumps flying off in all directions from his touch. "Just the thought of you gets me hard, Ari. The way you took your pleasure that night, using your toy exactly how you wanted. It was so hot. So perfect. The way you let go the second time. Your pussy was so hungry for it, I could feel it. Mmm," he purred into her ear. "It's making me ache just thinking about it now."

Ari's hand drifted from his waist down to his warm, hard cock, still trapped inside his jeans.

He pushed into her touch, a low rumble growing in his chest. "I had to jack off like three times this weekend just to keep my cool around you, Ari. I don't know what it is, but it's like a flip switched. Your scent on my skin. Your taste on my lips. It's made me crazy."

"I touched myself thinking about you, too, Gid."

He groaned, this time as if in pain, tortured. "Can I touch you now?"

She nodded, their foreheads coming together, as he popped the button of her jeans and ripped down the zipper. There wasn't much room in the back, but there was enough. Gid didn't waste any time plunging his hand into her panties and finding the seam of her lips. He tickled her there, teasing for a moment, before splitting her and finding her clit. With a moan, she ground her hips into his touch, desperate for more.

"Greedy little girl," he laughed.

Their shared breath mingled between them, until, when he entered her with one finger, Ari tipped her chin up and their lips just barely touched. Gid pumped in and out, rubbing on her clit with this thumb. Suddenly, she needed more of him. She wanted to touch him while he touched her.

"Can I touch you, too?"

When he nodded against her lips, she undid his pants and pushed his briefs down around his thick erection. His heat filled her palm and she moved her hand up and down his silky length slowly, torturously.

When he ground out her name, he dove into her cunt with another finger, stretching her just a little more. Rocking his palm as he made a coaxing motion inside her, her orgasm grew, tightening her pelvis, but she didn't want to come on his fingers.

"Fuck me, Gid. I want to come on your cock."

With those words, he sucked on her bottom lip. "Yes ma'am."

He shimmied his wallet out of his pocket then pulled out a condom wrapper. Gid held the package between his teeth as he and Ari wriggled out of their jeans.

They laughed as they knocked foreheads. He grunted when she elbowed his stomach. The blankets crinkled as they kicked their legs.

"This is absolutely ridiculous," Ari said as she curled up with uncontrollable giggles.

Gid silenced her with a quick kiss, clutching onto her at the collarbone, running a thumb along the soft hollow there. "Laugh now, pop tart. You'll be screaming my name in a couple minutes."

"Is that a promise?"

His gaze darkened. "It's most definitely a threat."

"Game on," she said.

Before she could get in another word, Gid had pinned her underneath his body, bracketing her shoulders with his upper body. In a deft move, he ripped the condom package and rolled it on.

He positioned himself at her opening, rubbing the tip up and down, coating him in her wetness. Even the shallow spreading of her opening felt good. So good that she was already softly mewling and eager for more.

"Ready?" He asked and she nodded in response.

Gid pistoned his hips forward, pushing into her a little more. Forward and back, forward and back, inch by inch burying himself deeper inside her until he was fully sheathed and she was fully stretched.

He paused there and she clutched onto his back, relishing his weight on top of her and girth inside of her. Everything tingled as he rested his forehead against hers.

"Gid," she whispered.

"Ari," he responded, his whole body quaking.

Then he started to fuck her. Slow at first, but gradually picking up speed. She matched his rhythm, rocking her hips up and down to meet his thrusts.

"So good, Ari. So good," Gid praised her through gritted teeth and her entire body flushed with the compliment.

Gid rolled just slightly, bracing himself on one arm

and reaching down between her legs, rubbing her clit in firm circles.

"Oh god, Gid."

"That's right," he said, increasing pressure of his fingers and his thrusts.

Her body tightened, just about to the crest the hill of her orgasm. As stars sparked through her every nerve ending, she screamed his name—just like he promised she would.

NINETEEN

GID

IN THEIR POST-SEX HAZE, Gid rolled off Ari and brushed her hair off her face. She was gorgeous. So gorgeous.

In some ways, he couldn't believe that this was only just happening between them now.

And in other ways, *this* wasn't anything that was happening at all. It was just sex. Just getting it out of their system. That's what they agreed.

But something twinged inside of him when he thought about this ending when they got back to Starling Hills.

"Don't move," he murmured to her, kissing every spare inch of her soft skin that he could manage as he arranged their space blankets and clothes in a little cocoon of warmth.

He didn't intend for them to spend the entire night in

the backseat. After all, it was barely after five o'clock, but it was pitch dark with the early sunset, heavy cloud cover, and the blizzard. But as he lay on his side, Gid brushed his fingers through Ari's long, dark hair and within minutes she was asleep.

Of course, he was exhausted too from the stress of the wedding weekend and the day. The snow wasn't supposed to let up until midnight anyway. He grabbed his phone. Thankfully he had signal, so he mapped the route to their stay. Only about an hour to go. In good weather conditions that is. They might as well just wait it out at this point. Getting there this late, they would just go to sleep anyway.

Gid set his phone alarm for midnight. He wrapped an arm around Ari's belly, and she cuddled sleepily into him. Within minutes, he was asleep, too.

* * *

WHEN THE ALARM blared them both awake, the first thing Gid realized was that his body was very unhappy about sleeping in a cramped makeshift backseat bed.

Ari groaned, her eyes still closed. "Oh my god everything hurts."

"Hard same. But at least we're warm."

A thin layer of sweat covered both their naked bodies, especially where they touched—which was everywhere, considering their close quarters. He turned his phone flashlight on and looked around the car. The windows were completely covered in snow.

"What a disaster," he mumbled.

"Still snowing?" Ari asked, not daring to open her eyes.

"Can't tell. We are apparently encased in snow." Gid turned off the flashlight and dropped his phone, instead nosing up Ari's arm, neck, and into her hairline.

"You still smell so freaking delicious." His hand around her waist drifted down her stomach to her hip bone and he grabbed her there.

"Gid," she laughed. "Stop it."

But she said it without conviction as her fingers laced through his thick hair.

"I can't," he mumbled against her skin.

Which was true. Being this close to Ari and this naked, he couldn't keep his hands off her. Keep his lips off her. Every fiber of his being screamed for her body against, under, and touching his.

Ari tugged his hair, sending a shock of delicious pain lancing through his scalp, and pulled him back to look into his eyes. "How about we see what the situation is outside, and then if it's stopped snowing, get to where we're staying and continue this there. Where it's, ideally, warm and a little less centered around crinkly space blankets."

"Deal."

Gid maneuvered into his clothes and tugged his

beanie down over his ridiculous sex hair before shoving open the back door and tumbling out. He landed in snow up to past his ankles before slamming the door shut behind him and sending more snow raining down on his pants.

His breath puffed in tiny little clouds as the world around him glittered in sparkling snow. Ice crystals clung to the trees that lined the parking lot of what looked like a massive grocery store somehow in the middle of nowhere. It reminded him of the days when he'd wake up as a kid on a snow day, only to bundle up against the snow and go exploring in the winter wonderland. If they weren't trying to get somewhere in the middle of this storm, it would pretty much be a Christmas miracle to wake up to this kind of sparkling world on Christmas day.

The door opened behind him.

"What's the damage?" Ari called out, her hair falling over one shoulder.

"Well, it's stopped." The cold air stung his lungs when he took a deep breath. "But it's left about a foot of snow with the drifts and an inch of ice in its wake."

"Shit." Ari fell head over heels out of the Suzuki, wearing boots trimmed in faux fur.

"Where'd you get those?" Gid said, raising his eyebrows toward her footwear.

"Packed them." She shrugged. "Basically the only practical thing I packed, apparently."

Ari crossed her arms in front of her and rubbed her upper arms. "Fuck, it's even more freezing than before."

Gid pulled her into his chest. Another car took the curve in the road, lighting them up with their headlights. "But it's so freaking pretty."

"Remember when we took the cafeteria trays to go sledding?" Her voice rumbled straight to his center.

"After that massive snowstorm freshman year?"

"You pulled me up all the hills because my stupid Ugg boots had absolutely zero traction." Ari kicked a boot in the air. "Learned my lesson."

"Then we got lost."

"But that was some of the best sledding of my life."

"Who knew cafeteria trays made such excellent and dangerous sleds."

"Only every college freshman ever." Ari laughed and broke away from Gid, twirling in the cold.

Something shifted inside Gid's chest as he watched her. Ari had such a lightness to her that he could never access, despite whatever shit she was going through that they were decidedly ignoring. At least for now. For the next couple of days, there was only them.

She waltzed up to him, pausing a couple inches away. Her mouth scrunched to the side and one hand plunged into his pocket, coming up with the car keys. Ari shook them in the air as she walked backward toward the car.

"Gimme those!" Gid grabbed at them, but Ari bobbed

out of his reach, running around the car to the driver's seat.

He couldn't see what she was doing, but he had a suspicion she was putting on music. And when the *A Charlie Brown Christmas* came on, his suspicions were confirmed. Her favorite Christmas album and one he knew she had downloaded to her phone. The opening piano chords filled the cold air and nostalgia flooded his veins. His family used to listen to this album on vinyl around Christmastime. When the holidays were still fun, and his parents weren't submerged in their work.

After a moment Ari resurfaced around the side of the car, two snow brushes hoisted into the air like victory trophies.

"These rental cars come stocked," she said, tossing a snow brush to Gid. "Many hands make light work."

"That sounds like something a mom would say to get her kids to do chores."

"Funnily enough that's exactly what my mom would say to me and my brothers to get us to do the worst chores. Like weeding. God, I hated weeding as a kid." She frowned at the window she brushed off.

"I think it was mostly that my mom never wanted me to help with the chores that I hated."

"What do you mean?"

Gid swallowed, his chest hollow. He stepped up to the car and scraped ice where Ari had already cleared snow.

"My parents were just always working. Too busy with their careers and research to be interested in what I was doing. Or not doing. I got away with bloody murder in high school, but they never taught me how to do my own laundry or how to cook macaroni and cheese. I shrunk way too many sweaters before I figured out laundry."

He didn't like thinking about his family life. The things he missed out on in his youth. Most of the practical things that Gid knew, he taught himself that chaotic freshman year of college.

"Oh," Ari swallowed a giggle, the heaviness of the moment snapping with the strangled sound. "I remember some of those casseroles you made junior year."

"Hey! You all always complimented my food."

"We didn't want to hurt your feelings, Gid."

"This changes everything!" he said, pausing his brushing. "What if I'm not even a good cook at all?"

Ari grimaced a smile in his direction that turned quickly into a laugh. Snow clung in her hair and the way the white sparkles contrasted against her raven locks made his heart stutter.

He dropped his snow brush to the ground and scooped snow from the vehicle's hood, forming it into a ball. "You better duck," he growled, stalking a step toward her.

"You wouldn't dare!" Ari squealed, sprinting around the car, her boots digging into the snow for traction.

He chased her for a minute, and then stopped, letting her keep running. When she careened around the front end of the car again, he was there to grab her. She screamed with laughter as Gid snatched her around the waist, smashing the small snowball onto her back between her shoulder blades as he laughed, too.

"Oh my god, you ass!" She squirmed in his arms, trying in vain to break his iron grip around her.

Now that he had her, he wouldn't let go.

After a moment, she stopped struggling and allowed herself to be held.

"Merry Christmas, Ari," he murmured into her ear, nosing through her hair.

Her scent was like a tonic, running thick like honey through his veins. He could smell her all day.

She pulled her head back and looked up, meeting his gaze. Now that the storm clouds cleared, the inky black sky and the stars from above reflected in her eyes. Gid ran a thumb along her cheek, flushed from the cold and the exertion...and maybe something else.

"Merry Christmas, Gid."

* * *

IT TOOK another hour and a half on the still slick roads in the middle of the night to finish the drive. Their reservation in their rented guest house had automated check-in, so all they had to do was punch in the key-code into the door's lock, and they were in.

"It's roasting in here," Ari said, falling onto the couch. "I'm in heaven. I never want to sleep in a car ever again."

"But we made it worth it." Gid smirked at her as he shut the door behind him and deadbolted it.

"Mmm," she murmured, her eyes already fluttering closed.

Gid let her rest there while he went around, checking out the little home and moving their bags into the bedrooms. One queen bed in the actual primary bedroom, and one twin-sized day bed in the office.

Of course, they made this reservation months ago, before they had any inkling what would happen between them on the trip. Even so, it would be presumptuous of Gid to assume that just because they'd had sex a few times that they would be sharing a bed for the rest of the trip.

But he would be lying to himself if he didn't admit that was exactly what he wanted.

Boy, was he screwed when they got home. Were they just supposed to go back to being friends? After he knew how perfectly her pussy molded to his cock? The way she squirmed when she orgasmed? He stiffened in his jeans, his head swimming as he remembered her taste.

Gid peeked out at Ari, who had fully passed out on the couch, and he decided to slip into the shower.

The hot water pelted his back as he grit his teeth, one

hand holding him up against the shower wall, the other stroking himself. He imagined that he plunged into Ari's warmth instead of his fist with each motion, but even with his release, he didn't get any relief.

Instead, a mild amount of self-loathing washed over him: the kind that usually came after he masturbated. Similar to the kind he always associated with the holidays and being home.

The feeling that was a major reason why he'd accepted Ari's invitation to her brother's wedding in Ireland. At Christmas. Why he was so keen to plan this trip afterward. If he could avoid his parents and their pseudo-bonding activities over the holidays, he jumped at the chance.

He stood in the shower until it got cold, hunched against the world. Against the tight leash that he always kept on his emotions. Hiding it all from everyone else.

Gid sighed, pulling his hand through his wet hair. He never felt like he had to hide around Ari, but still, he did. She didn't know much about his family. About the years that they favored their research over their only son. How they moved around the country for their career but didn't seem to care about his schooling or his friends.

"Fuck." He slapped his palm onto the wall, the flat sound echoing through the bathroom.

Turning the water off, he stood in the shower, naked and cold and feeling every bit of the three in the morning exhaustion. He needed to dry off. Go to bed. Try again in the morning.

Christmas morning.

After Gid towel dried his hair, he pulled on his pajamas. He padded back into the living room, where Ari still lay on the couch looking awkward and uncomfortable. Her sweater twisted up around her ribs, as her belly expanded and contracted with each breath. Gid wanted to grab her around the waist and hold on tight, never letting go.

Instead, he knelt next to the couch and pushed her hair back from her face. "Ari," he whispered.

She groaned, a sweet little sound, scrunching her nose against the intrusion to her dreams.

"You need to go to bed. It's late."

"Mmno." Ari tried to roll over but almost fell off the couch instead.

Gid gripped the back of his neck, letting his head fall and stretching the tight tendons. God, he was exhausted. And he didn't want to leave Ari on this too-small couch.

There was only one thing to do: he snaked one arm under her knees and another around her shoulders, heaving her off the couch.

"Mmm." This time her groan was more like a sound she might make when biting into a piece of her favorite double chocolate cake. She nuzzled right in under his chin, like she was always meant to be there.

Gid's chest literally ached as he carried her down the

dark hallway, praying that he wouldn't run into anything with his shins. He didn't dare turn on any more lights and disturb her slumber even more. Keeping her comfortable —after the day they had—was more important than his shins.

He walked into the primary bedroom and tipped her into bed. The light from the moon and stars filtered through the window, casting her face in a silvery glow. Fuck, Ari looked lovely. He pulled her furry boots off, but didn't dare undress her any further, considering she was very much asleep.

A little noise of complaint escaped her lips and her tiny fist curled into his top.

"Stay." A tiny crease appeared between her eyebrows, though her eyelids were still shut.

Standing upright, Gid ran a hand over his face, his heart doing gymnastics in his chest.

Stay? Stay in bed with Ari tonight? Eyes on the ceiling, he wet his suddenly dry lips.

"Please, Gid, stay with me."

When he looked back down at her, she met his gaze with wide, pleading eyes.

"It's Christmas," she whispered.

"Well," he said, raking his fingers through her hair. "Just because it's Christmas."

Her sweet, sexy pout curled her lips, and she peeled her pants and sweater off, dropping her clothes off the side of the bed. In just a camisole top and underwear, she closed her eyes, nestling into the pillow. Gid walked around the bed and pulled back the blankets as Ari scooted underneath them. As natural as anything, he slid in behind her, notching his big spoon to her little spoon.

"Merry Christmas, Ari," he said, already half in a dream, floating on a cloud of her floral-sandalwood perfume.

TWENTY
ARI

THREE GENTLE KNOCKS rapped on the door. Or, somewhere nearby.

Ari's eyes flew open, but she didn't move, looking left and right before daring to lift her head from the pillow.

Some muffled words came from...some direction...but she could barely even figure out where she was right now let alone who the disembodied voice might belong to. Was the voice talking about *goats*?

As Ari turned onto her back, she realized there was a heavy arm draped over her waist.

Oh right, Gid was in her bed. Because she'd asked him to stay.

Groaning internally, she filed that away to dissect after she maybe got some caffeine in her bloodstream. She unfolded herself from under the blankets and her bare feet hit the ground and, *oh fuck*, it was freezing in here.

Shivering, she pulled her cowl neck sweater over her head, wiggled into her leggings, and took in her surroundings. They'd slept on a wooden farmhouse spool bed underneath a couple patterned quilts. A rocking chair sat in the corner and an antique travel trunk functioned as a bench at the foot of the bed.

This place looked exactly like the pictures when she picked it out online.

Except that she hadn't anticipated that Gid would be sleeping in the same bed as her. He looked good there, more peaceful than she'd seem him in some time.

Just as she was thinking of tucking back into the bed, the knock came at the door again.

Right, right, that's why Ari had gotten up in the first place. She padded on treacherously cold bare feet to the front door of the guest house and then peeked through the curtains.

A pink faced older woman—their host, Ari recognized her from the website—beamed back at her, waving a mittened hand in front of Ari's face through the glass pane.

"Merry Christmas, love!" she giggled. "If you celebrate, that is."

Ari already liked this woman and especially loved her Irish accent. She reminded her of an apple pie, sweet, innocent, and wholesome. Ari held up one finger before dropping the curtain again and unbolting the front door.

"Good morning," Ari said, smiling. "Merry Christmas."

"Oh, it's barely morning anymore! The goats have been bleatin' all morning waitin' for me to come out with the barley n' the oats for them. But I just had to have my Christmas breakfast with my fella Jack before heading out." She rubbed her hands on her corduroy overalls. "I'm being so silly. Bless me. The name's Bridget, your host here on the farm."

"Ari, and Gid is still inside sleeping," Ari said, pointing a thumb over her shoulder into the guest house.

Bridget squinted, as if trying to see Gid laying in bed and then nodded, smiling. "Wore him out, did you?"

Scratch that on the wholesome. Ari's cheeks heated. "Oh, it's not like that."

Though it absolutely had been like that last night in the back of the Suzuki.

But they had gotten it out of their system, right? Even though she had definitely asked him to stay last night.

Ari swallowed, certain that all of these emotions likely played out over her face, and she had the sneaking suspicion that their host could read her every last thought.

"Mmhm." Bridget smiled, jolly as Mrs. Claus on Christmas morning. She swung her pail. "Care to join me in the barn?"

"Absolutely!" The prospect of helping out with the goats was exactly why Ari had picked this stay. Who didn't love pygmy goats? Okay, there were probably a lot of people who didn't love goats, but Ari did.

Ari grabbed her coat, gloves, and Gid's beanie that he'd left on the kitchen counter before stuffing her feet into her furry boots. She wasn't exactly dressed for farm work, but she figured this would do for feeding the goats. "Is this alright?"

"Of course, love, the goats won't bother ya once they see ya have food."

In the soft morning light poking through wispy clouds, the farm was gorgeous. A thick blanket of crystalline snow hushed the entire landscape, sparkling in the sun.

"Quite the storm we had last night. Hasn't snowed like that since before the pandemic. Just glad you two made it in safe, even if it was late."

"I hope we didn't keep you up," Ari said as they trudged through the snow. It was over eight inches deep in some parts. A little bit of snow trickled into her boots, leaving a flash of wet cold behind.

"Oh." Bridget waved her off. "I don't sleep much these days anyway. When I got your message you'd be late, I said to Jack that I'd stay up with my Netflix and wait for you. Saw you pull in around three in the morning and then I tucked myself into bed. Wouldn't have been able to sleep not knowin' anyway."

"Well thank you." Ari smiled, remembering last night.

Everything about last night. The whole whirlwind

adventure and near disaster. The way Gid took control and took care of her. How his dirty worded confession still lit fire in her veins.

Bridget opened the barn door and let Ari walk in first. Inside was surprisingly warm and overhead a row of dangling Edison lightbulbs burst to life with a flick of a switch near the door.

"Oh my god!" Ari squealed as the little goats tottered over, bleating precious little *baas* in their direction. She crouched down to their height and stared at them through the pen in the barn.

"Hello little ones," Bridget said, scattering a handful of oat and barley mixture as the little goats sniffed the air. She handed the bucket to Ari and unlatched their pen gate. "Here you go."

"I can go in there?"

Bridget nodded, ushering her forward.

Their little black noses booped her legs and all Ari wanted to do was sit down and let them scamper all over her like puppies. But she suspected the ground was half covered in poop. She pulled off her glove and grabbed a handful of their food, opening her palm to the animals. They pranced up to her, eager for food.

"Their tongues!" she squealed as Bridget watched, leaning over the fence.

"Cute little buggers, aren't they? Let's bring them outside."

"Into the snow?"

"They'll be fine since it's not too cold now. They need some fresh air and then I'll turn the heat lamps on once we bring them back inside."

The goats hopping through the snow was almost more cuteness than Ari could bear. They bleated and jumped around, playing with each other, and nosing around for food that she kept scattering for them. One all black one walked right up to her and ate right out of her palm.

"Old Coal doesn't usually take to strangers," Bridget said. "He's usually quite a grump. He must really trust you to walk up to you like that."

Ari furrowed her brow at the goat. "You're not a grump, are you?"

"You'd be surprised." Bridget crossed her arms over her chest. "Nibbled quite a few heads of hair when we do goat yoga in the summer. Can't usually have Coal come out for that."

Tickling a finger under Coal's chin, Ari thought the two of them weren't so different. A little misunderstood but wouldn't cause any lasting harm.

"Are you and your partner coming up to the house for the roast dinner this evening?" Bridget asked as they corralled the little goats back into the barn.

"If the invitation still stands?" Ari asked, crouched down to give them all, especially Coal, a last little scritch goodbye.

"Of course, love, it's Christmas! Jack's been working all day on that turkey. It'll be nice, crispy meat when it's done.

Cocktails starts at four." Bridget beamed and Ari smiled right back.

"Well in that case, we wouldn't miss it."

* * *

WHEN ARI OPENED the guesthouse door, she was greeted by the smell of coffee. Probably the best smell in the world.

"Hello there," Gid said, sauntering around the kitchen in his pajamas, grey waffle Henley and low-slung flannel pants.

He looked freaking delicious.

"You made coffee?" Ari smiled, her cheeks stinging from the sudden warmth.

"Saw you outside with the goats, so I figured you'd need something warm when you came back in," he said, pouring them two steaming mugs. "Also, I needed the caffeine."

"After the day we had yesterday..." Ari snorted. She walked across the kitchen peninsula to grab her mug and had the overwhelming desire to smooth her hand around his hip. Instead, she stared into his eyes, warm and coffee brown like the steaming cup he put into her hand. "Thank you," she whispered.

"Merry Christmas, Ari." Gid took a deep breath, his chest shuddering as he did. Somehow the holiday wish sounded so sweet on his lips, she would never tire of hearing it. She had a sneaking suspicion that he couldn't help but say it to her multiple times. "I wouldn't want to be with anyone else today."

"Me neither." She was surprised to find that she actually meant it. Despite their mishaps so far this trip, their stumbling along the way, she wouldn't change anything. "Our hosts re-invited us up to the house at four for Christmas cocktails and roast dinner."

"That sounds fantastic." Gid checked the time on his phone then pulled his lips between his teeth, rolling them slowly. "Are you cold?"

"A little." But already the heat tingling in her cheeks had spread across the bridge of her nose, down to her fingertips and toes.

He traced her jawline with his knuckle, ending at her chin then running his thumb just below her lips. "How about I run a bath for us."

Her heart stuttered over the word *us*, but then realized that was exactly what she wanted. "That sounds perfect."

Gid went to draw a bath and Ari stayed standing at the counter, sipping her black coffee, until he hollered down the hall for her.

The bathroom had a massive claw foot tub, the kind she dreamt about in her wildest cottagecore fantasies. The room was already steamy from the hot tub water.

"Ready?" he asked, standing with a fuzzy, white towel wrapped around his hips.

Was she ever. Slowly she stripped off one piece of

clothing at a time, while Gid watched her like a man starved for sustenance.

Had he always looked at her this way? This reverently? Like her body was holy?

She couldn't remember now how Gid used to look at her. But she hoped that he would never stop gazing at her with this exact kind of hunger.

His chest heaved as she got down to her cotton bralette and undies. Her nipples stiffened as she ran her fingertips up her sides.

"Fuck," he whispered, running a hand down his own chest, and loosening the towel wrapped around his waist.

When it dropped down to the floor, all Ari could do was stare. There wasn't anything notably exceptional about his body—he was just a normal guy with a normal shape, slim hips and maybe a little bit of pooch from drinking beer and eating pizza—but he looked perfect to her. It was all the years of memories that made him so attractive. And his smile, he had the best smile. So sincere and friendly. It cut through the steam of the bathroom and hit her straight in the heart.

She reached around behind her and undid her bra, letting it fall to the ground, and then pulled her panties down from her hips. Once they hit the ground, she stepped out of them. They both walked to the edge of the tub, and he held a hand out to help her into the bath.

When her toe hit the water, she hissed at the heat.

"Too hot?" Concern washed over his face.

"No, it feels amazing."

Slowly, she lowered herself into the water all the way, enjoying the warmth that enveloped her. Then Gid got in across from her. For a couple minutes, they just sat there, both of their legs drawn up to their chests and playing with each other's hands in the water. Their toes touched under the surface.

"Never have I ever taken a bath with anyone," Ari said, a small smile turning up her lips.

"Me neither." Gid ran a wet hand through his hair and then caught her palm again in the water. "I'm really happy we're together today. I always hate this holiday with my parents. It's cold and awkward and I'm starting to think maybe they're still only together for their research. They're basically estranged from their siblings and it's just a quiet day. Like all the days with them. Nothing special about it. You make every day special though, Ari. Just being with you. And this tattoo."

Gid reached down, grabbed her left ankle, and smiled through the watery at the cartoon donkey.

"Eeyore," he said, raising his eyebrows.

Ari wiggled her toes. "My Eeyore tattoo. And still my only one."

"Why didn't you ever get more?"

"Didn't need more. Eeyore was enough." Ari giggled at the memory of going with Zahra to get it done.

He ran his palms up over her knees and down her

thighs and grasped on at her hips, his fingers indenting her soft skin.

"Thank you for sharing that with me, about your parents," she whispered as she wrapped her hands around his calves. It meant a lot to Ari that he was comfortable enough to open up about his parents. "I'm happy I'm with you, too, Gid."

"Yeah?" Hope burned hot in his eyes, like he was hanging off her words.

"Yes."

"Ari..." Gid started before he dropped his head to her shoulder, "I want to touch you again. As much as I tell myself it was just those one...or three...times, I can't accept it."

She swallowed and curled a hand around his neck. "What's going to happen when we go home?"

"Do we have to think about that right now?"

There were a lot of things she wasn't thinking about right now. About school. Her dad. Her friendship with Gid after this week. How long could they live in their fairytale bubble before everything collapsed in on them? Maybe, since it was Christmas, they could put it all off a little longer.

"I suppose we don't," she said.

"Because all I'm thinking about right now is being deep inside of you."

Ari stuttered out a laugh as her stomach clenched, hot and syrupy.

"But first I'm going to wash your hair and take care of you before I get you dirty again."

Using the buoyancy of water, he spun Ari around on her bum and pulled her between his legs. The faucet had a detachable head and he pulled it out, testing the water.

"Tilt your head back," he said, soft but firm. Another kind of command.

She did as she was told, her throat stretching long as the prickly water hit her scalp. Gid cradled the base of her skull with one hand. The ends of her hair floated in the tub around her, tickling her shoulders. Once all of her hair was wet, he picked up the bottle of shampoo; coconuts filled the air as he squeezed it into his palm. He massaged her scalp, varying the pressure points and the patterns of his fingers. Tingles ran down her neck and she shivered despite the warm water. Finally, he gathered all of her hair on top of her head to suds the shampoo.

"No one's ever washed my hair before," Ari whispered, staring at the exposed beam ceiling.

"Never have I ever washed anyone's hair before," Gid murmured behind her.

"No one's ever taken care of me the way you do, Gid."

When she said it, his fingers stilled on her tingling scalp. She couldn't see what he was doing, but she felt his weight transfer as he leaned forward and planted a soft kiss on the hollow of her clavicle. He straightened his legs beside her and pulled her back by the shoulders, leaving sudsy shampoo behind. Ari's ass nestled between his thighs and when he pulled her back a little more, she felt his erection hard on her back.

"And no one ever will, Ari Callaghan." He whispered it like an oath he intended to keep.

It settled in her belly, but not before a little kindling of fear sparked up in response, and Ari wondered how the hell she could mess this up, too.

TWENTY-ONE
GID

GID HADN'T MEAN to come on so strong, but around Ari, he suddenly couldn't help it.

Every bit of his body screamed to keep her. Keep her just like this. Maybe if he could, then he might be able to drown out the little voices in his head that screamed he was not enough. Not enough for his parents, not enough for anyone. Why he was so alone.

They held hands as they walked up to the main house, electric candles in the windows guiding their way, trudging through the snow as the sun set and the dusk grew purple and shadowy around them. Christmas cocktails and dinner would be enough to drown those voices out for now.

"Ye made it!" The older woman pulled Ari into an immediate hug, which Ari accepted with a little surprised oof. And then she pulled Gid in, too, introducing herself as she did so. "I'm Bridget, and you must be...?"

"Gideon. But just Gid is fine."

"Of course. Ari's sleeping man."

Gid raised a questioning eyebrow at Ari, but she shook her head, brushing it off.

"That's Jack over there mixing the gin and tonics." Bridget pointed across their cozy living room to the warmly lit kitchen bar, and the man waved. "We use our own sloe gin."

"Sloe gin?" Ari asked, unwrapping her scarf, and kicking off her boots.

"Ah yes, we infuse the gin ourselves with sloe berries from the farm."

"Makes a gorgeous cocktail," Jack laughed from the kitchen.

"Sign me up." Ari waltzed through the living room and into the kitchen, immediately at ease as always.

"It smells amazing in here," Gid said to Bridget as he took in the cozy space.

It was decorated in the same kind of vintage farm-house style as the guesthouse. Which wasn't so much a style, he supposed, as how these kind of older homesteads came together. So much more realistic than the Scandi-modern style that his parents favored growing up. Sure, he could appreciate Marie Kondo as much as the next person, but he loved to see all the little crocheted blankets and quilts thrown over the backs of sagging couches and rocking chairs and the knick-knacks that sprouted up on every horizontal surface.

Soft Christmas music played in the background, and he immediately caught the familiar *All I Want For Christmas Is You*. Apparently, the song was a universal holiday experience, even across the Atlantic.

"I can't take any credit for the smells, love, that's all my Jack. The blessed chef in this partnership."

"She does the drinking for the both of us!" Jack called.

"Oh hush." Bridget took off toward the kitchen, too, and smacked her husband on the shoulder when she got there.

"Ah yeah, I can't let her take all the credit, of course. How do you think I got to this size?" When he laughed, his stomach shook. Though he wasn't really fat at all. Kind of a beefy, farm-raised size of a person.

"Okay this drink is amazing," Ari said, sipping.

"Now," Bridget said, eyeing Gid over her own cocktail. "Tell us your story."

"Oh," Ari laughed. "There isn't much to tell. We met in college and have been friends ever since."

"Friends first is always the best way to go about it, right Jack?"

"That's not— " Gid started, but Bridget cut him off again.

"We've been *friends* since primary school."

"Has it really been that long?" Jack said, peering down into the oven. "Sometimes it feels longer."

Again, Bridget smacked him lightly on the shoulder. "Be careful now, Mr. Murphy."

"Always careful with you, love." He bent over and kissed her cheek.

Inside his chest, Gid's ribs ached from wanting something so badly that had never seemed so out of reach.

Across the kitchen, he met Ari's gaze, twinkling brown in the warm kitchen light. She had her berry lipstick on again and she had never looked so kissable, so fuckable. His stomach twisted at the thought of holding her hair back in a tight, one-handed ponytail and moving in and out of those perfect lips.

He locked that thought down for later. Maybe that could be their little Christmas evening activity.

"Dinner's almost ready," Jack announced with another gander into the oven.

"Can we help with anything?" Gid asked.

"Oh, don't be silly. You two are guests. And anyway, everything is done." Bridget said, shooing them both into the dining room.

A massive farmhouse style table sat covered with a festive red and white runner down the center of the table, which was dotted with glowing white candles and miniature pine trees. Their white place settings were topped with plaid cloth napkins that looked soft from years of use.

"This looks amazing," Ari said, sitting down.

Bridget and Jack followed them out with the roasted turkey and a number of sides: roasted root vegetables of all kinds, gravy, potatoes, and—Gid recognized with a thrill—

"Yorkshire puddings! You make them in Ireland?"

"Jack loves to make them, but especially at Christmas. His mother was born in northern England." Bridget smiled, pouring red wine in all of the glasses around the table.

Everyone else found their seats.

"This is really something else," Ari said. "Thank you for inviting us into your home."

"It's nothing," Jack said. "We love hosting on the farm and having guests into the house whenever we can. And it's Christmas, after all."

"What's this?" Ari asked, picking up the large Tootsie Roll shaped object sitting on her plate. It shimmered in its holiday wrapping.

"Ah Christmas crackers," Bridget said with a smile. "You don't have those in America?"

"No," Ari laughed.

"Well, you take one end, Gid here will take the other, and you pop them open for a little treat inside," Jack explained.

Ari grasped one end and Gid dutifully took the other.

"We'll countdown?" she asked, with a serious look on her face.

"Three...two...one..." Gid said. And Ari grit her teeth, eyes shut, as they both pulled.

With a soft pop like a party popper, their cracker came apart.

"Oh!" Ari's eyes lit up with childlike excitement as she looked inside the canister. She pulled out a bottle opener, slip of paper, and folded piece of crepe paper. Undoing it, she found the paper crown and put it right on her head, pretty as a Christmas princess.

"And we have to keep them on for the whole meal," Bridget said, putting on her own.

"This is fun," Ari said as she picked up the slip of a paper and giggled. "Oh my god this joke is perfect. 'Which of Santa's reindeer has the best moves?'"

Gid smiled, warmth spreading out from the center of his chest. This was how Christmas should be. Warm, cozy, with his favorite person at his side, clearly enjoying the silly little traditions of the day.

"Dancer," he said. "Of course."

"Of course." Ari knocked her shoulder into his, looking up at him with those wide eyes.

After they cracked his, Gid put his own crown on his head, reading out his joke with a chuckle. "This one is also perfect. 'What kind of car do elves drive?'"

"Hmm..." Ari thought before she sat straight up in her chair. "Ooh. A *toy*-ota. But probably not my ancient Corolla."

After the crackers, they passed dishes around the table, spooning more than enough food onto their plates.

Gid's stomach grumbled as he took a deep inhale, the food smells warming him from the inside out. "This looks fantastic."

Everyone tucked into their plates, the quiet music their only companion as they ate. Ari made soft, happy noises from beside him that sounded suspiciously like the noises she made while Gid's fingers traced patterns over her body. He suppressed a groan and adjusted his hips in his seat.

"So...when did you two become *more* than friends then?" Bridget asked, mischief dancing on her face.

"Oh—" Ari and Gid both jumped in at the same time, apparently both eager to dispute the claim that they were more than friends.

That's what she was going to say, right? Gid's stomach plunged as he doubted for a quick second what her next words would be.

"Go ahead," he said, with a little, hopefully casual, laugh.

He couldn't take his eyes off her. In the artful lighting of the room, combining vintage lamps, a couple candles on the table, and the warm glow of the multi-colored Christmas lights, Ari was cast in stunning relief. The sight of her in her red sweater as she considered her next words nearly took his breath away.

"We've been friends for a long time," she whispered, staring only at Gid.

"Well, that's clear enough." Jack laughed, a warm rumble. "Bridget and I have been friends a long time, too." He laughed again, quite pleased with himself.

The rest of dinner passed companionably. Gid couldn't remember a warmer Christmas than this one in recent years. Even though Ari always tried to get him to go to the Callaghan Christmas, it was always too much and he felt too different. Especially last year when the family was still wrapped up in their grief.

Did Ari miss that this year? Her siblings and Mom? They were just together a couple days ago—and that wasn't all completely smooth sailing—but still he wondered... Would he be enough for her this year?

Bridget and Jack told stories around the table about their Christmas tree farm, explaining how it came to be and when Bridget's goats came along. It was clear the two were deeply in love, with each other and with their life on the farm. Gid wondered if he'd ever find that kind of cozy comfort with his decisions, the choices he made and would make. If he could ever feel truly comfortable in his skin.

His gaze kept wandering to Ari, and each time he did, his stomach lurched.

God, that was dangerous. How had he suddenly fallen in so deeply? A beast, now awake inside him, calling for her. She smiled when she caught him staring, dipping her eyes back down to her plate, in an uncharacteristic show of demureness. It made Gid want to be even closer to her.

After the plum pudding—which Jack doused in whiskey and Gid, as the youngest at the table, set on fire— Ari and Gid sauntered, unhurried, back to the guest house. Gid pulled Ari close, tucking her under his arm, as the snow sparkled in the moonlight. He leaned his head back, taking in the expanse of sky. A cloudless night, and the stars exploded across the sky like glitter.

"Wow," he said, tongue thick after the couple drinks they had at the house.

"I know," Ari whispered. "It's like a fairytale."

"What is?" Gid asked. He knew she meant this place, the rows of perfect Christmas trees covered in snow, the dinner they just had, the stars cascading across the sky. But he wanted to know what else she was thinking, if anything. He needed some kind of confirmation of what they were doing here.

Was it just a week-long thing? Was it something they could come back from? His brain spun with possibilities.

"This," she said, twirling out from underneath him, her arms stretched wide. The snow crunched under her boots, her mittened hands flying through the air. She smiled wide.

She looks so happy, Gid thought. Something she didn't look all that much since her dad died. Something that, he thought, maybe he'd given her on this trip. With a jolt, Gid realized he was happy, too. Maybe it was something that they'd found together.

"Come here," he laughed, grabbing one of her hands and pulling her close. Her scent came with her, mingling with the fresh cold air. With the illuminated farmhouse in the background, he couldn't help but agree with her. "You're right, you know. Being here with you...it's like a fairytale."

The word, one he wasn't sure he'd ever said before in his life, came out clunky. In response, Ari smiled, the one she gave when she thought something was unbearably cute.

With one hand, Gid curled around her waist and pulled her closer. The other nestled against her cheek, his fingers stroking into her hair.

"What are we doing?" He hadn't intended to ask the question and it floated between them, thin as tissue paper.

Ari didn't answer. She shrugged one shoulder, shaking her head. *I don't know.* He heard her say the words in his mind.

Gid nodded, licking his lips. He didn't care, not really, if there was an answer or not. Maybe there wasn't supposed to be. Maybe this was just what they were now, week-long parameters be damned.

"I want to bring you inside and warm you up. Would that be okay, pop tart?" The words puffed in frosted clouds.

"Yes," she said. "More than okay."

Gid leaned down and kissed her cheek. She closed her eyes, her eyelashes fluttering against his nose. He led them into the guest house, turning on the electric fireplace before either of them took off their jackets. Helping her take off her outer layer, he hung their coats next to the door.

She looked so beautiful standing there, her cheeks red from the cold and hair whipped from the wind. This country suited her: the wilds of Ireland.

Clear as day, he knew he wanted to keep her. Which he knew all too well would scare the hell out of her. But he had to try.

"Ari, I—" he started to say, unsure how to put it into words without frightening her.

"Don't," she cut him off, as if reading his mind. "Let's just...get warm."

She pushed him back toward the couch and he fell onto it with an *oomph*. Reaching up, he grasped her waist before she settled down on top of his lap. Rolling her hips, she brushed herself over him, and his cock stirred. Ari pushed up his sweater and her cold hands met his abs.

Gid hissed before breaking into a laugh. "You're evil."

She flicked an eyebrow. "Oh, I know," Ari said before pulling his sweater all the way off.

He ran his hands up her knit stockings, over the curve of her muscles, digging in knuckles where she felt tight. When he found a particularly nasty knot, she groaned, a sound hovering between pleasure and pain.

"Ow," she pouted. "That hurts but ohmygod feels so good."

"Hmm," Gid murmured, taking note.

"I want to make you feel good," she whispered.

In the next moment, she stood and stripped off her sweater dress and cable tights, standing naked except for her black, lacy bralette.

"You weren't wearing any panties under those tights?" Gid bit his lip.

"Nope." Ari winked before kneeling between his legs in front of him. Her long, dark hair fell over both shoulders, shining silver-black in the starlight that came in through the window. The electronic fire casting a thin, purple glow.

Gid reached for her cheek, cradling her. She leaned against his palm, eyes closed, for a moment before reaching eagerly for his belt.

"May I?" Ari asked, blinking up at him through her lashes.

"Yes," he breathed, aching for his pants to be off. His breath caught as she popped the button of the waistband and slowly drew the zipper down. He wiggled the rest of the way out of his clothes.

"Fuck my mouth, Gideon." Her words landed hot between his legs.

"I—what?"

"Fuck my mouth. Hard."

"You want that?" His heart raced at just the thought.

"I need it. I'll squeeze your leg if it gets too much, okay?"

Gid swallowed, or tried to. His throat was so dry.

"Yes," he damn near panted. God what a mess he was for this woman. "You're perfect, you know that?"

She snorted, pulling all of her hair over one shoulder and licking her dark, inky lips.

"Hardly." Ari scooted forward, nestling between his legs. "Hold my hair?"

Gid nodded and fisted her hair, his fantasy from earlier coming to life right before his eyes. How had he gotten so lucky?

"Don't be gentle." Her eyes flashed with the words and the next second, she swallowed him.

Eyes wide, she held his gaze as she swallowed his length until he felt the back of her throat.

"Fuck," Gid moaned at the erotic sight of his cock entirely sheathed between Ari's lips. "You're so pretty, baby."

She hummed in response, the sound vibrating around him. He bucked, pushing deeper. "Oh, are you alright?" Gid asked, nervous to hurt her.

Another murmured response and Gid relaxed. Though her eyes watered and her lips were stretched wide, Ari appeared blissful. How much she enjoyed it notched his pleasure up that much more.

Suddenly he wasn't afraid to do as she so crudely asked: to fuck her mouth. He smirked, tightening his grasp on her hair and her eyes darkened. "Here we go, baby."

With a lift of his hips, he thrust deeper down her throat. The base of his spine tingled in response. Ari hummed approvingly. As he pulled out, a ring of her dark lipstick stained the base of his penis; fire raced through his veins at the sight.

Gid tightened his fist on her hair, velvety in his hand, and pulled her closer to him this time instead of lifting his hips. Eyes watering, she took him deeper and Gid groaned.

"Jesus, baby, look at me fucking your mouth." He grunted with another thrust.

She whined, the high vibrations tickling all the way to his balls. But then—that was her nails there, too, tracing along his sensitive skin, the other hand still firmly in place on his thigh.

Snaking his hand around her neck, he moved both her and his hips as his rhythm kept a steady pace.

Christ, she really did look fucking beautiful with her eyes watering and still glued obediently on him. He could get lost in those eyes, the ones he'd stared into a million times during dance rehearsals and performances. Her reassuring gaze reminding Gid he was safe. That Ari had him. Partners.

Gid swallowed, his heart pounding in his chest. With each plunge, he inched closer to an abyss—his orgasm, yes, but of something else. Something that scared the shit out of him.

Because he couldn't *love* Ari Callaghan. No. This thing, what they were doing right now, was temporary. That's what they agreed.

But when he thought the word, he murmured, "I'm gonna come."

She nodded, never breaking eye contact and Gid came, buried deep in Ari's throat.

TWENTY-TWO
ARI

ARI GASPED, sitting back and wiping her mouth with the back of her hand.

"Gid," she whispered as her heart leapt in her chest. She began to laugh. "Wow."

He cradled her cheeks and lifted her up, curling her around his waist.

Could he feel how wet she was? Soaking. There's no way that he couldn't feel her dripping down her thighs and onto his.

"Baby," he murmured, thumbs ghosting over the insides of her thighs and drifting toward her core. "That was fantastic. You got this wet doing that?" He tutted. "Such a dirty girl."

She had to be careful. Because with each passing second she spent in Gid's presence, she realized how freaking perfect he was. To be fair, she'd always known that, but not like this. Not like *this*.

"Now it's my turn," Gid said, his thumbs parting her slick lips. They both moaned as he traced her slit. One hand snaked back into her hair, grabbing a fistful. "Let's lay you down."

He repositioned her over his lap, her heart fluttered as her bum went into the air, exposing her completely to him. Ari felt explicitly on display.

"Fuck I thought you looked pretty before, pop tart, but I might like this angle better." Gid stretched her ass cheeks apart, massaging the muscles, before plunging a thumb into her pussy.

She grunted, the intrusion surprising. With his other hand, Gid smacked her behind. Ari bucked back into him, pistoning herself on his thumb.

"Fuck," she moaned.

He spit onto his fingers and repositioned, his two middle fingers plunging into her and his thumb circling her clit. Heat built in her core as she squeezed her eyes shut, letting her body chase the sensation that was quickly overwhelming her.

"That's it," Gid murmured, encouraging her closer to the edge.

From her angle over Gid's legs, she leaned onto the armrest and could see the sparkling snow out the front window. She knew how cold it was out there as they neared midnight, marking the end of Christmas Day. But here in Gid's lap, she was warm. Held under Gid's control, she wasn't afraid. He cradled her, guiding her to oblivion and allowing her to give herself over completely to the sensation.

Ari realized she hadn't worried all day, in fact. Since she woke up in his arms under the heavy quilts, her academic probation hadn't crossed her mind once. And now, instead of unraveling under that pressure, she let it go and focused on the sweet words Gid muttered behind her.

"That's my girl," he whispered, licking his lips. His arm clamped across her hips, holding her in place as he stretched and teased her closer to her orgasm. "Let go for me, gorgeous. I got you."

She didn't doubt it. As she pushed back her hips one last time, forcing his fingers deeper inside her, she crested her climax.

"I'm coming," Ari whispered, clamping her eyes shut. Awash in a waterfall of pleasure, her entire body tingled.

Gid slowed behind her, tracing her spine with his free hand. Exploring the crests and valleys of her body, his fingertips memorizing her topography as they cuddled on the couch.

She would allow herself to be claimed by him, if that's what he wanted. His gentle markings along her back all seemed to spell *mine, mine, mine*.

When had they gone from best friends to *this*? And was there any going back?

* * *

THE QUESTION LINGERED with Ari through the night. Even as she woke, once again completely wrapped up in Gid, she wondered if what they'd done could be *un*done.

And did she even want to go back to the way things were?

They agreed: this was an isolated thing. This was a week abroad with her best friend. This wasn't real life.

Soon, she'd be back in her apartment in Everdale, getting ready for her academic probation meeting and then what? Then her life could look totally different.

"Good morning," Gid said, ducking his head to kiss her bare shoulder. "Last night was...something."

"Something, eh?" Ari smirked, looking back at him.

"Yeah." He nodded, a dreamy, contented look on his face.

"Best Christmas ever?" she murmured with the world still shrouded in darkness, her mind still clouded with fear.

"Never have I ever had a better Christmas in my entire life," he said, his voice still muffled by sleep and layers of blankets. He nuzzled closer. "You're far too tense for Boxing Day morning," he laughed. "What's Boxing Day anyway?"

His half-hearted attempts at joking didn't get much response from Ari. She was already far away, back in

Michigan, even though her body still lay in bed in the Irish countryside.

They lay in bed until the sun rose and as the darkness slowly became a pre-dawn blue, her dreams floated back to her. But, really, they were more like...nightmares. Mazes and running and falling and darkness. Half snippets her imagination had concocted overnight as her brain worked through all the shit in her life. But she also remembered something that was clear, golden.

"I had a nightmare. Nightmares all night. But you were there, Gid." She reached over and stroked his cheek knowing that things would be okay because he was by her side now, too.

"Hey," Gid said, frowning as he pushed up on his elbow. "I'm joking...but also serious. What's going on, baby?"

"It's hard to take you seriously with that hair," Ari smiled despite herself. His bedhead stuck up at all angles like a cartoon caricature of his daytime self.

Gid smiled his dopey little grin and ran a hand through his hair, which wasn't much of an improvement.

Ari sighed, the light-hearted moment passing as quickly as it came. Because soon she'd be back to Real Life.

"That right there," he said. "Where did you go?"

"Home," she said. But the word didn't feel right. Instead of relief at the thought, dread spiked her heart rate. Laying here with Gid, she felt more at home than she had in a long time. She swallowed. "I'm not ready."

Still, she hadn't told anyone about school. It seemed impossible, humiliating, that her life had amounted to this.

This. Nothing concrete to show for her twenty-six years. She covered her face with her hands, foolishly wishing she could hide from the embarrassment. But there was nowhere for her to go. She couldn't hide from herself, from the inky blackness that swirled inside of her.

It was now or never. Ari was just sated enough that she could share her secret with Gid. There wasn't time to worry about what he'd think. In truth, she hadn't stopped considering what everyone would think from the moment she first got the email. A special kind of self-inflicted torture.

"I'm on academic probation," she said, the words finally tumbling out.

Gid's brows furrowed. "Academic probation? What are you talking about? You're studying all the time."

Ari shrugged, wrapping herself tighter in the quilts. "I'm not. I try to. Pretend I am. Go to the library, get all set up, and then...nothing. I just stare into space for hours, Gid. *Hours.* I have no idea where the time goes."

"Okay," he said slowly, processing. "It's okay." He paused. "What does that mean? Do you want to talk about it?"

"No," Ari groaned. "I don't know. I...I just feel off. Since

Dad died. Like, I thought I was okay. I thought things were fine, that I grieved before he died and all that. But the one-year mark hit me bad. After the summer in Chicago, getting a taste of what the rest of my life was going to be like. Just—" she gestured into the air, an attempt to convey the fruitlessness of it all. "I don't know."

Gid nodded along as she spoke.

"I know what you mean," he whispered, curling an arm around her waist, and pulling her close. "Sometimes, I just wonder, what's the point of it all?"

The way his body felt so near to hers was intoxicating, dangerous.

"Yeah." Ari swallowed, laying flat on her back, and staring at the ceiling. "It's so absurd that life just keeps going, regardless of what bullshit is going on in the world. I still have to study and work, pay taxes, and go to the dentist, but people are dying, the economy is collapsing, and Earth is getting hotter. And I'm stuck. I'm grieving. I'm lost. Nothing makes sense anymore."

"Does it have to make sense?"

Ari frowned, the gaping hopelessness sitting heavy in her chest. "I guess it doesn't."

"Is that a comforting thought?" Gid laced his fingers with hers under the blanket.

"Sort of," she sighed, a big deep thing and gripped his hand tighter. Maybe it was comforting, here in this bed with Gid at her side.

But what would happen when they left the warmth of

this bed? Left the cottage? This country? Ari groaned. "But it doesn't help me figure out what the hell I'm going to do if I get kicked out of school."

Gid huffed a laugh and nestled into her shoulder. The moments passed in silence, the big grandfather clock in the living room ticking the seconds by.

"Okay," Gid said, voice still soft where he was tucked against her skin. "We can figure it out. What now?"

"Now...I don't know." Ari covered her face, unsure if she felt better or worse for finally having shared her secret. For so long, it had weighed her down, and so far, she didn't feel better having shared.

"Well, what happens next?" He wrapped his arms around her waist and Ari felt safe.

God, bless Gid. She didn't deserve his kindness, his patience. She didn't deserve anything good—hell, it made sense that this was happening to her. "It's all my fault," Ari said, breathing through the weight on her chest.

"Come on." Gid circled his fingers around her wrists, pulling her hands away from her face. "It's gonna be okay."

"I've worked for this for years, Gid. Years I've been on this path thinking there'd be some kind of fulfillment at the end. But it's just all the same shit over and over." Icy dread lanced her heart and for a moment it was difficult to breathe.

"Okay," he nodded, letting her word vomit.

"I'm twenty-six and all I can see is the rest of my life

stretched out before me, working in some corporation I don't give a shit about, that's probably contributing to the burning of this planet. I just don't care anymore. I can't pretend to." Ari rolled onto her side, making eye contact with him, his face heavy with sleep and lined with pillowcase creases.

"The happiest I've been in a long, long time has been the last twenty-four hours in this cottage. With you." She tore the words from the depths of her soul, so difficult to admit.

What were they even doing here, anyway? Admitting to her happiness meant that Gid now had that power over her—but she wasn't scared. She trusted him.

His gaze didn't leave her face. "Me too."

"Yeah?" Her heartbeat fluttered. *Is this really happening?*

Ari didn't want to think about it. For once in her damned life, she didn't want to worry about something. And she was always fucking worrying. This, this was easy. This was Gid. The man who had already been with her so much, here lying in this warm bed with her. With him, Ari could just let go.

Somehow, the future wasn't so scary with him by her side.

"Yes, baby." Gid laced his arms around her neck and pulled her close.

Ari squealed as her naked body slid across the flannel sheets.

"Come here," he whispered, gathering up a fistful of her hair. "I'll take care of you."

"You always do."

Gid pulled her hair, angling her chin upward and exposing her neck. Her pulse thrummed along her taut skin and in the next moment, his tongue caressed the epicenter of her beating heart in her neck.

The delicious juxtaposition of her tightly pulled hair and the softness of his tongue along her neck sent prickles of pleasure through her veins. Spreading like wildfire in her blood.

A small gasp escaped her lips and Gid chuckled in response. "Like that, eh?"

"Yes," she breathed.

"And I'm barely touching you."

Certainly, they'd been in more incriminating positions while dancing—albeit with more clothing—but he was right. Gid was barely touching her, and Ari's core pulsed with need. The fingers of his free hand ghosted along her waist. Goosebumps pulled the hair on her arms upright. Lower and lower Gid trailed, so slowly that Ari wasn't sure at first it he was going to move down her body.

With his lips still focused on her neck, Gid pushed her hip back so that Ari lay flat on the bed. Her legs fell open and he wasted no time in trailing his fingers over her bare pussy. Now it was his turn to groan as he rut his hips forward, his stiff length rubbing against her hip.

"You're so soft," he said, nipping her clavicle between the words. "I can barely contain myself."

"Then don't," she said, wriggling underneath his touch. "Make me yours."

Ari wanted to give herself completely over to him— not that they hadn't already a couple of times. But now, in the same bed the day after Christmas, the walls around her heart softened.

What if she just let herself be had? Be loved by another?

Love. A word once so scary didn't seem so heart-wrenching now.

"Mine," Gid mumbled over and over against her skin between kisses.

Instead of fear, Ari melted into the bed under his touch. Slowly, Gid explored her curves and ridges. Getting lost and finding her in the dips of her bones. He mapped her and Ari had never felt so revered.

Finally, Gid entered her with his fingers. Already she was so close to the edge, so blissed out on his touch, his fingertips leaving behind little burning beacons along her frozen veneer. She thawed, unfurling like a snowdrop blossom peeking through the frost in early spring.

With his thumb, he coaxed her most sensitive spot. He knew, after years of dancing together, how to watch for her little responses, making him already familiar with what she liked.

"Gid," she gasped, wrapping an arm around his shoulders and clutching onto him as her body began to quake.

"Come on, baby," he said, focusing his gaze on hers. "You're gorgeous like this."

His words spiraled her tighter, a spring priming for release.

"Come on my fingers," he whispered, notching deeper inside her.

She willed her body to obey. The storm inside her calmed, like the eye of a hurricane, and in the next moment, everything shattered. A million pieces of herself scattered in as many directions. Gid worked her through it, wringing out every ounce of pleasure from her orgasm before slowing down. He brought her back to earth, stroking her long, dark hair and pulling her body next to his.

"That's it," Gid murmured. "I've got you, baby. Whatever happens next, I'll be there."

Ari curled up in his arms, trusting every single word he said.

TWENTY-THREE
GID

GID SHUFFLED barefoot across the cool wood floor of the cottage. He didn't really know what to do with himself. Pacing the cottage, he checked out the views from the different windows. A quaint red barn—promised in the advertisements for the place—stood between the guest-house and the main house. That must be where the goats lived. Ari had already met the little rascals, maybe he'd get a chance, too.

And of course there were the rows and rows of neat Christmas trees. What in the heck did it take to sustain them all? He hadn't the foggiest clue, even after Jack had painstakingly explained the process over Christmas dessert. The farm was a marvel of agricultural engineering, that much was clear. Lots of moving parts he would never be able to understand.

All that to say: Gid was very glad he went into the manufacturing field.

But he could admire the beauty of it all. The orderly rows. The evergreen boughs weighed down with glittering snow as it melted off. Today was considerably warmer, and Bridget had mentioned it was a perfect place for a walk.

Maybe Ari and Gid could get out there sometime in the next day or two. The cottage even came equipped with massive rubber boots in a couple different sizes. Which was lucky, considering neither of them had very appropriate footwear for all this snow, which was quickly becoming slush. The yard was more mud now than fresh, white snow.

Finally, Gid made it back to the kitchen and he put on the kettle for some tea. Bridget and Jack kept the place stocked with an assortment of teas, goat milk, bread, butter, and jam. All of which, he assumed, was homemade considering the dinner they had last night.

As the tea steeped, he tried not to let his mind wander to the last few days with Ari. He didn't want to question it. He wanted to revel in it. Like the coziest pair of flannel pajamas, it just felt right. Nothing had ever felt so natural in his entire life—other than when he started dancing with her, which should have been an indicator in the first place.

But Ari had her rules. She always said, she knew what kind of trouble could take root between partners who slept together. And for years, he didn't doubt it. The line was clearly drawn, and he didn't begrudge her for it.

Until this trip. Until the flip switched between them. Until being across an ocean with this woman reminded him of everything that he adored about her, and had for years, if he was being honest.

And being honest right now was frightening. Because Ari had drawn another line: this was just for now. For this week. Once they were back in Starling Hills, their relationship would snap back into its usual shape. Or he would force it to, if that was what she wanted.

He would do anything for her.

With Ari still asleep, Gid pulled out his creased crossword puzzle book and his pencil. Mechanical, since he didn't want to travel with a pencil sharpener.

Before sitting down on the worn couch with his tea, he clicked on the electric fireplace. Truthfully, he would have preferred a wood burning fire, but since that was more a chore than anything, he was thankful for the easily adjustable electric burner.

Within minutes, his feet were toasty.

It wasn't long before the sun rose and streamed warm, golden streaks through the front window. After he finished three puzzles in the quiet cottage, sipping one cuppa then another, the floorboards creaked across the room.

Gid looked up and his breath caught. *Fuck.*

Ari had pulled on a pair of his sweatpants and his

sweatshirt, both of which were huge on her. But holy shit he loved seeing her in his Michigan State gear. The rolled sweatpants waist band reminded him of when she used to do that in college at their practices. He didn't find it attractive then, but the memory of it was so sexy now.

"Afternoon, pop tart," he said, putting aside his crossword book as she plopped on the couch and snuggled up to him.

"Mmm," she moaned, tucking her hands under his hoodie, icy against his skin.

"You're freezing!" he hissed and then laughed, pulling her closer.

"I just left the warmest bed. It's cold and bright out here." Ari squinted against the sun.

"Let me make you some tea," Gid said, standing up and grabbing a knitted blanket from behind the couch. He tucked it around her, making a warm little cocoon.

"You're the best." She smiled up at him sleepily and he leaned down to kiss her nose.

"Need any crossword clues, babe?" she asked as Gid moved to the kitchen to reset the kettle.

Babe. It felt so good to be called that. He wanted her to mean it. He wanted to hear it every day.

"Take a look at the next puzzle. You can add in anything you know."

Gid watched her from the couch, her hair still in its messy bun as she chewed on the end of his pencil and considered the clues. The domesticity of it all made his heart squeeze. What had he expected for this trip? He didn't even know anymore. They were always going to have a great time together, but he never expected *this*.

"You feeling well rested?"

Gid hadn't meant the question to carry any implications, but when she looked up at him with her eyebrows raised, he had to laugh. The two had gotten quite a workout between last night and this morning.

"Yes, Gideon, I am very well rested. Thanks to you." She gave him a tilted smile that hinted at exactly what she was thanking him for.

The way she said his full name threw him for a loop. A good loop. Really freaking good.

Gid walked around the kitchen counter back into the living room space, carrying a steaming mug of tea.

"Pop tart," he said and even to him, her old nickname felt loaded with emotion.

With her free hand, Ari picked up her fresh paperback from the side table, a recent Georgie Adler release she'd grabbed on their layover.

Gid started back into the crosswords. She tucked her feet between him and the couch and eventually they ended up in his lap, so that he absentmindedly massaged the arches as he considered the puzzle clues.

They spent the next couple of hours like this, snuggled on the couch, as the grandfather clock ticked away the time. Gid couldn't remember the last time he felt so content and relaxed. And he wondered if she felt the same. If, inside, she still worried about school and the real life they hurtled toward in just two days.

Two days, and they'd be back in Starling Hills.

He swallowed, trying not to think about what that would mean.

The grandfather clock eventually chimed four in the afternoon. Shortly afterward, there was a knock on the door. Gid stood to answer and found Bridget standing there.

"Gid! Happy Boxing Day," she laughed, her nose red, presumably from working on the farm. "Jack and I are going into the village for a pub dinner. You two care to join?"

"Pub?" Ari perked up at that.

Bridget poked her head through the doorway, talking directly to Ari. "We're walking, but it's a lovely walk. Perfect for the day after Christmas. They usually have a trad session on, too."

"Music?" Ari jumped off the couch now, excitement clear in her voice.

"That sounds perfect," Gid said. "Thanks for the invite. We just need to get dressed."

"Bundle up!" Bridget said as she turned to trudge through the snow back to the house. "We'll meet you down at the mailbox." She pointed with a gloved hand.

It was a lovely walk. Thankfully they had the boots to borrow from the house as they crossed a field before getting to the paved road that weaved its way into the village.

The cool air filled Gid's lungs, clearing out the dark cobwebs from the corners of his body and mind, invigorating his steps.

Ari seemed to enjoy it too. He kept sneaking glances at the smile that stretched across her face, the way her eyes tingled with warmth despite the cold.

After a half hour, they came to O'Brien's Inn, with the pub on the bottom and accommodations on top. Before Jack even opened the door, the clear sounds of fiddle and bodhrán bounded through the walls, as if the pub wasn't big enough to hold it in.

Ari's eyes widened and she clapped her gloved hands. Gid loved to see it, this excitement that seemed to displace the heavy feelings she secretly held on to earlier in the trip. He placed a hand on her lower back and guided her through the door, following Bridget to an open table in the back.

It was warm inside with a roaring fire in the fireplace and so cozy as if they'd just stepped into someone's living room. Tea and coffee mugs hung from the rafters in rows, a collection built up over the years. The mahogany interior kept the place dark despite the warm lighting at even intervals. Combined with the music and a small space where some folks danced, Gid felt perfectly at home here in this little pub across the ocean.

The beat of the music filled his bones. Jack brought

four Guinness to the booth and Gid drank deeply from his, settling back into his seat.

"This is amazing," Ari said, leaning toward him, her breath warm on his neck.

"I was just thinking the same thing." He squeezed her knee under the table, and she laced her fingers with his.

"Thank you for this," she said.

"For what?"

"Everything."

Gid looked down at her and they held each other's gaze.

"For being here," she continued. "For this trip." She swallowed. "It's nice to have a friend."

Ari smiled, small and sad, causing the corners of Gid's lips to pull down before he kissed her on the top of her head.

"Always," he said.

Across the table, Bridget and Jack smiled and laughed, clapping and banging their fists on the table along with the beat of the music. It was too loud to really have a conversation, but Gid didn't mind. The place was warm and homey, and the Guinness delicious.

Part of him couldn't believe that he was, in fact, sitting in this booth across the ocean, with this gorgeous woman at his side. He already knew that he'd leave a piece of his soul behind in this exact spot, where he pulled her close, felt her body fitted into his, relaxed and warm. It was a moment he knew he could never return to.

It wasn't long before four servings of seafood chowder landed at the table with a side of brown bread and butter. It was an ideal dish after walking through the cold snow.

Gid insisted on covering the next couple of rounds of Guinness as the music continued to bore its way into his brain. It pulsed through his limbs, his veins, as intoxicating as the alcohol flowing through the same channels.

"I want to dance," Ari whispered after a couple pints.

"Oh yeah? I'll always dance with you, pop tart," he said, squeezing her hip.

When they stood up, Bridget and Jack cheered, raising their pints to them.

It wasn't dancing like their favored West Coast Swing. It was loose and relaxed. No set steps or slots. The couples already on the small dance floor swung each other around, stomping their winter boots to the beat of the music.

Ari was warm underneath his palms. Laughter coursed through her, and he picked up the vibrations.

Could they stay in this moment forever? Frozen in time in this pub in the Irish countryside?

Ari had said she didn't want to go back to Starling Hills, and he didn't either. Not if he couldn't have her, like this.

Loose, happy, free.

Instead of saying any of that, he held onto her tighter, hoping that his solid grip and strong arms said everything that he couldn't.

TWENTY-FOUR
ARI

WITH A BELLY FULL of soup and stout, Ari spun through the door of the cottage. They'd only been there a couple days, but somehow it felt like a home.

Their home.

As she unwrapped her scarf, her eyes caught on Gid, his soft, dark hair poofy as he pulled off his beanie.

No, she thought. It wasn't this place. It was this *person*.

The thought struck her like a lightning bolt. After all the years they'd known each other, flying across an ocean together is what made her see things differently. See *him* differently. And she didn't want to go back to the way things were before.

But that wasn't what they agreed.

"What?" he laughed, catching her staring. "Does my hair look awful?"

"You look wonderful," she murmured, stepping closer to him, and wrapping her arms around his waist.

Ari tilted her head up and their lips met, cold from the walk but soft and gentle. Gid cradled her cheeks, his palms warm from his woolen gloves. Ari smiled, her cheeks squishing up against his hands.

"Let's go to bed," she said the words against his lips.

"Yes ma'am." Gid picked her up and Ari squealed at the unexpected lift.

He put her down on her side of the bed and he walked over to his. With the lights off, they undressed, staring across the expanse of bed at one another. Piece by piece, their layers came off and dropped to the floor.

Ari ran her fingers over the lace of her lingerie before reaching back to unclasp the bra. The dark purple florals were one of her favorite sets. Goosebumps erupted as she anticipated Gid's hands ghosting over her bare skin. She bent to pull off her lace panties.

From across the bed, Gid groaned, staring at her naked now. She returned the sound of pleasure as she took in his body. The one she memorized from years of dancing together, but now knew in such a different way. Her eyes dropped to his erection, and she licked her lips.

"Come here, pop tart," he said, rolling onto the bed and opening his arms to her.

"There's nowhere else I want to be," Ari said, snuggling into his embrace.

"I like to hear that." Gid's lips brushed across hers,

pulling her naked body into his, their middles flush. "What else do you want, Ari Callaghan?"

There were so many ways she could answer that question.

She wanted her dad back.

To not have missed her midterm earlier in the semester.

To not be facing academic suspension.

She wanted to know what the rest of her life was going to look like.

She wished she knew if she made the right choices— any right decisions—along the way.

With each passing second, she wanted something else. She wanted so much that it scared her.

Her heart was a black, bottomless void, and she couldn't fill it.

"Hey," Gid whispered. "Come back here. Back to me. What can I give you, Ari?"

"You," she said, reaching down and fisting his stiff length.

"I can help you with that," Gid mumbled against her skin.

He rolled on top of her, arms bracketed on either side of her shoulders, and stared down at her. Ari was sure that he could see straight into her soul. It scared her. She felt more than naked with him; she was bare, stripped down. With Gid, Ari didn't have to hide what she was thinking. There wasn't a role that she had to perform.

"You don't have to hide from me, Ari," he said, giving words to her thoughts.

"I don't want to," she said, her voice small. And it was true. Even though it scared her, she trusted Gid.

He kissed his way down her body, caressing every sharp edge that he found, polishing it smooth. Ari rolled up into his lips, meeting him at every contour. His lips would forever be imprinted on her body. She didn't know how there was any way she could let him go after this week, back to just being *friends*.

As he teased his way down her body, she wound tighter, ready to spring.

When he pushed her thighs wide open, Gid groaned at the sight. "Look at you, so pretty."

God, she loved the way he spoke to her.

That night, in the queen-sized cottage bed with the moonlight streaming through the windows and starlight reflecting off the snow, they made love. Slow and sweet. The kind that didn't have a climactic ending, but that felt like one long, luscious orgasm.

Guided by her soft moans, Gid touched her in all her favorite ways.

"Can I keep you?" she whispered the words into the night, unsure if he was even awake.

Gid took her hand and squeezed it against his chest. "I'm already yours."

TWENTY-FIVE
GID

ON THEIR LAST morning at the guest house, Gid slipped out of bed.

The cool air shocked his system as he padded on his bare feet over to their suitcases. He pulled out his traveling clothes, joggers and a fresh Henley.

Moving slowly through the cottage, he passed the second bedroom they never used, the bedding still neatly made. The aged floor creaked underfoot as he gathered up pieces of their stay.

Her cashmere sweater tossed over the sofa in the front room, his beanie discarded on the dining table after coming in from the cold.

Her paperback that somehow had made its way to the kitchen counter, his creased crossword puzzle book and favorite mechanical pencil hooked over the pages.

Bits and pieces of the little life they had over the last couple of days.

Gid washed the mugs, stained with last night's hot chocolate and Ari's berry lipstick. They had spent the day exploring the tree farm. He met the pygmy goats and Ari's little favorite, Coal.

Weaving in between the long rows of fir trees, they snuck kisses in secluded spots and stayed out there until their noses froze. Afterward, they warmed each other up with searing touches and endless mugs of hot cocoa in front of the electric fireplace.

How was it that this place existed in the same universe as Starling Hills?

He emptied the countertop compost bin of the days' coffee grounds, a whoosh of cold air coming in from the outside as he dumped the bucket out the side door. Across the snow, Bridget waved as she ducked into the barn.

What a life Bridget and Jack lived out here. A Christmas tree farm and their herd of pygmy goats, quiet and blissful. So different from the speed of life he lived back home.

It made Gid wonder: *what do I really want?*

Which wasn't an entirely convenient question, because at this exact moment, every single little thing that he wanted was wrapped up under thick quilts and flannel sheets in the primary bedroom of this tiny guest cottage.

It wrenched his heart, recounting the last couple of days with Ari. Had these been feelings that they both had for years? Was he one of those dopes who'd been lying to himself all this time about other people? When his whole world had, apparently, been in front of him all along?

No, he thought. No. Maybe Ari had always been the right person, it had just never been the right time.

Or, more likely, the right place.

It had taken them flying across an entire ocean together to see what had been clearly in front of them for the last eight years. A switch had flipped, and suddenly Ari Callaghan was it. Endgame.

Staring out the window, the thought ricocheted around his mind and then settled in his stomach like their Christmas roast dinner. Whatever would come with her academic probation, Gid wanted to stay by Ari's side through it all. He would support her, cheerlead her, like they'd already been doing for years. But he wanted to do it as her lover, not just her friend. Her best friend.

In his bones, he knew there was no going back for him. Did she feel the same?

The floor creaked behind him, and he turned from the window.

"Hey," Ari said, her voice heavy with sleep.

He smiled in response, a million puzzle pieces clicking into place as she tiptoed across the floor, minimizing the contact of her bare feet on the wooden floors.

"You need some socks," he said as she snaked her arms around his waist and held him. Her head pressed against his chest, his heart thumping against his breast-bone. Could she feel it?

She was one of the few people who never made him feel wrong or broken. One of the few people who never required that he change to fit some preconceived notion of himself. Ari simply accepted him for exactly who he was at any given moment.

Gid loved her for it.

He tightened his arms around her back, bringing her closer. "Are you ready to go home?"

Ari groaned, the sound vibrating through him. "No."

"Listen." Gid disentangled them, stepping back and grasping onto her shoulders. "Everything is going to be alright."

She frowned. "How can you know that?"

"Because I'll be right there with you. Nothing will happen that can't be undone or fixed. It's not the end of the world."

"But it's humiliating. I'm not ready to face the music."

"That's what we do, pop tart. Whatever song comes on, we dance, right?"

"That easy, eh?" She smiled half-heartedly.

"We'll make it look that way, at least."

"I suppose we always do."

"Our trophies didn't win themselves."

Ari sighed, stepping away from Gid. It wasn't a rejection, but he immediately wanted her body back close to his.

"I'm going to shower," she said, squeezing his hand before she walked away.

Somehow it seemed like their week-long spell was already over. He wasn't ready. They agreed *just for the week* but now that seemed so absurd. How had they ever really thought this could work? How did he think he could come out on the other side unscathed?

Once packed, they said goodbye to their cottage, the door snicking shut behind them with finality that echoed in Gid's chest. They said goodbye to their hosts and the farm, everything that would soon be nothing more than a memory.

"Goodbye," Ari crooned as she scratched the chin of the coal black pygmy goat.

God, he loved to see her happy and smiling. He would do anything to keep that wide, contagious grin on her face. After the year she had, she deserved it.

"Thank you for bringing us here," she said, sidling up next to him and hooking her arm around his elbow.

With Ari at his side, everything felt right. With her. Always with her. For the last eight years, every brilliant, shining moment had been with her.

"Seriously, can we stay here?" she asked, her eyes wide and shining.

"You know we can't, pop tart." Gid almost leaned over and kissed the tip of her nose. He wanted to kiss her properly, so badly, but as they inched closer to home, he wasn't sure what was allowed anymore.

"I don't want to go back," Ari whispered.

* * *

THE DRIVE to Dublin was entirely different from the one they had on the way out. The snow from a few days before had all but melted and the roads were clean and clear. Overhead, the sun shone bright in a cloudless blue sky.

As the landscape passed, Gid could hardly believe that they'd be back in Michigan in less than twenty hours and he'd be all alone in his empty, lonely apartment. Their trip already felt like a hazy fever dream and, somehow, they would go back to business as usual once in Starling Hills, even though that was the last thing he wanted.

Maybe they could just stay in this in-between state forever...not friends, but not necessarily more. Even though the thought broke his heart.

They'd been mostly silent for the drive beyond asking if either of them needed to stop for the restroom or confirming directions. But the drive wasn't long at all without the white-out blizzard they had just days before.

"I want to stay in that cottage," Ari said, adjusting herself in her seat. "Our cottage. Live on a Christmas tree farm. Forget my problems."

"Problems don't just go away," Gid said softly. "It's a hard lesson of growing up, I guess. I've tried to outrun...so much over the years, and I'm still stuck with it. My parents and all that. Wherever I go, it's still with me."

"Mmm," Ari murmured, staring out the window. "Everything on the farm seemed perfect, ya know? Real life is scary."

What did she mean? It almost sounded like a rejection, an ending to their fragile arrangement. But he still wasn't ready, not yet, maybe not ever, for this to end. Instead of asking Ari what she meant—afraid of what she might say—Gid reached over and laced his fingers with hers.

"It will be alright," he whispered.

She squeezed his hand and, for now, he believed it, too.

* * *

STANDING in Ari's apartment parking lot Thursday evening, Gid looked down into her wide brown eyes. Eyes that he could lose himself in. *Had* lost himself over the last week.

The return flights were quiet, their hands clasped between them as they watched *The Office* and took naps on each other's shoulders. He held onto her like she was his life raft.

But now, saying goodbye to her, Gid couldn't bring himself to touch her. He wasn't sure if it would be for the last time. Like this, anyway. Whatever *this* was.

"Goodbye, Gid," she said, no hint of the nickname she

started to call him. *Babe...* Over before it even really started.

Gid thought he saw it flicker in her eyes, but the next moment she squashed it.

"I had a great week," he said.

Sadness flit across her face. "The best week."

"But now it's over?"

Ari sighed, catching his meaning. "That's what we agreed."

He almost broke then, but the words wouldn't come out. He couldn't force them past his mangled tongue.

Gid nodded. Cleared his throat. "Alright."

She gave him a thin-lipped smile and returned the nod. "I'll text you later."

They always texted. Good mornings and goodnights. Have a great day and don't forget an umbrella. He imagined her text later would be about the ridiculous amount of laundry she had to do. He wouldn't tell her that his was already done, and he was sitting on his couch bored and alone. That he was eating one of her Pop-Tarts just because he missed her.

No, he wouldn't tell her any of that. He would just send a sad face emoji.

Now he watched her walk away to her front door.

She didn't turn back and that was fine. He didn't need her to. She'd text him later.

* * *

GID UNLOCKED his apartment door and it opened to silence. His shoulders literally dropped. After his last week, he already missed Ari's giggling, the Callaghans chatter, Irish accents, trad music, fir trees...he could go on. He was really good at hurting his own feelings.

Coming home was the hardest part about traveling. Everything is the same in the real world.

The Christmas tree farm was just a memory. Another ache to tuck away.

And, fuck, it was freezing in his apartment. He'd picked up the habit of turning the temperature down when he was out of town, just like his parents did. Something he distinctly regretted as he talked himself up enough to take off his beanie and jacket.

Gid moved around the apartment like a ghost. Listless, purposeless. He'd cleaned the damn place top to bottom before their trip so there weren't even any chores to do. Other than unpack. But, in truth, he wasn't ready for that. Not yet.

* * *

THE FEW, short days since Ireland passed in a blur. He tried everything he could to not think about Ari, but the fact was that their lives were twined together tight and had been since they met. Something he only recently realized.

Gid kept spotting things around his apartment that

reminded him of Ari: the ballroom trophies he still kept on his bookshelf, the cherry Pop-Tarts he stocked just for her, a worn t-shirt of hers that somehow ended up in his dirty laundry.

He distinctly did not want to think about her but found it impossible.

They had only texted since they landed in Detroit. And they had left things, a lot of things, everything unsaid.

But what was there to say? The stipulations of their arrangement—*situationship*, as Zahra would say—had been clear from the beginning. Until the end of their trip and that was it.

Gid had held back the truth of what their time on the Christmas tree farm had meant to him. So, when he finally pulled out his hoodie from this luggage only to catch her smell on it, it bowled him over. He sat on the edge of his bed and stared into space for...well he wasn't sure how long. Long enough to lose track of time.

He did all his laundry after that, only mildly ashamed that he hadn't done it immediately after getting home, as he'd planned. Mostly because it said a lot about what kind of a chump he was. A damn lovestruck fool, despite the clear parameters they set.

Unpacking was torture. Her damn perfume clung to all his sweatshirts, pajama pants, and even his boxers. That was the hardest one to endure.

It all went straight into the wash. If her scent still hung

around his apartment, he wouldn't be able to resist saying the things he wasn't supposed to say.

He didn't even have work to distract him.

Knowing Ari, she'd spend the Friday and Saturday since Ireland curled up on her mom's couch wrapped in a fuzzy blanket, drinking hot chocolate non-stop, with her vape clutched in hand.

Was she thinking about him, too? *Trying not to* think about him?

Ari texted, like she promised, but she didn't bring up school again or anything that had happened on the trip. Gid didn't dare bring any of it up either. He almost couldn't bear to ask about school because then he'd have to remember how she told him: when they were naked in the guest house bed on Boxing Day.

Standing at the kitchen window, he sipped his pour over coffee and mentally prepared himself for that night. On Saturday, his mom texted to invite him over for dinner the next day, New Year's Eve. And afterward was Thomas and Julia's New Year's Eve party. It was an anniversary of sorts for them, and now it was their "coming out as a wedded couple" party. And the first time Gid would see Ari since their trip.

Gid wasn't entirely sure he was ready for that, but he would face the music, just like he always did.

TWENTY-SIX
ARI

"CAN you be hungover from traveling? Because I think I am." Ari frowned and pulled her blanket tighter.

"I think you can in Europe," Zahra quipped, popping a sucker from her mouth.

Even though she quoted one of their favorite movies, *10 Things I Hate About You*, Ari's frown creased deeper.

"Alright, alright no jokes, got it," Zahra said. "Seriously are you okay, dude?"

Ari groaned in response.

The two sat nuzzled on Mom's basement couch on Saturday, wrapped in the fuzziest blankets and slipper socks, drinking hot cocoa and watching *Taylor Swift: The Eras Tour: Extended Version* concert film. Ari had rented it Friday morning after she was back in Starling Hills. She had it on loop in an attempt to distract herself from thinking about Gid and everything that happened over the last week. Hopefully she'd have her head on straight by the time she saw him tomorrow at Thomas and Julia's party.

Of course, she hadn't told anyone anything about what had happened. Mostly because she wasn't sure what it meant and what would happen next. Not to mention, it wasn't the only thing contending for her brain space. There was still that looming meeting on her calendar that would determine her academic future.

Zahra finally invited herself over after she hadn't seen her friend in the two days since she landed back stateside.

"I'll take that as a no," she said. "Do you want to talk about it?"

Did Ari want to talk about it? She definitely didn't want to talk about school and putting what happened with Gid in words would make it real. If she didn't tell anyone about it, maybe she could convince herself it was just a dream. But it was actually more like a nightmare. Because when she opened her eyes, he wasn't there.

"Gid and I hooked up in Ireland." Ari furrowed her brow as her brain caught up with her mouth. She hadn't intended to say that. At least, definitely not so bluntly.

Zahra shrugged. "And?"

"That wasn't the reaction I was expecting."

"Not like that's a new thing."

"Excuse me?" Ari shifted on the couch to stare down her friend.

"I mean you guys have been hooking up since that summer after junior year."

"Umm, no we absolutely have not."

"Well, that's news to me," Zahra laughed. "I swear to god you two were fucking like bunnies that entire summer!"

"Mmmm, no," Ari said. "I mean, yeah, everyone *thought* we were, and we didn't stop those rumors and maybe stoked the fire a little with a couple drunk, sloppy kisses, but I can promise you that never happened."

"Huh," Zahra said, sipping from her mug of hot chocolate. She was silent for a couple of minutes. "Well, I guess the general state of things," she gestured to Ari, "would suggest that things didn't go...well?"

Quite the opposite. Everything had been perfect. The way he took care of her, even through his anxiety, how he washed her hair in the tub, and the sex...well, there was no denying the sex was outstanding.

"I wouldn't exactly say that," she said.

"What would you say then?" Zahra was all ears, focused only on Ari and completely ignoring the stunning blonde singer strutting around on screen.

Ari chewed her thumbnail, her black nail polish now well chipped. "It was good... Really good. But we agreed it would only be something that would last the week, something to get out of our systems. And now the week is over."

Zahra gave a thin-lipped smile. "That sounds dangerous."

"Trust me, I know. We tried to ignore it but something about being in a foreign country together woke something up inside me that I didn't even know was there. I can't explain it."

"I think I understand. Being abroad just hits different."

"Yeah, and just a lot happened. There was some drama with my family and the travel plans."

"Callaghan family drama? Shocking," Zahra laughed, always making little jokes to try and lighten the mood.

"I know." Ari rolled her eyes. "And Gid was...there. By my side through the entire thing and never once judged me or my family and I was there for him, too."

"Partners, just like you've always been."

"Yeah," Ari said, sadness weighing down her body.

"I'm failing to see the problem here," Zahra said after Ari didn't continue.

The more Ari thought about it, the less she saw a *problem* either so much as just another perfect thing that she could royally fuck up.

Like what would happen if they did get together and then broke up? Would she lose her best friend? Her dance partner? She couldn't see a way around it.

Her stomach tensed. Because, if she didn't fuck things up, and they had a long, happy life together, still one of them would die first, just like her dad and mom. And then what?

"I think you're scared," Zahra said, reaching over to squeeze Ari's hand.

"I think I am, too."

"And, hey, that's okay. Being scared is normal. I'm scared like 90% of the time thanks to my existential dread."

"Preach."

"But climate change and economic collapse and war all over the world, it's fucked up, but that's all going to happen whether you're happy or scared or getting dicked down by your best friend."

Ari laughed, her first real belly laugh since back at the cottage on the tree farm. "What are you saying, Zahra?"

"I'm *saying*, we gotta find happiness where we can and if Gid makes you happy, then that's a good thing."

"Yeah…" She wasn't fully committed to the idea, even though what Zahra said made absolute sense.

But there were a lot of steps between where Gid and Ari were now and this *happiness*. She didn't even know if they were still friends and she was reluctant to find out.

"You don't have to figure it all out right now, you know." Zahra knocked her shoulder. "Let's finish *The Eras Tour* and then we can play with pole routines, yeah? Forget about Gid for now. I know he'll still be there when you're ready."

If she was ever ready. And Ari wasn't sure she ever would be.

* * *

LATER THAT NIGHT, Ari lay in her childhood bedroom, tears streaming down her face. After Zahra left, Ari couldn't bring herself to go back to her apartment in Everdale. It was so quiet and full of all of her textbooks that she couldn't bear to look at.

Even though Mom had started re-doing all the kids' rooms after Dad died—her little project to keep her busy —this room felt more like home than her own place did. She loved and hated that so much. Shouldn't she, at twenty-six, be ready to be away from her family home? Ready to be on her own?

But she couldn't quite shake the bottomless feeling inside her. Between school, the risk of losing Gid, and the lingering grief from her dad, everything felt impossible.

There was a soft knock on her door.

"Ari?" her mom said softly. The door creaked open. "I didn't realize you were still here."

"Yeah," Ari sniffed.

"Oh, pumpkin, what's wrong?" Mom asked as she crossed the room, the light from the hallway illuminating her from behind.

Ari sat up in her bed and scooted up to the headboard. When her mom sat down on the side of the bed, she pulled her daughter close. It was just the right thing for her to do to make Ari's tears come on harder.

"Everything."

"That can't be right. What do you mean?"

"I fucked everything up."

Mom tutted, hugging Ari's shoulders tighter.

"No, I did," Ari insisted. She took a deep breath. If she didn't spill the beans now to her mom about *everything*, she wasn't sure she'd ever be able to. She started with the worst thing. "I might be getting kicked out of school."

To her credit, Mom took a second before responding. "Why?" was all she asked, without any hint of judgement in her voice.

It made Ari cry harder. "I failed a class and did awful in the rest. I missed an exam earlier in the semester and everything just spiraled out of control from there."

"Missed an exam?"

Ari picked at the blanket. "It was the day after the anniversary of Dad's death," she whispered.

"Oh, Ari." The words were so heavy. "I'm sorry, baby girl."

That was unexpected. "Sorry?"

"I'm sorry things have been so hard. I'm sorry you're going through this. You and your brothers, it's not fair."

Ari's chest tightened. "But what about you?"

"What about me?" Mom smoothed Ari's hair down the back of her head.

"Isn't it hard for you, too?"

"Of course it is. But I got years with your father. We had every day together. Good days and bad days and the in-between mundane days. We had a life. I won't say his death was easy, but we had years to prepare, to make the best of it. And I'm at peace with it now. Especially since I know we all finally got to Ireland together." Mom rocked them both side to side as she spoke.

"I thought I was ready for his death, too," Ari said. "I was here helping all the time and we knew how it would end. For a while, I *was* okay. But it's all been messed up since the summer."

Mom nodded along as Ari talked. "Has there been any time that you've been happy in the last year?"

Ari's stomach dropped into her toes. *Yes, oh my god yes.*

The memories of her time in Ireland flipped through her mind. Cuddling with Gid on the couch as she read her book and he did his crossword. All the cups of hot chocolate he made her. Feeding the goats together and exploring the farm. The way he looked at her as if she were truly something precious, despite the real-life mess that she was.

"Mmm," Mom hummed. "Want to tell me what you're thinking about right now?"

"Not really," Ari pouted.

"Why not?"

Because I'm scared shitless.

"You don't have to, pumpkin, if you don't want to," Mom whispered. "But I will tell you, if you've found something—someone—who makes you happy, who sees you and respects you and cares for you... Someone who loves you? That's worth its weight in gold."

Was she really that transparent? Could her mom see how much she loved Gid written on her face?

"I'm not blind," Mom said. "I saw you and Gid in Ireland. That boy adores you, and I think you're sweet on him, too. You've been miserable since you got home, and I know you haven't seen him since."

"But what if I mess it up?" Ari asked, afraid to even hear the answer.

"Relationships are a two-sided thing. You work together, build together, and love each other fiercely. It's not something you can mess up all on your own if you two really care for each other and want to fix things. And I have a sneaking suspicion that you both do."

Ari untwined herself from her mom and got out of bed, her bare feet dragging on the carpet as she paced back and forth. It was all too much, everything coming to a head all at the same time, and she needed to burn off the energy.

"Ari," her mom said, a stern edge to her voice.

"Hmm?" She halted mid-stride.

"This school thing, it's okay, too, you know? Your dad was so proud, we're all so proud of you, but not because of some degree. We're proud of the wild, bouncing, dancing, caring woman you've grown into. Whatever happens, it'll be fine," Mom said.

Ari nodded, but that wasn't the only thing on her mind.

"I miss Dad," she said, the confession raw in her throat. "And I'm scared to lose someone else. To lose Gid.

What happens if I give him everything and then one day he's just gone?"

"One day we'll all be gone. What happens if you give him nothing and then one day he's gone?" Mom stood and took both of Ari's hands in hers. "The last couple years with Dad were hard, really hard. But I wouldn't change a single second of my life with him. He was a good man, and he loved me with his whole entire heart. He knew me. He saw me for who I really am."

Ari recognized the feeling, the peace inside her soul at being known.

"We don't always have all the answers. We can make plans for life and the universe can muck it all up," Mom said. "But just know that whatever happens, whatever you do, your mom will always love you."

Her mom kissed the top of her head and Ari tucked back into bed.

For the first time since Ireland, she didn't cry herself to sleep. For the first time in a long while, her mind was quiet, and her dreams were easy.

TWENTY-SEVEN
GID

GID WALKED UP TO HIS PARENTS' front door carrying a bottle of white wine, the expensive one he knew his mom loved, and he squeezed the handle to push open the door.

Except it didn't budge an inch. It was locked.

His heart squeezed. They knew he was coming over and yet hadn't unlocked the door. It was a little thing, really, but the Callaghans kept their front door perpetually unlocked and he was accustomed to walking straight into their house. Something he apparently couldn't even do in his own parents' house.

Instead, he had to ring the doorbell.

His shoulders slumped and he tried not to think about everything else that made him feel truly awful over the last couple of days. In his mind, snapshots of the last week clicked by like a viewfinder toy. With each blink, he reset the image. The memories haunted his waking hours as much as his dreams.

But as he heard the door unlatch on the other side, he stood up straighter.

"Gideon!" his mother said. "Happy New Year."

She stepped back and pulled the door open with her.

"Hi, Mom," Gid said, stretching out the bottle of wine to her.

She took it and looked at the label. "You remembered, my favorite."

As if he didn't bring that same bottle every time he came over.

Gid toed off his loafers and lined them up neatly at the door on the mat.

"Your father's just finishing up some work in his study," his mom said leading the way into the dining room.

"On New Year's Eve?"

She gave him a piercing look over her glasses. "You know how he is."

Boy did he ever.

"He'll be done in just a second. You go sit in the front room and I'll just finish up things for the dinner."

"I could help you." Gid stepped toward the kitchen instead of the living room.

"No, no, don't be silly. Put the TV on. That show you like, *Office Space*, right?"

She turned around without waiting for his response.

After his week with Ari followed by a couple days of her absence, being at his parents was like being a stranger in their home. He barely recognized it anymore from when he himself lived here and most times it seemed like his parents didn't even recognize him.

He counted down the minutes until he would get to see Ari again; tonight, at Thomas and Julia's wedding celebration/New Year's Eve party. Hopefully that wouldn't be as terrible as this, but he had no idea what to expect.

Gid sat down on the couch but didn't turn anything on. In truth, he'd watched *too much* of *The Office* over the last couple of days. He needed a break from Michael Scott for his own sanity at this point.

He snorted a laugh. That would be a kind of joke that Ari would like. If only he hadn't already texted her too many times in a row today without receiving an answer. He checked the text thread to count how many. Only three times, but that felt like too much, given the circumstances.

"Oh," his dad said.

Gid jumped and turned on the couch just in time to see his dad recovering from a fright too.

"Didn't know you'd got here, Gideon," he said, pushing his glasses up his nose.

"Didn't hear you coming down the hall." *I was busy obsessing over texts I sent my best friend.*

"Yes, well, just finished up my work. Deadline coming up, you know how it is."

Gid nodded along.

Yes he knew, he knew. For years, that's all it was with his parents. Their work, their research, their papers, their conferences. Always about them.

They were the kind of people that if Gid saw them out in a restaurant or at the grocery store, he'd assume they were childfree. He couldn't explain it. Not that there was anything wrong with that, it was just this aura they projected, and it made it awkward when he tried to fit into their life, too. If his mom hadn't texted to invite him over for dinner, it could have been weeks before he saw them again.

"How was Ireland?" his dad asked, not stepping any closer, but instead bouncing on the balls of his feet across the living room.

"Uh, yeah, it was good." And for the most part it was. It was amazing, really. It was being back in Starling Hills that was not so great. God, he missed that warm, tiny cottage in County Cork.

"Good, good." Now his dad nodded along.

"Oh, there you are," his mom said, coming out of the kitchen. She put a hand on her husband's shoulder. "Dinner's on the table."

The three of them sat down around the too large dining table which, Gid noted, was set with the fancy china and the crystal glasses. His favorite squid ink pasta sat in front of his place, which meant the meal was catered in.

Something about that tightened his chest. Like, yeah

he loved the dish itself and was grateful that his parents had invited him over for it, but it felt so sterile. Just like the rest of their Scandi-modern home and their stilted relationship.

"So," his mom started before digging into her own dish, a hefty portion of filet mignon. "Tell us about Ireland."

Gid swallowed a drink of his chardonnay. "It was good."

Could he really find nothing better to say about it? He cleared his throat. "The wedding was beautiful. I think the Callaghans are happy they got to spread some of Sean's ashes while they were there."

"Oh, I didn't know they were doing that, too," his mom inserted.

Yes she did. He told his parents at least a couple of times. That was half the reason Thomas and Julia had decided on an Ireland elopement anyway.

"Yeah, they did," he said, already too exhausted to remind her about their past conversations. It wouldn't make a difference anyway. "And the Christmas tree farm was great. Perfect, really."

But he stumbled over his words, no longer trusting himself to say anything more about that without hurting his feelings more than they already were.

"Well," his mom said, her usual signal that she was about to change the subject.

Of course, their interest in his trip was more like a formality than anything else.

"Your father and I have some big news to share," she finished.

Gid didn't say anything, just waited as his parents had a silent conversation across the table with the other.

You tell him.

No, you tell him.

Finally, his mom took the initiative. "Your father got a grant from Utrecht University for his research."

"Oh, congrats," Gid said. "That's great. What does that entail?" He hated that he was the one to carry this conversation.

"Their lab is world-renowned in our field, and it's been quite a long application process. It's a huge honor." His dad shook his head back and forth as if he couldn't believe he'd been selected.

"Very prestigious," his mom said, admiration sparkling in her eyes.

"We're leaving next month," his dad added bluntly.

There was a literal record scratch sound in Gid's mind. Utrecht... That was the Netherlands, right? And his parents were moving there? *Way to bury the lede.* "You're moving there?"

"It's just a temporary thing," his mom rushed to clarify. "Once the project is done, we'll be back stateside."

Gid noted that she didn't say back in Everdale or even Michigan.

"Okay," he said, still processing. He wasn't close with his parents—obviously—but this news blindsided him. Suddenly, he felt more like an orphan than he ever had. They were just leaving the country, and soon, and only told him virtually as an afterthought.

At least, that's how it felt, trapped at the dinner table and hearing this news. They couldn't have waited until at least dessert to tell him?

Gid sat through the rest of the mostly silent meal with a growing stomachache and desperately wanting to talk to Ari.

TWENTY-EIGHT

ARI

GOD, Thomas and Julia were so sickly in love.

Ari was happy for them, of course she was, but their cutesy little displays of affection needled under her skin tonight. Because, happy as she was to celebrate their marriage, she was only thinking about Gid and the conversations she had with Zahra and her mom yesterday.

She was scared shitless to see him, about school and her future. That hadn't changed.

Despite what her mom had said about Gid *adoring* her, Ari refused to believe it. She couldn't bear the heartbreak if he didn't, actually, adore her.

Instead, she decided to live in delusion. If they never talked about it, she could stay in her fantasy. Ireland would remain perfect in her memory, and they could continue to be best friends.

Ask me how well that's working out for me.

"Gid just texted the group and said he's on the way," Zahra said, referencing the group chat the three of them had.

"Great." Ari downed the rest of her Prosecco. She was definitely feeling it and was hoping to feel it more. "I think I need a whole bottle to myself," she mumbled, popping the cork on a fresh one.

The corners of Zahra's lips turned down, but she didn't say anything.

"Don't give me that look," Ari said.

"I'm not giving you a look." Zahra shook her head to clear it.

"You are. It's the same damn look everyone's been giving me lately." A look of worry, concern. She didn't need it. "Let's just celebrate. Thomas and Julia getting married and Danny finally giving Lacey those *Eras Tour* tickets he's been hiding from her, and me, well...me having you."

Ari hooked her arm around Zahra's waist and pulled her close with a little *oof* from her friend. "Something tells me I'm not the only person you have."

"Huh?"

Zahra nodded toward the apartment door where Gid kicked off his loafers into the pile near the door.

Had he always been so handsome? His windblown hair and pink cheeks made Ari want to nuzzle up against him and warm him up. How had she overlooked this man who had been beside her for years?

Her heart raced behind her ribs as he spotted them. He raised a hand in silent greeting before beelining it to the two girls.

"Well, Happy New Year, gang," Gid said, giving a one-armed hug to Zahra before facing Ari head-on.

Neither of them said anything, just stared into each other's eyes for a moment too long. A scene straight out of one of Thomas's romance books.

"Alrighty then. I'm going to go over there," Zahra said, pointing at some random spot across the room. She sashayed away, quickly getting pulled into conversation with Danny.

"Hey," Gid said when it was just the two of them.

"Hey yourself." Ari couldn't help but pull her lip between her teeth.

Gid tracked the entire movement. "Can I talk to you? In private maybe?"

She didn't like the sound of that. But what could he say to her that she hadn't already thought? Could he hurt her feelings more than she already had in the last couple of days?

"Sure," Ari said, even though her entire body screamed to run in the opposite direction.

They grabbed their shoes and coats and went out onto the balcony. The Christmas lights still twinkled below in downtown Starling Hills and the fresh, cold air cleared some of the buzz out of Ari's brain. Which was probably a good thing considering she was pretty darned buzzed already. Maybe an entire bottle of Prosecco to herself wasn't such a good idea. Not that Ari was known for her brilliant plans.

"How was dinner?" she asked, staying on a moderately neutral subject before Gid could say something that really frightened her.

"Fine," Gid laughed darkly, not looking at her. He kicked at the concrete of the balcony. "I mean, it wasn't fine. It was stupid, awful. It's like I'm a stranger in my parent's goddamned house and now they're moving to the Netherlands, I guess? Some big grant my dad got."

"The Netherlands?" Ari scrunched her face. "That's far away."

"You're telling me. And they just sprung it on me as we were *starting* dinner. I had to sit there through the rest of my meal, pretending I wasn't freaking out inside."

Ari clicked her tongue. "I hate that for you."

He snorted a non-laugh through his nose. "Yeah, I hate it for me, too."

They stood in silence for a couple of minutes. The Taylor Swift playlist that Danny and Lacey put on blasted over Thomas's expensive speakers and everyone was singing along.

"How drunk are you?" Gid asked, running a hand through his hair.

"What does that mean?" Ari asked, immediately on the defensive.

"I don't mean it like that, Jesus. It means..." Gid sighed.

"I mean I want to talk to you, and I want you to remember the conversation."

"I'm pretty buzzed," she shrugged, stumbling slightly into the balcony railing. Her conversation with Lacey at the hotel in Dublin came back to her. *They say you're drinking a lot.* "I might have drank too much. I'm stupid, okay? Is that what you want me to say?"

"No, Ari, of course not. You know I don't judge you."

"I got enough brothers for that."

"I just want you to be happy. Safe." Gid stepped toward her.

She was desperate for his touch, for him to hold her, love her.

"Don't, Gid." She moved away from him, her Prosecco bottle swinging. "You can't fix me, you know? I'm not some *thing* that you can fixate on and forget about your own problems."

"That's not what this is about at all."

How had things gotten so twisted between them?

When Gid turned his gaze to her, her breath caught in her chest. His brown eyes shone with such hope she was stunned to the spot.

"Don't look at me like that, Gid," she mumbled before taking a drink from her Prosecco bottle.

He grabbed it from her hands and took a swig of his own then wiped his mouth on the back of his hand. "Like what?"

"You know."

Gid stepped closer to her, caging her against the railing with his body and his warmth. "Pretend I'm not smart. Explain it to me."

Ari raised her chin in defiance and a groan rumbled through Gid. He stepped even closer to her, bracketing her on either side as he clutched the railing.

"I want to hear you say it," he said, his breath hot on her neck.

The alcohol combined with her stubborn streak sparked through her. If he wanted to hear her say it, she was going to tell it exactly like it was.

"Don't look at me, Gid, like you love me."

The word hung in the air between them. *Love.*

They said it a million times as friends but that wasn't what she meant now, and he knew it. Ari could tell by the stiff set of his shoulders.

"Huh," Gid said and then laughed, stepping away from her and taking the bottle with him. "How else am I supposed to look at you then, pop tart?"

His words took her breath away but she wasn't ready to believe it.

"However you *used* to look at me. Like from...Before Ireland." There was no other way to describe it. There would forever be Before Ireland and After Ireland.

"What if they're the same way?"

"Don't be ridiculous."

"I'm not being ridiculous, Ari, I'm dead serious," he said. "Remember that very first night? In your dorm?"

"Of course I do," Ari whispered. How could she forget? It had been playing on loop in her mind for the last couple of days, remixed with her memories from the Christmas tree farm.

"I've been thinking about it a lot. I don't have any regrets. No regrets, zero. Our friendship means everything to me, and all those years dancing together were the best. I wouldn't change it." Gid took another drink. "But I think I hid something away after that night. Buried it deep down and Ireland shook it all loose."

"Gid, I—" she started, physically unable to finish the thought. She was scared. So scared. *I don't think I can do this.*

The words echoed loudly inside her, her body warring over them. Everything inside Ari screamed to cut him loose before she hurt him like she had everyone else in her life.

Gid put down the Prosecco bottle and stepped in front of her. His warm hands cradled her cheeks, thumbs running across her cheekbones as if she were something precious. Delicate.

"You can't hurt me," he whispered as if reading her thoughts.

But Ari knew it was a bald-faced lie. She was a monster, she could hurt anyone, everyone. Her family, the people who loved her most.

And the one person she never felt judged by: he was gone. The bottomless pit inside her stomach reminded her of that every day since the one-year anniversary of her dad's death. How silly that she thought she could escape the grief that had haunted their family since last fall.

Gid's hands tensed against her face. Maybe he was realizing it, too: that she absolutely could destroy him.

"You know that I can," she said, her voice hoarse.

They had to stop. But how? They were too far gone, too far down this road that they'd agreed years ago they wouldn't go down.

She fooled herself that the high from Ireland, their one-week arrangement, would be worth the pain—the pain of going back to real life.

"Baby," he whispered, his voice edged with pain.

"Don't. Not unless you mean it."

Gid stared into her eyes. Those eyes that she'd known for years, stared into as they practiced and performed, studied and partied.

Lord how she wanted him to kiss her. Her desires, her wants, her needs... They scared her. They were in direct opposition to everything she was saying out loud.

But then he smiled. "I do. I do mean it, baby. I love you, Ari Callaghan. I'll give you time. I'll give you anything you need. But I'm not going anywhere. I'll be right by your side, just like always."

Tears sprung to her eyes, completely unexpected. He said exactly the words she didn't know she needed to hear.

"Pinky promise?" she sniffled and lifted her pinky in the air. Just like before all their competitions and every exam and when they walked for graduation. Before all four of their flights in the last week.

Gid laughed, linking his smallest finger with hers. "Of course, pop tart."

"So, what we just...we're a thing now? Just like that?" Ari laughed, too, the giddiness contagious.

"If you'll have me." Gid bit his lip and, for a moment, looked completely unsure what would happen next.

"My partner." Ari pushed up onto her tip toes.

"My babe. I love you, too, Gideon Sims," she said before their lips met. It felt good to finally say it out loud and mean it in the *more than just friends* way.

It was a quick, soft kiss, but even still from inside the apartment, she heard whooping. She craned her neck around Gid's shoulders to see Zahra, Lacey, and Julia spying on them through the sliding door.

"We have an audience," she said.

"Nothing out of ordinary for us."

And before she could protest, Gid caught her around the waist, twisting her body so gently into a delicate lift that she didn't have to do any of the work. Cradling her under her inner thigh and waist, Gid leaned his upper body forward and Ari curled back into him. Into his warmth.

"Impressive," he murmured as he put Ari softly back on stable ground.

"You always were," she sighed.

The little peanut gallery on the other side of the door

clapped and cheered before Zahra opened it. "Come inside for midnight, you lovebirds."

The two linked hands, their fingers interlacing, as they re-joined the party. For the first time in over a year, Ari wasn't scared.

TWENTY-NINE
GID

THERE'S something about the sunrise on New Year's Day. The first day of a brand new year.

Gid blinked his eyes open, that first sun of the new year blazing right between a crack in the black-out shades Ari installed in her bedroom.

Her smell was all over him and he rolled forward to nuzzle his nose into her long, dark hair.

"Mmm," Ari murmured, her hips rolling back into his. "Happy New Year."

"Happy New Year, pop tart." Gid pecked kisses along the back of her neck. He snaked his arm around her hips and up under her navy cropped tank.

His fingers ghosted along her under boob. Ari reacted with a wiggle of her hips that sent her ass back into his cock.

"You naughty girl," he purred into her hair. "My naughty girl."

Finally finding her nipple, Gid pinched, and Ari squealed.

Of course he'd slept over at Ari's apartment in Everdale tons of times. He slept on the couch, the floor, once the bathtub, but most often he shared Ari's queen-sized bed. Not once over the years did they ever get close to hooking up before Ireland.

Now, as Ari squirmed under his touch, Gid marveled at Past Gid's strength. How he ever resisted this woman, he had no idea.

As Ari rolled onto her back, she stripped her tank top off over her head. Her raven hair flipped, falling over her shoulders.

"I like seeing you in my bed," she said as Gid situated himself over her.

"I was just thinking how I've slept in this bed so many times and never once did this cross my mind."

"I know, it's weird, right? Like, how didn't this happen before?"

"My working theory is that we were never in the right place," Gid whispered, his pulse bounding through his veins.

"The right place... I like that." Ari hummed. "Man, this was a wild winter."

"The wildest winter."

"And you were there." Ari turned and kissed the inside of Gid's forearm.

"I'll always be here." Gid dropped down onto an elbow and kissed along Ari's jaw until she turned her head to him.

They met at the lips. Gid notched his hips closer to hers as their kiss deepened, mouths open and tongues exploring. There wasn't much fabric between them. Just Ari's cotton panties and his black boxer briefs. Neither of which did much to conceal their arousal. His hard length rut against her as her wetness soaked through to his balls.

Ari pulled back and met his gaze. "I love you," she said before pulling her panties down.

Gid rearranged as he stripped his briefs as well, both now completely bare.

"I want to kiss you everywhere," he said before diving to her clavicle.

"No hickies this time."

"Oh my god." Gid paused his worship of her body and rest his forehead against the spot he just kissed. "I can't believe I did that."

"Honestly, neither can I." Ari shook her head, but her body shook with silent laughter. "Like a couple of goddamn teenagers."

"So embarrassing," Gid said. "I'm sorry."

"Oh, it's fine. It's all part of our *story*." Ari wiggled her head.

Story. Gid liked the sound of that. They had a *story*. "I love you, too, you know. So much," he said.

He continued to kiss down her body until he made it to the crease in her hips. God, he loved that spot on her body. A place he knew intimately from dancing with her for years, but now knew just how ticklish she was when he licked the spot.

As Ari giggled, Gid dipped his fingers into her cunt. She was so wet that she took two fingers easily.

Gasping on entrance, she bucked her hips up and his fingers were forced deeper.

"Gid?" she whispered.

"Yeah, pop tart?"

"Never Have I Ever... had a guy put a plug in my butt."

Gid froze. "Oh?"

"Nope." Ari bit her lip. "But I have one. Just in case I could do it with someone, you know?"

He remembered the vision he had of her back during the original game of Never Have I Ever: Ari with a pretty pink crystal plug sticking out of her ass. He swallowed. "Did you want to use that right now?"

"I was hoping we could."

"Oh, baby, hell yes."

Ari leaned over into her bedside drawer and pulled out a tiny velvet drawstring bag. She put it right into Gid's hand and he was surprised by the hefty weight of the plug and how cool it was. In her other hand, she grasped a small bottle of lube.

"Go slow and be gentle," she said.

"Pinky promise," Gid said before ducking down to kiss her nose.

Ari flipped onto her stomach and tucked a pillow under her hips, boosting her bum in the air. He reveled in the sight of her laid out like that for him.

"The safe word is pygmy goats," Gid said as he clicked open the lube.

"Got it," she said as he dripped the liquid on her opening. "It's so cold," she giggled, but went quiet when Gid began to circle her entrance with his thumb.

"Are you ready?"

"Yes."

For a few minutes, he softened her muscles with his touch.

"I'm going to start with the toy now. You're doing so good, baby," he praised her as he lubricated the cool metal, the handle of which was in fact a pink plastic gem, just like in his fantasy. He chuckled darkly. Things had certainly come full circle since a week ago and Gid was thankful it had.

Pressing the slim end to her opening, he applied a light amount of pressure, stretching her slowly until the piece hit its widest diameter. Ari gasped, her hips rising off the bed. And the next second, the toy popped through the tight ring and poked out prettily, just as Gid knew it would.

"Whoa," she said. "It's in?"

"It's in, baby." He leaned over and kissed just below her shoulder blade. Another of his favorite spots on her body.

"And?" She shimmied her hips at him.

"And it's very pretty." The sight of it drove him wild.

"Thank you, babe," she said, peeking over her shoulder. "Now please make love to me."

"Make love? I like the sound of that." He ran a hand down her spine, pausing at the plug to move it in a circle with his thumb.

After rolling on a condom from Ari's bedside table, he lined up with her pussy, pushing in as she stretched for him.

"You feel so freaking good, pop tart." Gid grit his teeth as he sunk into her as deep as possible.

"Everything feels so freaking good." She whined a little on the last word.

Grasping onto her hips, Gid started to move, slowly at first but quickly establishing a rhythm. Every time he bottomed out, Ari moaned, coaxing him closer and closer to the edge.

Her orgasm seemed to surprise her as much as him. She laughed through it and Gid thought, not for the first time, how much he loved that sound.

Gid didn't last much longer, falling forward over her as he came. "Holy shit."

"That was fun," Ari said as he rolled off and back onto his side of the bed.

"Everything's fun with you, pop tart."

This time she leaned over and kissed his nose.

After Gid eased her plug out, they showered together. Ari dressed in a knit leg-warmer and rolled cotton short combination that made him want to spend the rest of the day in bed. Even the big, wobbly dancer bun on top of her head lit a fire inside him.

On the little kitchen island, Gid found their Polaroids from the night before. Julia had passed around the camera that Thomas had gotten her for Christmas, changing out the film multiple times so that everyone could take and keep whatever pictures they wanted.

"Last night was fun," he said.

And it had been, counting down to the New Year with all of his favorite people in one room. He passed around his little flask of Buttershots and everyone took a symbolic sip to ring in the new year.

In the end, he went home with his most favorite person. After midnight, he stopped drinking and drove them back to her place in Everdale, the more comfortable of their two apartments.

"Those pictures are cute, eh?" she asked, hopping onto a barstool clutching a mug of steaming coffee.

"Very," Gid said, grasping onto her exposed bit of thigh and pushing her legs apart. He slotted himself right up against her, nosing against her neck. Something he couldn't seem to stop doing.

"This one's my favorite."

Ari flipped it around. It was of the two of them, Ari beaming into the camera with her arms around Gid's neck while Gid looked only at her. The angle of the camera caught his gaze, full of adoration, forever memorialized on film.

"You're my favorite," he said.

"Mmm," she sighed. "I could get used to hearing that."

"Let me make you breakfast," Gid said as he stepped around the island.

"I won't say no to that. But can your girl get a lil Pop-Tart appetizer?"

Your girl. She was his alright.

"Of course," he laughed, pulling down the box. Once he ripped open the package, he kept one of the pastries for himself.

The taste was full of memories. Her cherry chapstick that very first night, all of the Pop-Tarts he'd seen her eat over the years—as breakfast, study snacks, and drunk food—and most recently of the package she found at the gas station in the middle of the blizzard in Ireland.

If Ari Callaghan had a taste, she was absolutely cherry flavored. He'd never look at cherry pie the same way again.

She was quiet as he soft scrambled some eggs and served them with mixed greens, lemon, avocado, and a healthy sprinkling of Maldon Sea Salt.

"You know," Ari said, breaking the contemplative stillness. "I've danced with a lot of people over the years... but I don't want to dance unless it's with you, Gid."

He smiled around his fork, chewed, then swallowed. "Are we talking about dancing or *dancing* now?"

"I don't know," she laughed. "Both? I guess."

"Well don't expect me to learn burlesque."

"God, babe, I would pay money to see you twirl around in my platform stilettos."

"That can be arranged."

"Don't make checks ya can't cash, Gid." She knocked against his shoulder. "And please let me invite Zahra if you do ever put them on. She would literally pay to see that."

"In that case, she's more than welcome."

After a few moments of silence, Ari spoke up again. "This year's going to be great."

"Is it?" Gid couldn't help but think about all the awfulness January had in store for them. Ari's academic probation hearing, his parent's international move.

"I think so." She nodded as she sipped her coffee. "And I think I'm going to do dry January with you."

"Oh yeah?" It was something he started doing after college, a little reset with every new year. "It's not so bad, really. It actually feels good."

"Yeah... I think I need to just cut back on alcohol and weed. Take a break, figure my life out."

"Whatever you do, I'll support you," Gid said, planting

a kiss on the top of her head. He meant it one-hundred percent.

"Mmm," Ari hummed before giggling.

"What's so funny?"

"It's just... *All I Want For Christmas Is You*... You were all I wanted on Christmas Day, and I wasn't sure what would happen," she said with a shrug. "My wish came true."

"As you wish," Gid said with a lopsided grin. He knew in that moment he would always do anything he could to make Ari Callaghan's wishes come true every day, for the rest of their life.

SIX MONTHS LATER

ARI

GID DID up the final laces of Ari's pole dancing shoes and tottered around like a newborn giraffe.

"Oh my god, Gid," Zahra squealed. "Yes, this is absolutely worth the iced coffees and Isa's lecture about leaving him at Folklore all alone during the Saturday morning rush."

Ari sipped her drink: Zahra's payment for getting to see Gid in the shoes. She couldn't stop smiling as her man practiced moving around in her favorite purple-green metallic pair with a seven-inch heel and three-inch platform. The things Ari could do in those shoes defied the natural laws of physics, but Gid could barely put one foot in front of the other. Not to mention they made him truly giant-sized.

"How do they make my ass look?" Gid asked, posing in front of the wall of mirrors at Rosales School of Dance.

The girls howled with laughter. It had taken six months to actually get him in the shoes after he agreed to wear them on New Year's Day.

And so, it was also six months since she stopped drinking. Dry January had gone so well that she didn't feel like starting up again. Not that it was a strict thing, but she found that her brain was way nicer to her when she wasn't drinking a whole bottle of red wine at a time. She also stopped vaping, but she wasn't opposed to taking a weed gummy here and there.

That meant it was also nearly six whole months since Ari had been put on academic recess.

The hearing had gone exactly as her advisor predicted and Ari had to admit that taking a break from school really did help her mental space. She committed to more consistent therapy, worked every day at Callaghan's Coney Island, and made dance-related TikTok videos just for fun. School would start back up in the fall, but it felt good to just *live* for now and not be constantly busy with school stuff.

Of course, their weekly dance dates continued. Gid had been entirely supportive of her not drinking and only had non-alcoholic drinks when they were together. Thankfully, Cam and Angus had developed an extensive mocktail menu at Salt Cellar this year, so their dance dates never suffered. Ari had to admit that her choreography had really popped off since the beginning of the year.

Not every day was easy, but most days it was more than worth it to remain present in her body. Finally, she allowed her therapist to help her process all the heavy grief still lingering from losing Dad and she was re-learning how to measure her self-worth.

Having Gid as her partner certainly helped, too.

Well, they helped each other. Just like on the dance floor, they took turns leading. When Gid felt more alone than ever after his parents moved away, Ari made up for their absence as much as she could.

"God, I love you two," Zahra said, giving both of them a kiss on the cheek. A complicated feat seeing as Gid was well over six feet tall in those shoes. "But Isa will unalive me if I don't get back to the shop soon."

"Say hi to Danny for me; he's at his workshop this morning," Ari said.

"Will do," Zahra called as she skipped down the stairs two at a time.

"Your ass does look fantastic, babe," Ari said inspecting her partner's backside. "But to be fair, I always think that so I'm not sure how much it's the shoes."

"You flatter me." Gid hobbled awkwardly to the bench at the side of the room. "I'm taking these off now but maybe you could put them on for me later." He winked and unlaced the boots.

They practiced their in-progress routines for the rest of the morning as the sunbeams burned through the windows, catching dust motes. Closing it out, they ran an improvised dance to Gid's song of choice: "Dive" by Ed Sheeran.

After their session, they walked through downtown Starling Hills to the little house that Danny and Lacey had bought last year. The Callaghan monthly Friday dinner at Mom's had evolved a bit into Saturday brunch at a rotating location. When they walked up the front porch steps, Taylor Swift's *1989 (Taylor's Version)* blasted through the open windows.

"Party's apparently already started," Ari laughed as the front door swung open and Lacey came bounding out... wearing a veil? "Excuse me, but what is this?" Ari pinched a small piece of Lacey's headpiece and let it float back down.

"We did it!" Lacey screamed and jumped at Ari, who barely caught her in a hug.

"Oh shit," Gid murmured from behind.

Danny, backward baseball cap firmly in place, meandered into the doorway, pulling the door open wider. Ari's eyes widened as she spied the gold band glinting on her brother's ring finger.

"You did fucking what!" she screamed, now matching Lacey's energy.

"Good old Elvis married us in Vegas," Danny said, his eyes glued only on his bride.

"Excuse me, what did I just hear?" Julia asked, climbing up the steps with Thomas and their mom.

"We eloped!" Lacey apparently couldn't stop yelling everything she said.

The two had just gotten back yesterday from a quick trip to Las Vegas, and while Ari knew those two would have a wild time there, she never expected them to come back a married couple.

"Oh my god," Mom said, storming up the stairs and pushing through her kids to get to the bride. "I'm so happy for you! My newest daughter." She pulled Lacey in for the biggest bear hug and Lacey immediately burst into tears.

Thomas pulled Danny in for a congratulatory hug and when Gid went for a simple handshake, Danny insisted on a hug for him, too. "We're brothers now, eh? Brothers hug."

Gid didn't respond before Danny moved on, but Ari caught the lingering smile on his face.

The brunch passed with Bellinis, non-alcoholic beers, and a non-stop loop of Taylor Swift vinyl; Danny and Lacey had curated quite the collection for their home. Eventually, the boys pushed aside the furniture and everyone danced around the living room.

After a couple songs, Ari and Gid moved to the kitchen to refresh their drinks.

"Do you want to get married?" Gid asked quietly enough for only Ari to hear.

Her eyes widened at the question, her heart immediately picking up pace.

He laughed. "I'm not *asking* you. I mean I'm just asking if that's something you want to do someday."

"Not really. Too permanent." Ari shrugged. "I'd get matching tattoos though."

"You need to re-evaluate your idea of permanent," Gid said. "But I'd get a tattoo with you, too, pop tart."

"We could get a Pop-Tart," he said, pulling her closer, keeping their bodies connected at all times. She noticed he loved that. To always be touching her, holding her, cuddling her. She didn't mind it. In fact, she found she loved it too.

"Or a pygmy goat? A black one with this little pink tongue?" Ari laughed, remembering her favorite grumpy goat, Coal.

"Both." Gid smiled and it was one of the most beautiful ones Ari had ever seen.

"Okay, okay, I need a family photo," Mom called as she stopped dancing. Her face glistened with a little bit of sweat and she looked so happy. Spreading some of Dad's ashes in Ireland really seemed to be a turning point for her.

The Callaghans were definitely on the upswing now.

Ari slipped her hand into Gid's and went to step into the living room, but he planted his feet firmly and didn't budge.

"I don't know if I should get in the family group photo." His words were tense, and a little sad, as he whispered them into her ear.

Ari was just going to let it be. If he didn't feel comfortable, she wasn't going to push him. It wasn't an easy thing to accept, that he'd found a new family in place of his birth one.

"You're family, Gid! Get over here." Julia beckoned him into the frame of the photo along with a chorus of affirmations from the rest of the gang.

And when Ari looked up into his face, she could see how much those words meant to him.

"My family, my favorite," she whispered, squeezing his hand.

Gid led the way across the kitchen, pulling Ari along behind. When they got in the right spot, Ari stood in front of him. He squeezed her shoulders as they smiled for the picture.

Over the past six months, they defined what home, family, meant to them.

With Gid, in this place—whatever place *he* was in— Ari had never felt more at home in her entire life.

THE END

* * *

Thank you so much for reading Wildest Winter!

I hope that you enjoyed Ari & Gid's love story. If you did, please consider leaving a review and sharing Wildest Winter wherever you like to talk about books!

Looking for Alaina Rose bonus content? Scan the QR code or follow the link below for all of the Alaina Rose Literary Universe bonus content!

https://books.bookfunnel.com/alainarose

Looking for more Alaina Rose books? Find them all on Kindle Unlimited, Kindle, & paperback now!

Relative Fiction
Thomas & Julia's Story

Happy Accidents
Danny & Lacey's Story

Next Chapter of Us

ACKNOWLEDGMENTS

Wow, blink, and suddenly you'll have three whole ass novels out in the world!

I couldn't be more proud of the work I've put into Starling Hills, Michigan and the lives of my characters. Living with the Callaghans for the last three years (when I first conceived of *Relative Fiction*'s plot), has been really special and I'm so happy Thomas, Danny, and Ari's stories are all with the readers now.

Thank you to A. Lloyd Spanton, Emily Shacklette, and Sophie Snow for being major cheerleaders and behind the scenes champions of this novel and the entire Starling Hills universe.

There are so many friends I've made in the literary world, and it would be impossible to thank you all. If we've ever DMed, if you've ever posted about my books, tagged me in a nice review, or left a like or a comment—thank you. It's the little things that keep a self-published author going.

Thank you to my beta readers Ash, Emily, Erin, Laura, and Sophie.

Thank you to my Advanced Review readers for reading, reviewing, and sharing.

Many thanks to my cat, Gary for always keeping me company in my office.

Thanks to my own boo, Andrew, for taking care of me when I'm writing (and everyday). Your support means the world to me.

Thank you to everyone who reads *Wildest Winter*.

Ari & Gid are yours now.

ABOUT THE AUTHOR

Alaina lives in Michigan with her spouse and grumpy cat, Gary. She self-publishes angsty & sexy romance novels.

Find me, memes, links, & more on my Instagram.

instagram.com/alainarosebooks

Made in the USA
Columbia, SC
22 December 2024

50490494R00200